Trail of Hope

DAN VANDERBURG

Copyright © 2010 Dan Vanderburg

Second Edition 2016

ISBN-13: 978-1523448999

ISBN-10: 1523448997

All rights reserved. No part of this publication may be reproduced, Stored in a retrieval system, or transmitted in any form by any means, electronic, mechanical, recording or otherwise, without the prior written permission of the author.

Printed in the United States of America.

Some actual historical events are depicted in this novel and some well-known historical persons are mentioned. Dialog and activities involving known historical persons are fictional. All other characters are fictitious. Any similarity of those characters to real persons, living or dead is coincidental and not intended by the author.

Dedication

This book is dedicated to the memory of those individuals; some known, many unknown men, women and children Native American, Mexican, Anglo, and African who lost their lives because of the culture clashes during the turbulent and frequently violent times developing the Texas frontier.

Acknowledgments

I want to thank my sister, Vicki Risinger and my daughters; Tina Vanderburg and Shannon Twitty for their continued encouragement and support in helping me see my writing projects through to completion.

Thanks also go out to Harvey Stanbaugh for his editing and to Vicki Risinger, Tina Vanderburg and Molly Dalton for their technical support.

Special thanks also to Debbie Lincoln for her top-notch cover art.

TRAIL OF HOPE

CHAPTER 1

Central Texas, Along the Colorado River, March, 1836

My lungs heaved, begging for air. My heart pounded as I raced along the river's edge, ignoring the mesquite thorns ripping snags in my homespun shirt. I fought panic trying to focus on reaching the cabin in time.

I first saw them as I worked my traps along the shallows where the wagon trail veered close to the river. Crouching in the water behind a growth of cattails, I heard bits of their Spanish conversation and occasional laughter filtering toward me from no more than fifty yards away. Their muskets repeatedly thumped against their canteens as they marched along the trail toward the cabin. Sunlight glinted off their weapons through the cottonwoods and tangled undergrowth. A dry, high-pitched squeal emanated from some of the wheel hubs of their heavily loaded ox carts. The three officers in blue high-collared jackets with gold trim rode in front of the marching soldiers, their saddle leather squeaking beneath them. Tobacco smoke from the pipe of the bearded one permeated the air. I knew who they were and why they were here. Oh God, my nightmares were coming true.

I'd been waking in a fit every night since the man from the Smith settlement came galloping up the road to the cabin three days ago on a heaving, frothy stallion. He was spreading the word about the fall of the Alamo in San Antonio and Santa Anna's sweep through the Texas countryside burning out all the white settlers. The man's final warning to Papa was still etched in my memory: "Mister, you take your family and get on outta here right now! Everybody's headin' east to get beyond the Sabine River, out of Meskin territory. They done killed almost two hundred good men at Fort Alamo. They ain't stoppin' till they run everybody that ain't Meskin outta Texas. They're burnin' ever cabin they find and ain't takin' no prisoners." I'll never forget the fearful look on the lanky man's face as he turned to me before he spurred his bay to warn more settlers to the north. "Boy, you help your pappy get the family outta here."

    I remembered the vacant, faraway look on Papa's face as the man rode away from the cabin. Papa stood in the yard, his arms at his sides, staring at the ground for the longest time. Then, head still bowed, he walked back into the cabin to take care of Mama.

    Papa had lost interest in everything but taking care of Mama. It seemed that he had lost touch with reality since Mama had gotten so sick. He didn't talk much to me or Rosie any more. He spent most of his time in the cabin, ignoring the planting that needed to be done, just looking after Mama. For the last couple of weeks he hadn't left her side.

    Mama had pushed to take care of the things that needed to be done for all of us as long as she could. But she collapsed on the floor of the cabin two weeks ago and had been in bed ever since. I rode the mule to the Smith settlement to bring back the doctor, but was told he was in Galveston. Nobody knew when he would be back.

    Rosie tried to talk to Papa sometimes but her questions usually went unanswered. She spent most of her time with me outside the cabin for the company, sometimes just following me around like a puppy. But on this day I was glad I'd told her to stay home when I went out to check the traps along the river.

    I was confident the Mexican soldiers hadn't seen me. I was

separated from the soldiers moving up the road by the boulders alongside the river and the thicket between me and the road. I grasped my side in pain as I ran, pushing harder, trying to put more distance between me and them.

Tears stung my eyes and rolled down my cheeks as I ran, remembering how I tried to get Papa to agree to load Mama and Rosie in the wagon and go east with the rest of the settlers. That was the first time I ever yelled at him and the first time I had seen him cry. I even tried to lift Mama from the bed and carry her to the wagon myself, but Papa overpowered me and pushed me away.

"Son," Papa said through his tears, "she won't last overnight in that wagon traveling cross country. She talked a little this morning. She might get well, Andy, she might . . . ."

Before Mama got sick, she was stronger than Papa in many ways and he depended heavily on her during all the years they were married. He told me once that he considered himself a lucky man to have attracted the beautiful, intelligent school teacher when they were younger. She had been courted by several men with better potential, but she had chosen him.

Now Mama looked nothing like she did before. She'd lost so much weight, I hardly recognized her. Her thin, putty-colored skin was draped over the angles of her face and her eyes were sunken into her skull. She hadn't been able to talk to anyone for over a week. Sometime she made noises in her pain, but most of the time she just slept.

Papa wouldn't listen to me when I tried to make a plan for what we would do if the Mexicans came. He just brushed me away. "The Lord will deliver us. The Lord will provide," he said. Papa was never a religious man, but now I guess it was his way to cope with Mama's illness and his inability to reason.

I startled Rosie from her play when I broke through the brush and into the cabin clearing. She was squatting, barefoot, in her threadbare cotton dress next to the rain barrel at the corner of the cabin, rolling out mud pies. I couldn't hide the look of fear on my face. It frightened her.

She forgot her mud pies and stood when she saw me. "What's wrong, Bub? Why you running?"

I bent over, resting my hands on my knees trying to catch my breath. I scooped a handful of water from the barrel and wet my mouth so I could speak. "Rosie," I gasped between breaths, "we gotta leave. We gotta get Mama and Papa outta here!"

"But Papa already said he's not leaving." She followed me as I headed toward the cabin door. "Are the Mexicans coming?"

"They're on the trail right now. There's not much time. Come on!" I burst through the door into the dimly lit cabin, shattering the silence of the room. "Papa, we gotta go." I was almost yelling. "The Mexicans are just down the hill! Must be thirty of 'em! We don't have more than a few minutes! You grab her up by her shoulders and I'll get her feet! We'll hide out in that cave back up on the hill behind the house." I threw the covers off Mama's legs, grabbed her feet and started dragging her off the bed.

Papa glared at me, his sad eyes red-rimmed and blood-shot. "Leave her be, boy."

"But Papa, we gotta go! We don't have time to talk about it!"

"I said leave her be!" He returned his gaze at Mama's face. His face softened, his voice barely above a whisper, "I talked to your Mama again this morning. She said we'd be fine right here." He swabbed her neck with a damp cloth and looked at me with a blank stare. "You take your sister and go up on the hill. Come back after they pass us by. Me and Mama ain't goin' no place."

"Papa, please!" I pleaded, snatching the cloth from his hand.

He ignored me, smoothing Mama's hair. "Every thing's gonna be all right," he whispered and kissed her on the cheek. "You'll be feeling better soon."

I stood beside the bed, helplessly looking from Mama to Papa, trying to make a decision. Rosie held Mama's hand and cried softly.

"Rosie," I was desperately trying to choke back tears, "give Mama and Papa a hug and tell them bye."

I reached for Papa's rifle, checked the load and leaned it against the foot of Mama's bed, then kissed her on the cheek and hugged Papa. "Papa, here's your rifle." I grabbed Rosie's hand, took another look at Mama over my shoulder, and then pulled Rosie reluctantly out the door.

Rosie was too confused and scared to fully understand. She only knew she was leaving her Mama and papa. "Wait . . . My baby." She pulled away from me to pick up the rag doll she'd earlier dropped in the dirt.

"Okay. Come on, let's go. Hurry!" I again took her hand and led her running toward the cedar breaks behind the cabin. Both of us wiped tears from our eyes.

We dodged the low hanging cedars and live oaks and avoided the jagged rocks and prickly pear as we started climbing the rise behind the cabin.

I knew the rugged hill country well. I'd explored the river and hills for miles around the cabin. There was a vertical cave covered with low brush near the top of the ridge, about a quarter-mile away. It would be a good hiding place.

I continued to pull Rosie up the hill, pushing our way through the small cedar brush. Twice her long skirt caught in tangles in the mesquite thorns. Once as I yanked her skirt loose it tore, causing her to cry harder.

I stopped and knelt, pulling her close, wrapping her in my arms, trying to calm her. I looked in her frightened, blue eyes. "Rosie, you've got to be quiet. If they hear you crying, they'll find us." I wiped her tears with my finger as she tried to choke back her sobs. Soon we were again running up the hillside.

"Here it is," I said, pushing aside a clump of brush on the rock-strewn ground. I parted more of the cedar bush, exposing the lip of the cave.

"I'm not going down there!" She looked down the dark hole in fright, struggling to pull away from my grip. "It's dark and scary. Bub, there may be snakes in there." She started crying again.

"Look, I've been here before. It's all right. Here, I'll go in first to show you it's safe."

"Oh, Bub! Don't let the snakes bite you!" She grasped her rag doll to her chest with both hands and watched me lower myself into the hole.

"Shhh! Be quiet!" I scolded. My feet touched the bottom of the pit and I stood still as my eyes adjusted to the near darkness. "Come on down," I called quietly. "There's nothing down here but me. Just grab hold of those roots and climb down."

"No. I'm scared." She stood at the edge of the hole, looking down into the darkness holding her doll tightly.

"Rosie, listen to me." I hesitated briefly before continuing. "I don't want to scare you any more than you already are but . . . if the Mexicans find us, they'll kill us. Do — you — understand?"

She didn't answer for a few moments. Then in a quiet voice she answered, "Yes."

"Look, I'll climb back up part way. Just grab the base of that bush up there and lower your feet to me. Please, Rosie, we've got to get out of sight."

"Here, catch my baby." She leaned over the hole and dropped her doll into the darkness. "Will you catch me if I fall?"

"Yes, I'll catch you. Now come on."

I cushioned her body as we fell the last couple of feet to the floor of the small chamber.

"There better not be any sna—"

I clamped my hand over her mouth and cocked my head to listen to the faint rattle of gunfire from the valley below. It lasted only a few seconds, but there must have been at least twenty shots fired.

We huddled together at the bottom of the pit, watching the light fade from the small opening at the top as clouds moved in. For the longest time neither of us said anything. Rosie broke the silence. She looked at me and in a quiet voice asked, "Bubba, what do you think happened to Mama and Papa?"

I knew what had happened, but I didn't know how to share it with Rosie. I struggled to get the words out as tears welled in my eyes. "I, uh . . . I don't know, Rosie. I just don't know." *Oh God, how can I do this? How can I tell my seven-year-old baby sister that Mama and Papa have just been murdered and we're totally on our own in the wilderness? All the other families left days ago and we're hundreds of miles from safety — in the middle of a war.*

CHAPTER 2

The rain started sometime during the night. Thunder and lightning startled Rosie from her sleep. I shushed her quietly and calmed her back to sleep by stroking her red hair as she cradled her head on my lap, hugging her doll. The rain soon turned to a downpour. Thunder rumbled and lightning flickered from the hole above, illuminating our cramped space with brief flickers. Water trickled into the chamber but flowed on down below us through a crack at the edge of the floor.

I sat awake all night, thinking of Mama and Papa, listening to the rain, staring into the darkness with the occasional flashes of lightning. I tried to make sense of what happened and what we would do, but I had no answers. All I was able to do at that point was just plan a few hours at a time. I decided we needed to wait out the night in our hiding place. For the time being it appeared safe. The small flow of water into the hole and down through the crack beyond our feet showed there were probably more caves below, but the bottom of our chamber appeared to be sound. At least we were out of the wind and rain.

I calmed Rosie as she slept by twisting her curls in my fingers as the rain continued through the long night. Daylight brought gray skies still filled with water.

"Rosie? Rosie, wake up." I shook her awake when I could tell that it was full daylight above the small opening leading to the world above our hole in the ground.

"I'm going down to take a look and see if the Mexicans are gone. I want you to stay here while I'm gone. You understand?"

"No, Bub! Don't leave me here by myself, please!"

I looked at Rosie and held her by her shoulders. "Listen, we've got to do some things that are going to be hard for both of us. I'm afraid of what I'll find down there, and I don't want you to see it."

"I won't look if it's scary. Just don't leave me." Her forehead wrinkled and her mouth took a downward turn as her chin started to quiver. I knew more tears were a moment away.

I hesitated, looking at Rosie's fearful expression. "All right. But you've got to do everything I tell you. We've got to be quiet and we've got to stay hidden till we're sure the Mexicans are gone. Can you do that?"

She nodded, still clutching her doll. "Bub, I'm hungry. Can we eat when we get back to the cabin?"

"I don't know. We'll see when we get there." I picked her up and gave her a boost toward the lip of the hole. I took her doll and tucked it in my belt and climbed the roots behind her, pushing her up through the muddy hole.

The driving rain saturated our clothes within seconds. After walking only a few feet in the cool, wet air, I couldn't control my shivering. I held Rosie close as we headed down the hill to try to protect her as much as I could from the rain, but her teeth were chattering too.

Approaching the cabin site, we moved cautiously between the cedars and mesquite, squatting and darting from one clump of cover to the next. We listened as much as looked for the Mexicans. Hearing and seeing nothing, we slowly walked into the clearing.

The cabin was a blackened ruin. The logs that weren't consumed in the fire were charred, almost burnt through and leaning into the collapsed rubble that had been our home. The rain had extinguished any remaining fire smoldering in the debris but left it with a strong, damp, burnt stench.

I knelt on one knee and hugged Rosie. She silently cried as I led her away from the cabin to the shelter of a thickly-branched cedar tree.

"Rosie, you stay here. Maybe this tree will keep some of the rain off of you. Don't follow me to the cabin. There's nothing there for you to see. Turn around, away from the cabin and think about all the good things that we all used to do before Mama got so sick. Think about Christmas and the Fourth of July.

Remember all the fun we had at that party down at the Smith settlement last Fourth of July?"

She nodded, sadly looking at her doll, attempting to brush some mud from its face.

"You just stay here and think about those things. Think about Mama laughing with us. Think about Mama teaching us the Christmas songs and bible songs we used to sing. You remember those songs about Jesus?"

Rosie nodded, her eyes still filled with tears.

"And think about Papa laughing and telling his stories like he used to. Now you just stay here and think of those happy times. I'll be back soon. Try not to look at the cabin."

Later that day, I, in my mud-stained buckskins and my little sister, barefoot in her faded and ripped cotton dress, both with our hair plastered to our faces in the rain, and our clothes soaked to our skin turned our backs on our burned-out home and the two mounds of freshly turned mud. We walked away hand in hand with nothing except each other into a world for which we could never have been prepared.

CHAPTER 3

After the initial feelings of shock, loss and anger had settled inside me, I knew what I must do. I felt a sense of responsibility like I'd never had before. Papa and Mama had taught me much in my thirteen years. Now I had to draw on that knowledge to find the right things to do. Somehow I had to see Rosie to safety. Even as I buried our parents, I started putting together a plan. I knew there was nothing more I could do for them, but Rosie depended solely on me now. First, I had to find shelter. It was still early March and we had just gotten over a late winter storm that had left ice along the edge of the river. The rain continued in a steady downpour with no end in sight. If we couldn't get out of the rain and cold air soon, I knew I may have another grave to dig.

We climbed the hill back to the cave where we'd spent the night. Approaching the lip of the hole, I heard water splashing into the hole as it surged down the hillside. All I saw as I looked down the shaft of daylight was a swirling pool of muddy water.

I knew we must keep moving. I didn't know if the army would turn back toward the cabin after they burned the last farm up-river beyond ours. The man who brought the news of the Alamo said they were running everybody out of Texas to the east toward the border, all the way to the Sabine.

I remembered Papa talking about the different rivers of Texas. He said the Sabine was the one that divided Texas from the United States. He also said it was a long way off to the east. He told me there were several other rivers and many more creeks and streams between us and the Sabine. The way it was raining, I knew we wouldn't be able to cross any of them for several days.

Rosie was quiet, holding my hand tightly as we climbed the hillside through the rain. I explained everything I knew that I thought she would understand about war and the people who get caught in it before we left the cabin. I'd also taken her to the graves I'd dug in the mud and we both said prayers and cried, standing together between the graves of Mama and Papa. She hadn't said much since.

I worried as I thought about what we would eat. I had no weapons except the little skinning knife I carried on my belt. I thought about the traps I dropped when I first saw the Mexicans, but they'd be covered by the flooded river now and would be either washed downstream or lost under gravel and mud. I looked for weapons around the burned-out cabin and found little. I did pocket a couple of pieces of flint that Papa kept as spares for striking a spark on his old Kentucky rifle. Both the rifle and Papa's large butcher knife were gone. Everything had been either taken or destroyed in the fire. The soldiers even caught and butchered the team of mules for meat and burned their carcasses along with the smoke house.

We walked for about an hour until we came to an outcropping of rock along the hillside. I found what I was looking for. There was an indention in one of the vertical rocks that would protect us from the rain. It was hardly a cave, but it was dry and blocked the wind. I also found a few pieces of dry wood under the overhang.

Rosie squatted and watched me anxiously as I prepared to make a fire. I pulled pieces of bark from the trunk of a nearby cedar tree until I reached the dry, fibrous sections. I then tore them into small pieces and wadded them into a ball. I also gathered some small, dry twigs, leaves and sticks from under small rock overhangs. I searched for dry firewood and found several pieces of rotten logs that broke up easily and were dry on the inside. I made a pile of my dry kindling and firewood in a protected spot next to the rock wall. I sparked the flint I had salvaged from the cabin against my knife blade over a tuft of the cedar bark fibers. Soon a small fire was crackling, smoothing the goose bumps on Rosie's legs and arms and calming her chattering teeth.

"Rosie," I said, rising from beside the fire, "I'll have to leave you while I find something to eat. You'll be all right here by the fire. I'll try not to be gone too long. Promise me you'll stay here and just rest and dry out some while I'm gone."

She was too cold, tired and hungry to argue. The fire felt good and she had no desire to go back out in the rain. After making sure she was as comfortable as her miserable circumstances would allow, I headed back into the storm to find food. Stuffing my pockets with several almost fist sized rocks, I strode away from the cluster of boulders that served as our temporary shelter. I didn't expect much movement of small game in the rain, so I decided I would have to seek something out.

Several fresh animal burrows had caught my eye as Rosie and I came up the hillside. I expected that some small animals would burrow to protect themselves from the rain. After cutting a long, forked stick, I started probing each burrow I discovered. Sooner or later I knew I would get lucky and be able to twist something out of its hole.

I was lucky sooner rather than later. Crouching on my hands and knees, I was probing on the third hole I'd tried when I felt something move. I thrust the stick, rapidly twisting as I shoved it farther into the hole. When I heard the high-pitched squeal, I knew I had a cottontail. I quickly withdrew, all the time keeping the tension on my catch by twisting the stick, tangling it in its fur and skin. I had a good sized rock ready beside the hole when the rabbit emerged kicking and squealing from the burrow.

Soon I was scrambling back up the hillside to my sister and supper. I found her standing next to the fire hugging herself, warming her skin and drying her dress.

I skinned and dressed the rabbit and within a few minutes had it strung across the fire, roasting on a green stick. After a few minutes more, the rabbit's juices were sizzling over the fire. Rosie finally spoke after eating some of the first bites of food she'd had all day.

"Bubba, where we goin' now? Where we goin' to sleep tonight? How we gonna stay warm?" She looked at me with hope for simple answers to those very important questions.

I stared into the crackling fire, hoping it would reveal a plan. "I wish I had some better answers for you. I'm just not sure myself yet. Rosie, I reckon all the rivers and creeks are up so high now, there's no way we'd be able to cross for a while. Looks like we'll just have to stay here till the rain stops and the creeks have time to go down. Then we'll head east — or maybe we'll follow the river south a ways and see if the Mexicans left anything we can use at some of the other farms."

"You think we'll find people there?" Rosie pulled another piece of rabbit from the sharp stick above the fire.

"I doubt it. Not Texans, anyway. They've all headed toward the border. The Mexicans may have already taken over. We'll have to be careful to steer clear if we see them."

"Bub, What if they find us?"

"They won't find us. We won't go near the roads. We'll do our traveling cross country."

"What about the Indians? 'Member? Papa always said there was Indians back out here, away from the river, roads and settlements."

"I can't promise there aren't Indians out here." I said, poking at the coals with a stick. "We'll just keep our eyes open. Rosie, don't worry about stuff like that. We've got enough troubles without thinking about Indians that may or may not be within a hundred miles of us."

I wouldn't tell Rosie, but as I sat, staring at the fire, I *was* concerned about the Indians. Papa had warned me about the Indians from the time I was old enough to understand. I even watched him shoot at a couple that stole his saddle horse last year in the middle of the night from the corral next to the old lean-to. He didn't hit any of them that night, but he still lost his horse. We'd had Indian scares a couple of other times while I was growing up. Any time Indians raided or made any attempt to raid in the settlements, word was passed to all the neighbors to keep a sharp eye out for them and stay indoors for a few days. Once, when they did attack a family about six miles away from our place and killed several of them including the children, a group of men, including Papa took off after them. He was gone a week before he finally came home. All Papa ever told us about chasing Indians was that they got their revenge.

My immediate concerns could not include worrying about Indians. I decided to take the advice I'd given Rosie. Texas was a mighty big place and from what Papa said, most of the Indians lived far to the north. I figured our chances of running across Indians were pretty slim. I tried to turn my thoughts to things closer to home like keeping us fed and finding safety.

In an effort to make good use of the five days we waited for the rain to stop and the rivers and creeks to go down, I started making weapons. Since I only had my small knife, I knew I must develop ways to not only protect myself and my sister but to bring down some larger game than rabbits and gophers. I started working on a bow and some arrows. I'd seen bows and arrows when Papa and I ran across a handful of civilized Indians and their women at the Smith settlement trading furs for staple goods. Also, several years earlier, I'd seen an arrow close up in what was left of the rotting carcass of a deer that had outrun the hunter, but not his arrow.

I spent the better part of two days whittling from the branches of a bois d'arc tree, making a bow and several arrows. Every once in a while I tested the straightness of the arrows by rolling them against the flat rocks where we were making our temporary home. If they were a little warped, I soaked the wooden shafts in water then heated them over the fire to develop the straightness that I was looking for. I robbed a bird's nest of the feathers that were needed for the arrows but I had no idea what I would use for arrowheads. Papa said the Indians used flint for their arrow tips because they could be chipped easily into the shaped needed. I only had the two pieces of flint that I'd salvaged from the cabin to strike a spark for fires. I didn't know of any flint deposits in the area, but there was plenty of quartz just lying around. I tried breaking some quartz rocks into small, sharp pieces suitable to tie onto the arrows. Several hours and a few bruised and bloodied fingers later, I'd fashioned a few slivers of rock that looked as if they might serve as arrowheads. I tied them to the arrows with intestines from the animals I'd twisted out of the holes.

All I was lacking was a strong bowstring. Trying different materials at hand, I made several attempts to string the bow. I tried cutting rabbit skins into thin strips and tying them together, but it wasn't strong enough. I tried a flexible vine that I'd soaked to make even more pliable, but it splintered as I tried to tie it to the bow. I even tried the hem of Rosie's dress. None of those were strong enough

I knew I needed the sinew from a buffalo carcass or some other large animal for a strong enough bowstring, but without a suitable weapon, I had no idea how I would bring down something as big as a buffalo.

"I guess there's nothing around here that I can use to get this bow working," I told Rosie, putting the bow aside. "We need to move on anyway. Maybe we can find something I can use if we follow the river south past some of the farms. The Mexicans probably didn't leave any more at the other places than they did at ours, but at least it's worth taking a look. We'll leave first thing tomorrow. Since the rain's stopped, I've been watching the river every day when I go hunting. It's gone down some and should be back to normal in another day or two. Maybe by the time we cut back east the water will be low enough so we'll be able to cross the other rivers."

The drier weather was not only going to allow Rosie and me to travel, but it had brought more animals out of hiding and on the prowl for food. I had seen deer the last couple of days but was unable to take one down with rocks I threw, so once again we had a dinner of rabbit.

Well after dark on a moonless night, which was the last at our temporary shelter, we sat by the dying fire watching the glowing coals. We were both into our own thoughts of our lost past and our unknown future.

Suddenly a piercing high-pitched howl came from the darkness at a distance off to our left. Rosie and I both jumped and stared into the darkness beyond the small ring of firelight.

"What's that?" Rosie whispered, squinting into the darkness and nudging closer to me.

"Sounds like a coyote, or maybe a wolf."

Like her, I followed the sound with my eyes and ears.

Again, another howl. This time it came from the opposite side of the fire, but farther away. I listened. The sounds of the night went silent with the piercing calls in the darkness. I started to rise to reach for more firewood, but Rosie grabbed a fistful of the back of my shirt and pulled me back to the rock ledge where we were sitting.

"Where you going?"

"Just getting more firewood." I reached for her hand and pried her fingers loose from my shirt. I took the four steps to the pile of dead wood and loaded my arms full. Returning to the fire, I started feeding fresh fuel in. Rosie was again at my side, clinging to my belt. As I pushed the second small branch into the fire, I heard another yelping howl, this time straight out from us and much closer than the other sounds. I dumped the whole load of wood onto the fire, hoping for an immediate increase of light. It took a few moments for the new fuel to catch and the fire leapt back to life with a blaze three feet high.

"Look! There!" Rosie pointed straight out from the fire, grabbing at me again. Sixty feet beyond the fire something grayish-brown moved away from the firelight. I put my arm around Rosie's shoulders and held her closer. I also grabbed an arrow with the other hand and held the shaft like a spear.

A couple of minutes passed in silence. Then we heard a low, throaty growl in the darkness, only a few feet beyond the glow of firelight. Rosie pressed her body into the narrow space between me and the rock ledge.

"Be still and quiet," I said, reaching for a stick of flaming firewood and pulling it from the fire. I threw it in the direction of the sound. "Get! Get out of here," I yelled. A high pitched yelp came from the space that was suddenly illuminated by the thrown torch. A coyote scampered away from the sparks flying as the torch hit the ground. I grabbed another good-sized log from the fire and threw it in the direction of the other sounds and heard a scampering of footpads on the rocks.

Ten minutes went by and I didn't hear or see anything else. The fire was beginning to die down from the large load of fuel. I moved my entire cache of wood closer and continued to feed it to keep the flames high and the creatures of the night away from our campsite. Some while later, perhaps an hour or so, I heard faint howling and yelping again, far away. This time the sounds were a distant reminder that we are all a part of the natural animal cycle of life. Some will eat. Some will be eaten. Tonight was not our night to be eaten.

CHAPTER 4

I was awakened by Rosie shaking me. The sky was just turning pink beyond the rocks to the east. "Bub, wake up. It's morning. I want to go now. I don't like it here any more."

After I wiped the sleep from my eyes, I reached for my bow and arrows to tie them into a bundle with a strap to sling over my shoulder. Rosie squatted next to me and hugged her knees and watched me tie the arrows into a bundle.

I noticed her hands as she watched me work. I saw the changes that had overcome my little sister in just the few days since the world we had known before had ended with the murder of our parents. Her hands were no longer the chubby, dimpled little hands of the carefree child that my baby sister used to be. They looked almost animal like, with dirt and soot under her nails and ground into her knuckles. I looked up and saw the curly red hair that Mama had so lovingly brushed and kept tied up in a bow now hung in dirty tangles about her neck and shoulders.

Her face looked little better than her hands, streaked with dirt and soot from living in the mud next to the fire.

Rosie noticed me staring at her. "What?" she asked, bringing me back to my present time and place.

"Oh . . . nothing," I glanced away. "I was just thinking that I must be a real mess living out here, sleeping on the dirt and not washing up the way I've been for the last week. Soon as we get to the river, I'm going to wash some of this ole Texas dirt off me."

Soon we left our temporary home and headed south. We were gone over two hours before I noticed that Rosie had left her rag doll behind. What I didn't understand then was that she had left her little doll with her childhood and the life she used to live.

The worried look across her tired and dirty face that I saw when I stole sideways glances made me wonder even more if I could handle the unknown that lay ahead.

CHAPTER 5

Had the ground been drier, the thirteen horses and mules and eight riders would have kicked up a cloud of dust. But with all the rain, they moved through the damp, rangy hill country leaving only faint tracks while dodging the mesquite, prickly pear and rocks, angling their way toward the river.

They'd been traveling for eight days, looking forward to raiding the white settlers' farms along the river when they heard from a French trader the news of the large army of Mexican soldiers pushing the white settlers out of Texas. Their raiding party turned into a salvage operation when they started finding abandoned animals around a few of the burned-out cabins. They had already found and rounded up two horses and three mules as they rode southward, roughly following the river from one burned-out cabin to the other. They learned that the hated Mexicans had left little around the cabins. However, many of the fleeing settlers turned what livestock they didn't take with them loose before they left.

The Comanche warriors were gleaning the benefits of the Texan's losses. They had added two more mules to their herd just that morning when one of the younger men sensed, as much as smelled, the freshly doused campfire. He and one of his companions left their ponies with the others and cautiously approached the rock outcropping on foot.

The almost-naked, dark figures blended perfectly with the scattered boulders and vertical outcroppings, making them practically invisible as they moved silently toward the scent that caught their attention. Only the few eagle feathers tied in their hair and on their weapons and the red and black face paint betrayed their presence as they crept into the abandoned camp.

Cautiously walking into the campsite, the two men gestured and pointed to different signs they found. The footprints, the fire ring, wood shavings and scraps of animal fur and bones told them much about the former occupants. After commenting on the small footprints and the whittled shavings next to the still-warm ashes, the taller of the two walked to the vertical rock wall and found the rag doll leaning against a smaller rock. He picked it up with one hand, bringing it to eye level. His cold eyes looked beyond his large, twisted nose at the limp figure in his hand. He grasped the doll's head and tore the head from the body, flinging both parts to the ground. He and his companion scrambled away from the rocks and quickly joined the others, leapt on their ponies and continued their journey with a new urgency, following a new set of tracks.

Rosie lagged behind as we tramped through the scattered clumps of buffalo grass and skirted around the low growing cedars and mesquites. "Bub, how much farther are we going before we rest? I'm tired and hungry. We still haven't had breakfast."

"Not too much farther. We'll see the river in a little while. I'll find a critter burrowed up in a hole soon, or maybe I can take something down with a rock. We'll eat soon."

As we continued toward the river through the rough country I frequently stopped and waited for Rosie, who seemed to slow even more as we approached the river. "Come on, there's fresh water up here. Aren't you thirsty?" I called, picking up the pace after I heard the trickle of moving water ahead.

Rosie heard it too and ran ahead of me, over a rise to see the river. The vegetation changed toward the water with thicker grass, cottonwood trees, willows and a few scattered pecan trees along the river banks.

Although I was as thirsty as Rosie, I was distracted from the river as we approached the trees. Two large pecans held promise of a squirrel or two that I could possibly bring down with a well-thrown rock.

I saw Rosie disappear beyond the river bank toward the water as I looked for a couple of good-sized rocks to hurl at the first squirrel that was foolish enough to poke his head from behind cover.

The peacefulness of the river valley was shattered with Rosie's scream, "Bub! Help me!"

Rosie's terrifying scream propelled me across the sixty yards and over the ridge to the river's edge where I found her screaming, biting and scratching one mostly naked but brightly painted Indian and kicking at a second.

I had just drawn my arm back to let a fist-sized rock fly when the blow came to the side of my face. The last I remember was pain in my jaw, Rosie screaming and my legs crumpling under me.

I woke in a fog. I didn't understand the voices and the rough treatment. My head hurt. *Cold . . . Under water . . . When will it stop? Got to breathe!* I was being held under the water, struggling against my captors with my hands tightly bound behind my back.

They pulled my head from the water with a horse hair rope that was tied around my neck. I cleared the surface gasping and opened my eyes against the pain and swelling on the right side of my face. Rosie, totally nude, was bound at the arms and feet and sitting at the edge of the water, sobbing and screaming as she watched my near fatal abuse.

"Let him go! You're killing him!" She screamed. "You can't do this! Stop, he's gotta breathe!"

When my tormenters realized I was alive and conscious, they pushed me under water again, laughing at their game of seeing how much I could stand before they did indeed drown me. I struggled against my bindings as long as I could. When I stopped struggling, they again pulled me above the surface.

After what seemed an hour of this watery torture, but was probably only a few minutes, they tired and dragged me from the river, coughing and gagging. The wound on the side of my face where I was clubbed was still bleeding. I realized that I also had been stripped of all my clothing.

"Oh Bubba, are you alright?" Rosie cried, her eyes wide with fright, her body shaking with terror. "They tried t' drown you! Make 'em turn us loose!" She struggled against the binding holding her hands behind her back. Her legs were pulled back behind her and tied to her wrists.

I tried to answer, but was struck in the belly by the fist of the frightful looking Indian with the black paint on his face. I went to my knees, vomiting water, gagging, struggling for breath.

"Don't hit him! Leave him alone!" Rosie screamed, louder than ever.

I turned my face toward her, still on my knees, gasping, shaking my head, trying to mouth the words *no, no be quiet!*

One of the Indians strode to Rosie, pointing his finger at her, angrily shouting something in his language. He then struck her several times across the head and face with a woven leather strap.

I finally got my breath as the Indians jerked me to my feet and started leading me to a mule. I managed to get out just a few words to Rosie before I was struck in the face with the same leather strap that Rosie got her beating, "Don't cry. It's worse when you cry."

There was little delay before Rosie and I were lifted onto separate mules, our feet bound tightly under each animal's belly and our hands still tied behind our backs.

Before any of the Indians mounted, one of them, the tall one who scared Rosie the most from the hideous black and red paint on his face, stepped toward me with the bow and arrows that I had worked on for so long. He showed them to the others and said something as he laughed and gestured to me. He broke the bow over his knee and repeated the process with the arrows. He threw the broken pieces at me and laughed as the pieces fell harmlessly off my chest and to the ground. Turning, he strode to his pony and mounted in an effortless leap. He walked his pony to the mule where Rosie was tied. She pulled away from him as he grabbed a handful of her hair and jerked her head closer to him. Rosie twisted her face away and refused to look at him as he fingered her curls and stared at her hair and her fair skin. He forced her face toward his by twisting her hair in his fingers and stared into her blue eyes, grinning at her. She was too frightened to scream or cry. Finally, he released her, turned away and took a position at the rear of the caravan, behind Rosie and me. We quickly moved out, following the river southward.

I soon realized just how hopeless our position was. Rosie's pleading and calling for me caused her more pain and suffering from the lashings she received from lengths of rope or leather switches that each of the Indians carried. Any effort that I made to answer or comfort her brought me more blows from whoever was close at hand. Several times during the first hours of our capture when I tried to answer Rosie I was beaten with the horse hair rope belonging to the warrior wearing the black and red face paint. It appeared to me that this particular Indian had assumed responsibility for disciplining both of us. I began to understand that this one human being with the crooked nose had control over whether we lived or died.

Once in the early afternoon, when I screamed at my captor for striking Rosie again with his leather strap for crying, the Indian dismounted, cut a mesquite switch five feet long and at least an inch thick and gave me a thrashing while another Indian held the mule. Then he turned on Rosie with the spiny switch when she screamed watching me being beaten.

When the Indian tired of the abuse and withdrew, heaving from his exertion, we were both left bleeding with cuts and scratches over most of our bodies.

The sun was only a few minutes from going beyond the

trees when we reached a stream where the Indians dismounted to water their horses and slake their own thirst. Rosie and I watched, still mounted and bound to our mules while the Indians and animals drank their fill from the cool, clear stream.

Neither of us had tasted water all day. We were attacked at the river before we'd had a chance to drink. Dehydration from exposure to the sun and loss of blood left us only half-conscious as we sat, still bound hand and foot on the mules standing in the middle of the stream in foot-deep water. Our once white, naked bodies were caked in blood and red from sunburn and starting to blister. We were unable to brush the flies away that buzzed around and crawled on our skin, biting us, attracted to the blood from our cuts.

I listened to the brisk sounds of the cold, clean water gently splashing and sliding over the smooth rocks, and the slurping of horses, mules and Indians sucking up their fill. I tried to moisten my cracked lips with my dry, swollen tongue. All I managed to accomplish with the movement of my mouth was to make my cracked lips bleed again.

Surely they'll give us water. How long can we live without water?

I shifted my position on the mule as much as the leather bindings would allow so to ease the pain from the galling on my inner thighs and looked at Rosie. We were separated all day and the ten feet now between us was as close as we had been since our capture. She was as bloody and sunburned as I. Her little legs were galled like mine from the constant rubbing of the sweaty mule against her bare skin. She had a far-away look in her eyes, as if she had removed her spirit and left only the shell of her body slumped on the mule.

"Rosie," I whispered. "Rosie!" She lifted her head and turned her face in my direction. The sparkle that always lit her normally bright eyes had died. Her eyes were cold and lifeless, but they stared at me nonetheless. "Rosie, believe me," I whispered, "We'll get through this. I know you can do it. Just try to be strong."

There was a long silence, and then she whispered, "Bubba . . . are we . . . are we gonna die?"

"No, Rosie," I whispered, glancing at the Indians who were finishing filling their bellies with water. "Don't ever think that. If they wanted us dead, they would have already killed us. Shh, they're coming. Just be strong."

After drinking his fill, the tall Indian who had given us so much punishment approached my mule. I watched helplessly as he pulled his knife from his waistband. He hesitated a moment, staring hatefully at me, then cut the bindings at my feet that held me onto the animal and shoved me head-first into the stream. He then repeated the action with Rosie.

Our fevered and sunburned bodies fell into the frigid water. We'd barely wet our tongues and sucked in a little water before the Indians pulled us, shivering from the stream.

They hauled us out of the creek by the horsehair ropes still around our necks. The rough treatment and Rosie's uncontrollable shivering from the sudden temperature change to her skin caused her to lose her footing. They dragged her by the rope around her neck the last five feet to the tree where she and I were tied for the night. It took several minutes for Rosie to regain normal breathing from being choked after she fell. I felt so helpless because I couldn't comfort her or help her in any way.

Later, after dark, we sat silently and watched as one of the Comanches built a small fire while the others butchered one of the captured mules that had gone lame.

Lying at the edge of the firelight, forty feet from the others and still bound hand and foot to a large tree, shivering, and naked on the bare earth, we watched as our captors feasted on the red meat, barely heated over the fire.

Rosie whispered, "Aren't they gonna let us eat?" She had leaned as close to me as she could, pulling against her ropes as we watched the savages wolf down large chunks of meat while they sat around the flickering campfire.

I glanced at the Indians, making sure they were occupied with their eating and it was safe for us to have a whispered conversation before I answered. "I don't think they'll let us starve. They wouldn't drag us along all day if they were just going to let us starve."

"But... why did they beat us that way?"

"I reckon they just want to be boss over us."

"I don't want them to be my boss."

"Rosie, I promise, it won't always be this way. We'll get out of this somehow."

The moon was midway across the night sky when one of the Indians pitched some scraps of meat into the dirt at my feet.

I managed to pull a piece of meat toward Rosie with my toes, and finally worked the other piece, a bone with a little meat attached, to my own mouth.

My face ached where I had been clubbed each time I chewed, but I still managed to suck some nourishment from the raw, gritty bone.

Later when the fire had died to coals and the Indians and Rosie were asleep, I tugged at my bindings, trying to find a position comfortable enough to sleep. I thought again about Rosie's question from the back of the mule before we were thrown into the water. *No Rosie, they didn't kill us today. The time may come when we wish they had. But for today we're still alive. We'll deal with tomorrow, tomorrow.*

CHAPTER 6

At daylight, my body jerked violently as Broken Nose kicked me savagely in the ribs. Something snapped along with the intense pain in my side as I was startled back into the same nightmare I had finally dozed away from a few minutes earlier.

I was yanked, painfully, to my feet by the hair rope still around my neck. In less than a second, I was stretched against the rope held over my head by the thick, bare arm of the Indian. For endless seconds, ignoring the pain in my side from the broken ribs, I defiantly looked into the cold, black eyes of the young man with the large, crooked nose. The Indian, only a few years older than me, was enjoying this challenge of will being played out in his hands. The rope was taut enough to make me dangle on my toes, trying to support my weight enough to loosen it so I could breathe. Even though I was almost choking, I continued glaring into the Indian's cold, black eyes.

My breathing choked even more as the tension of the rope increased. With his other hand, he removed his knife from his belt and pushed the cold steel point against the side of my neck.

I sucked what little air I could manage through my clinched teeth as the knife pressed harder and harder into the flesh of my neck. When I felt its point sliding through flesh and warm blood trickling toward my collarbone, I lowered my eyes in submission. A few moments after I dropped my gaze, Broken Nose released the pressure on the knife and the rope, dropping me back on my feet. I staggered momentarily, regaining my footing, only to realize the Indian had reached behind me and severed the bonds around my wrists.

Before the bindings could fall away from my hands, the knife was once again at my throat. This time I kept my gaze to the ground. I held this subservient position for several seconds as the Indian stood over me, humiliating me, dominating me, and silently challenging me to try to fight or escape. Then, as quickly as the knife had appeared at my throat, it was withdrawn and replaced in Broken Nose's leather belt.

I understood the message as clearly as if the man had screamed the words in perfect English: If Rosie and I are to stay alive — we must do exactly as we are told and always remember who's in charge.

We followed the trail of the burned-out settlers' homes for another four days, seeking out and gathering stray livestock before leaving the river valley to head north. By the time we turned north and away from the settlements, our herd consisted of six draft horses, five good mules, and seven decent saddle horses besides the Indian ponies.

Our first day with the Comanches was the only day of our journey that we got to ride. From the second day on, even though most of the horses and mules we'd captured had no load, they made us walk and carry supplies in skin bags attached to straps slung over our foreheads and shoulders. The pace was slow with the extra livestock collected along the way. Our loads were heavy and we were still naked and barefoot. We had to ignore the cuts and bruises on our feet.

"Yes, I know you're tired," I told Rosie during our walk the morning of our second day with the Indians. "I'm tired too, but we're gonna have to stay up with them. We can't complain or cry out." I looked over at Rosie and saw her slowly nod her head. "As long as we do what they want us to, maybe they'll treat us better."

After the first day we were allowed to eat what and when the warriors did. There was always meat at night from the kill that was brought in. Usually we had deer, but on a couple of occasions, it was buffalo.

We were expected to do all the work when the group stopped for the night. I started the fire while Rosie collected wood under the watchful eye of Broken Nose. We weren't allowed to skin or butcher the meat, because we weren't trusted with a knife, but we were expected to do everything else. \

As the days passed, we began to adjust to our new roles. We were eventually given some hides to protect ourselves from the sun and keep us from shivering at night. Rosie was thankful to finally be able to hide her nakedness. I was just glad to have something to throw over my shoulders and back to keep my skin from cooking under the merciless sun.

One evening after twelve days on the trail, Rosie and I lay next to each other, trying to gain warmth from each other's bodies before we fell asleep. Rosie whispered, "Bub . . . what's going to happen to us?"

I was silent a few seconds, trying to think of something that could give her hope. Coming up with nothing, I said, "I don't know Rosie. I wish I did. I wish I could tell you everything will be all right tomorrow, but I just don't know. I know I haven't done a good job protecting you, but I've done the best I could. At least we're still alive. They won't kill us as long as we work hard. Just hold on. It won't always be like this. Remember, I love you and I'll take care of you. You'll be all right, you'll see." Rosie snuggled closer to me and I felt her tense body relax as she fell asleep, trusting in me as she always had.

Three days later, something changed with the Indians. While they were usually quiet and surly during each traveling day, they were now talking among themselves and even occasionally broke into laughter. They also took time to bathe in a creek and apply fresh body and face paint that morning before starting the journey for the day.

By counting the days from the time we'd turned north from the settlements and estimating the distance we'd marched every day, I calculated that we'd traveled almost two hundred miles from where we were first captured.

We always traveled in a northwesterly direction. As we traveled, I tried to fix notable landmarks in my mind.

I noticed that the landscape and vegetation changed as we traveled. The rolling terrain covered in live oak, cedar, mesquite and hackberry trees of the hill country changed to flat prairie carpeted with patches of range grass, prickly pear, grease bush and brushy mesquite with larger trees along the creeks and streams. I suspected we were approaching our destination when I saw large cottonwood trees in the distance, skirting a river. The Indians pushed the herd of animals and Rosie and I to a trot as we picked up our pace for the last mile or so. We saw dozens of conical, rawhide lodges scattered along the northern side of the river along the high side of a bluff.

Approaching the village, we wove our way through a scattered herd of horses of all colors and sizes with children tending them along the river. The children yelled and ran to greet us as we splashed through the shallow water on the south side of the village. The Indian children stared at Rosie and me curiously, pointing at our long, curly red hair as they rode their ponies past us. The racket of scores of barking dogs announced our arrival to the rest of the village. Soon several young women approached to walk with the warriors. Before long, there were dozens of people of all ages greeting and walking with our group as we entered the village.

Then we noticed the stink and saw the buzzards.

"What stinks?" Rosie asked, making a face and holding her hand over her nose.

"I don't know," I answered, looking around for the source of the odors. I reached for a corner of the hide that was draped over my shoulders to hold over my mouth and nose.

We'd become used to the odors of the raiding party. The smells of wood smoke, horse, mule and human sweat, body and face paint and old leather had become a part of us as we'd worked, traveled and lived with our captors. We barely noticed it any more. But the odors that wafted from the village in the simmering heat of midday were awful. As we approached the village, I realized the stench came from dung of several hundred horses and mules, a good sized village of people and their waste and almost as many dogs as the people. The discarded bones and other rotting by-products of buffalo, deer and other animals were lying around wherever they were discarded. Buffalo hides, some with stinking meat still hanging on were being processed throughout the village. Buzzards hung over the village and scavenged the rotting bones on the ground.

One particularly old and ugly woman greeted Broken Nose with an embrace. She gestured several times toward me and Rosie and the horses and mules, jabbering something in their language and pointing to a location up ahead. Broken Nose nodded and picked up his pace.

The old woman lagged behind to get a closer look at us. We moved away, but she grabbed Rosie by her hair before she could sidestep out of arm's reach. The procession came to a halt as Rosie stopped and stubbornly glared at her. The woman said something to those around her as she looked Rosie over. She held onto Rosie, turning her hair over in her hand, examining it carefully. She finally let go of her hair and went back to Broken Nose with more loud discussion, gesturing toward Rosie.

Rosie looked at me, her eyes wide, more in question than in fear. "What was that all about?" she asked.

"Maybe they've never seen anybody with red hair."

"Well, whoever she is, she's ugly and mean, and I don't like her."

In the center of the village, we came to a large open area with a fire pit in the middle. About twenty men were clustered in small groups, standing next to buffalo hides spread on the ground and covered with colorful wool blankets, knives, hatchets, mirrors, several piles of black pieces of flint, and small, colorful beads sorted by color and neatly piled on the robes.

Another group of six warriors were loading bags of goods on their horses. Several other horses were tied nose-to-tail and looked like they were being readied for travel. All the people around the buffalo robes and working with the horses stopped what they were doing to look at us as we entered the clearing.

It looked like a big trading event had taken place and the traders were preparing to leave.

Broken Nose walked into the clearing ahead of his caravan and made loud greetings to those packing their horses. One man stepped away from his horses and came forward ahead of the others. He wore leather leggings, a beaded vest and had several eagle feathers in his loose hair. He and Broken Nose had a discussion loaded with wide arm gesturing and pointing. He walked with Broken Nose into the herd of livestock we had brought from the settlements. The other men that were loading their horses followed them to get a closer look at the newly arrived horses and mules. Broken Nose stroked the manes and legs of several horses and lifted the horse's lips to show the other man their teeth as the two Indians talked.

"What they doin' Bub?" Rosie asked in my ear.

"Kinda looks like ole Broken Nose is trying to sell that other fella some of the horses," I whispered to her.

Broken Nose led the Indians through the entire herd so they could see all the horses and mules. He then steered them toward Rosie and me. We stood with our arms around each other. We must have been a pitiful sight in our skimpy loincloths, our fair skin burnt and peeled and burnt over again by the sun. Our curly red hair was matted from days of grooming not being a priority. There was a fine coating of trail dust over our entire bodies with rivulets of sweat caked on our faces and rings of dirt around our necks. After each of the group of men with Broken Nose passed by us looking both of us over, Broken Nose pushed us onto the red dirt to sit in the sun next to where the horses and mules were held. Broken Nose and his warriors and the traders circled the fire pit, sat and smoked from a pipe that one of the traders pulled from his bags and they bargained. The traders pulled goods from the bags on the pack horses and displayed them on buffalo robes as they argued, then ultimately agreed on the price of goods to be traded.

"Whatcha think they're doin' now?" Rosie asked.

"Looks like they're bargaining for the horses. You saw how close they were looking 'em over."

"You see the way those men looked at me?" She asked.

"I guess they were kinda looking at both of us."

"You think they were lookin' to trade for us?" Rosie clasped my hand tighter.

"No, they don't trade for people. They just trade for horses."

"Are you sure?" As she looked at me for reassurance, a look of fear once again spread across her face.

"Well, kinda. I guess I really don't know, but I don't think so anyway."

"Bubba, I think I'm scared again." She huddled closer to me. "What if they want to take us away?"

I thought for a moment and shrugged, "I guess it couldn't be much worse than what we already have. Besides, none of those other fellers look near as mean as ole Broken Nose. Just don't worry. You know I'll take care of you."

After most of the afternoon passed, the group of Indians rose from their smoking circle and started exchanging goods. They put more knives, hatchets, beads, flint, mirrors, several cooking pots and some ribbon and calico on buffalo hides. Then they collected several horses and mules that Broken Nose had offered and tied them with the others that had been readied to travel earlier.

One of the traders, the one wearing leather leggings, a vest and several eagle feathers in his long hair approached me and Rosie. He wore no paint on his face or body so he didn't scare Rosie as much as Broken Nose had when she'd first seen him. He stood over us for a moment, looking at Rosie, and then reached for her, grabbing her by the arm and pulled her away from me.

Rosie screamed, "Bub, Bubba, what's he doing? Don't let them take me!"

I jumped to my feet to reach for Rosie as the Indian pulled her away. Several hands grabbed me before I could get to her and held me as the traders lifted her onto a pony. They quickly tied her hands together. She screamed and kicked at the Indians as they worked.

"Stop it! Leave me alone! You can't do that! No! No!" She screamed.

The Indian in the leggings tied her legs securely to the horse while a second man held her still. All the time, she continued begging, screaming and pleading for me.

"Help me, Bubba! Don't let them take me. Please . . ."

Several men held me as I fought them, struggling to go to Rosie. "Rosie, I'll find you if it's the last thing I ever do!" I yelled. I pulled against those holding me until the old woman I had seen talking to Broken Nose picked up a two foot long stick of firewood and hit me in the stomach as hard as she could, knocking the wind from me and taking me to my knees. Bent over with pain, my face almost in the dirt, I struggled to catch my breath. Looking up, I saw my little sister straining against her bindings on the pony to get a final look at me. Her face twisted in terror as she pleaded and screamed for me. "Bubba, you said you'd take care of me! Please help me! Please, don't let them take me! Bubba!"

The sounds of her screaming, begging for me and pleading for help burned deep into my heart. Those sounds returned to haunt me over and over again long after the echoes ringing from the bluffs above the river faded to silence.

CHAPTER 7

Slumped on my knees, I struggled to regain my breath against the stabbing pain of my re-injured broken ribs. I tried to ignore the physical pain, but my face twisted in agony as it reflected my tortured soul while I watched my little sister being taken away on horseback by her new set of masters.

Mine and Rosie's lives had once again changed in the blink of an eye. I had no idea where they were taking her, or whether she would live or die. *I'm such a miserable failure. I ran instead of protecting Mama and Papa and let the Mexicans murder them. Now Rosie's gone. I promised her comfort and safety, and she trusted me. It's all my fault. All of it!*

I watched the departing trading party through my tears, still on my knees, crying in anguish, pounding my fists in the dust until I was once again struck by the old woman wielding her stick of firewood. This time she hit me on the back, and then again on the side of the head. When she wasn't hitting me with her stick, she waved it in the air, poking at me with it, yelling and pointing. I understood that she wanted me to go with her. I struggled to my feet and turned for one last look at Rosie in the distance as the group taking her rode over a rise and disappeared from view. The old woman's club arced toward me again. I managed to dodge the blow and stumbled backward to follow my new master and take up my new life.

In time I learned the old woman's name was Coyote Den and she was the mother of the young, but respected warrior, the one I had called Broken Nose. His tribal name was Strings Bow Tight. I found that my job — my only reason for living — was to make Coyote Den's life easier. Then, as she saw fit, after I had accomplished my tasks for her, she frequently loaned me to her friends to perform their tasks. I worked sometimes eighteen or nineteen hours a day and was given no real shelter. I wasn't allowed to sleep in the lodge with the old woman like some of the dogs, nor was I allowed to have my own lodge. I had to find whatever I could to cover myself during rainstorms. Sometimes I crawled under a buffalo hide that I was working to soften for Coyote Den to use as a new sleeping robe. Other times, I made a shelter for myself from sticks and leaves.

I was not allowed to eat with my masters. Many times I provided food for the old women and the young men by picking berries and wild plums or gathering nuts and seeds or honey with the women. But after the hard work of gathering and processing the food, the women took it all into their lodges without leaving me even a scrap. I learned that in order to stay alive, I must steal and hide food for myself.

Abuse was heaped on me as I tried to learn the Comanche ways. Most of my mistakes were met by beatings or lashings. If my muscles were bruised or bones fractured during the abuse, I had to find ways to work around my injuries.

I was thankful that I already knew about slaughtering and processing animal meat and hides from my work on the farm because working with buffalo products became some of my most time consuming duties.

I did all the traditional work that the women usually did. What meat wasn't cooked and eaten immediately after a successful hunt was cut into strips and dried as jerky to be stored and eaten later when hunts weren't successful. Spring and summer were months of plenty. The buffalo were easy to find during the warm season.

There was little of the buffalo that the tribe didn't use. The heart and liver were claimed by the hunter who killed the animal and was eaten raw and steamy immediately after the kill. The tongues were also considered choice parts and were eaten before the other meat. I processed the stomachs and bladders into containers for holding and transporting everything imaginable. I removed the brains from the skulls and set the brains aside for use in the tanning process to make hides soft and pliable. Sinew was collected and processed into bow strings. The bone marrow was considered tasty and I worked many hours breaking open the bones to scrape it out. Even the hooves were boiled and rendered down into glue for saddle making and laminating the many layers of rawhide together to reinforce the strength of the warrior's shields.

Processing and preserving meat was the most critical of the jobs associated with the buffalo because it meant the survival of the tribe. They thrived or suffered based on availability of the buffalo. Preserving buffalo hides required the most time and labor of all the buffalo tasks and the uses of the hides were endless.

The days and nights during the spring and summer of 1836 blurred together. I didn't have time during my work to mourn the trading away of Rosie or to punish myself for my failure as her protector as every waking moment was focused on trying to please the old women of the tribe. During the first few months, I frequently misunderstood their commands or made mistakes in my tasks. I was punished for whatever mistake or misunderstanding happened, no matter how minor. Usually it was old Coyote Den that lashed out at me with whatever was handy for her to beat me with, but occasionally she called on her son, Strings Bow Tight to give me a thorough thrashing to remind me of my status. After every beating, I silently resolved that someday, I didn't know how or when — I would get my revenge. I knew, however, that until I developed a perfect plan to escape and was able to find my way back to civilization, I could not attempt it. If I tried to escape and failed, it meant certain death.

I did, however reserve a few minutes every night before I fell into a fitful sleep to think of Rosie and to pray for my escape and her safety. *Rosie, you've got to be strong. Just hold on. I'll be there soon as I can. I'll come get you, I promise. Wherever you are, no matter how far, no matter how long it takes, I'll find you and bring you home.*

CHAPTER 8

Rosie's screams faded to sobs as the trading party rode beyond the ridge and out of sight of the encampment. No amount of twisting and turning on the horse's back gave her another view of her brother. Never in her life had she been away from her family. Her mother was always with her until she became sick, then Andy was almost always with her. She became used to the hard work and harsh treatment of the other Indians, but with her brother she'd learned how to avoid some of the beatings. Now she was taken by a new group and may never see her brother again.

She cried until she had no more tears. She was miserable during the first hour with the new Indians. Her whole world ended beyond the horse she was riding. Now looking around, she saw that there were six riders, each leading at least one horse. Some led several tied head to tail. The man leading the horse Rosie was riding was the one who had pulled her away from Andy and tied her to the horse. He occasionally looked back at her. Each time she immediately looked away to avoid eye contact.

They rode all afternoon. There was little conversation between the men until late in the afternoon when two of them gave the horses they were leading to other men and rode away. The group rode for another hour, then stopped by a stream to camp for the night. Rosie's captor untied her feet and lifted her from the horse to the ground. He removed the buffalo hide pad she had been sitting on and put it on the ground, then motioned for her to sit. He removed the bindings from her wrists. Rosie didn't know what to make of her treatment, especially when he offered her a drink of water from a bladder with a wooden stopper in the spout.

The two Indians who had left earlier soon rejoined the

group. One of them was balancing a large buck in front of his saddle.

Everyone but Rosie busied themselves around the camp, gathering firewood and starting a fire, watering and then hobbling the horses and skinning the deer. Soon venison was roasting over the fire. When it was done, Rosie was given more than she had eaten in weeks. She kept waiting for the beating and rough treatment, but it never came.

Several times during the evening the Indian who was caring for her spoke to her as if she understood him, but she silently looked down, embarrassed by the attention she was getting. As the evening wore on, she found herself stealing glances at the man who showed interest in her. His skin was almost the color of the old copper kettle that her mother used to make tea in when they could trade for it at the settlement. He wore his long black hair loose, hanging beyond his shoulders with three eagle feathers braided into it. His deerskin loincloth hung to his knees and his leather leggings covered his bowed legs and protected him from mesquite thorns as he rode through the prairie. The leather vest he wore was decorated with colorful glass beads. She noticed that his moccasins looked to be almost new and they too had red and blue beadwork designs all over the tops. His high cheekbones framed a large nose and full lips. She noticed that he had even, white teeth when he spoke to her and laughed during dinner with his friends.

She tried to guess his age. He was older than Andy, but not nearly as old as her papa. *He looks pretty old though*, she thought. *Maybe twenty-five or thirty.*

Later, with a belly full of venison, she sat hugging her knees. She listened to the men talk while they smoked from their pipes. As their voices droned, her eyes got heavier and she started nodding. Soon the man in leggings left the circle of firelight and went to a large, leather bag that he had earlier removed from one of the horses. He returned with two trade blankets and spread one on the ground next to Rosie, motioning for her to lie down. Then he spread the other blanket over her.

In the twilight between wakefulness and sleep, Rosie was bewildered by the behavior of this new Indian. All she had known of Indians had been hard work, torment and abuse. These men were treating her with kindness. As she drifted to sleep, she wondered what her new life would be.

CHAPTER 9
Eight months later

I ran toward the large bull buffalo lying on its side. Its heaving breath spewed steamy blasts through the bloody foam around its nose and mouth, leaving small red splatters in the thin layer of snow. The fourteen foot lance that Strings Bow Tight thrust between its ribs, piercing its lungs, snapped apart as the huge beast fell to the icy ground. I knew I must work fast as there would be several other animals to skin and butcher before dark. I also knew I must carefully avoid the horns and thrashing hooves of this still alive bull, struggling with his last painful breaths. My first cut circled the buffalo's throat, severing the windpipe and the major arteries. The dead bull's lifeblood formed a puddle, staining the snow around its head. I sliced deeply from the throat to the groin, then down the legs to the hooves. I automatically went through the process of gutting the carcass, separating the usable parts from those I would feed to the dogs. The always present skinny dogs snapped up any part that was thrown their way and fought among themselves for what little was offered.

Expertly separating the skin from the carcass, I thought of the many times I'd done this during the months since I was captured. I'd butchered many buffalo, lots of deer, some antelope, and even a few wild hogs. Earlier in the winter when the hunters couldn't find the buffalo and deer had become scarce, I'd butchered a couple of mules.

Every few minutes as I worked, I held my hands inside the steaming carcass or between the skin and the body to warm them as the cold, wet blood on my hands numbed my fingers. I'd learned my jobs well and worked fast and efficiently. Out of necessity I was learning the language and already knew the words and phrases necessary to get my jobs done, plus much more. I knew the routine of camp life and had learned to anticipate the needs of Coyote Den.

She lashed out at me less frequently — not because she liked me anymore, but because she could find little about my work to criticize. She surprised me in the fall. When the weather started turning cooler, Coyote Den gave me her old, leather jumper and skirt, heavily stained with grease and dirt to make myself a jumper, leggings and moccasins. Because of her large size, there would be plenty of leather for my garments even though several places would have to be patched because of the holes she had worn in them. I'd recently finished tanning several nice doeskins for her and she put together a new outfit for herself from the leather. It took me several thorough scrubbings in the river with suds from yucca root to remove the old woman's stench and much of the grease from the leathers before I could start working on my own garments by my little fire at night. She also gave me her oldest buffalo robe to help deflect the cold winds at night. I still had no formal living quarters like the tribe members. Only twice during the winter had I been allowed to sleep inside Coyote Den's lodge. Those had been on extremely cold nights. The old woman wasn't getting soft. She was only protecting her investment in her slave.

The tribe moved frequently, following the buffalo for food or following the warriors on long raiding trips. It was one of my jobs to break down Coyote Den and Strings Bow Tight's lodges, pack all the belongings, load the travois and horses or mules and then control the animals while traveling, following the rest of the tribe and eating dust in my position as the lowliest tribe member.

A few months earlier I stopped stealing and hiding food. I started openly setting aside a small portion of whatever I gathered or butchered for myself, then built my own small fire and cooked my food after work was finished for the day. Since I wasn't punished for assuming responsibility for feeding myself, I assumed my behavior was accepted.

After the tribe enjoyed an abundant spring and early

summer with plenty of rain, which resulted in good grass to fatten the horses and buffalo, the late summer brought stifling heat and drought. The tribe moved time and time again following the herds as they sought water on the dry plains.

Even though frequent moving meant more work for me, I was always glad to move on, especially in the summer. The stench of the camp became overwhelming the longer we stayed. The Indians didn't bury their trash or their waste — they left it where it lay, close to the lodges or not. They knew that once they moved on, the prairie, their Mother Earth, would reclaim itself over time, much richer than it had been before their visit.

As the leaves on the cottonwoods started turning yellow, then brown, the cooler weather of fall and winter arrived. We were faced with longer periods of travel, unable to find buffalo or even deer. Now, during the month the People called The Moon of the Starving Horse, we had been on the trail for six days looking for a herd of buffalo. We'd found a small herd of two hundred or so, and the warriors had killed no less than twenty before the remainder scattered, to regroup again miles away. I was working on one of those bulls now.

After I completely removed the skin from the carcass, I spread the hide, hair side down and started butchering the meat from the bones, placing the meat on the hide. While I worked, my thoughts drifted to the place in my mind where I could block out pain, cold, stress and hunger; the one place where love still lived within me. It was the place I went to talk to Rosie.

Rosie, do you get enough to eat? I hope you have warm clothes and a robe for winter. I pray the work you have isn't as hard as mine. Rosie, can you hear me? I think about you so much. Do you ever think of me? I'm so sorry. Just be strong. I'll come to you. I promise . . . .

CHAPTER 10

Running Stream watched as her daughter snuggled deep inside the thick buffalo robe with the soft hair of the robe pulled up over her nose. Just her closed eyes and that curly tuft of red hair stuck out. The sun was already up but she tried to be quiet to allow the child to get a little more rest. She knew her daughter was awake. But it was so cold, she wanted her to stay deep inside her warm, thick robe as long as possible while she rekindled last night's fire. Running Stream busied herself folding and putting away her sleeping robes. She quietly hummed a tuneless song, poking at the fire until flames started licking at the dry sticks.

She thought of her man, Sharp Knife, as she folded the sleeping robe they shared and wished he would sometimes spend the entire night with her. He slept some nights in the lodge with her, but was usually gone before daylight to the lodge he shared with his father. She was so thankful that now after six winters of being with Sharp Knife, she finally had a child. She thought her world had ended each of the three times her children had been born dead. Now she had such a beautiful daughter.

She could hardly believe her eyes last spring when Sharp Knife brought her daughter to her. Her work stopped as she smiled and gazed once again on the child, now stretching every muscle in her body but keeping her eyes closed to the morning light. Oh, how she enjoyed working with the little girl, teaching her the language and the ways of the People, and how she loved brushing and braiding that beautiful red hair.

She went about her morning chores inside the lodge, organizing her storage bags. Lined along the walls of the rawhide lodge were bags of all sizes made from animal hides containing all of her things. The larger bags held extra sleeping robes and trade blankets. Other bags held her clothes. Several bags held foodstuffs that would not spoil like jerky and the grain she ground from mesquite beans. She would use those later in the winter when food was scarce. Hanging from the lodge poles were small bags stuffed with dried herbs and plants that she used for medicine to cure everything from a tooth ache to fever and infection. Her cooking utensils were kept close to the fire for convenience. Her daughter had recognized a fire-and-soot stained porcelain chamber pot that Sharp Knife had proudly given his wife as a cook pot after a raid on the white settlers far to the south earlier that fall. Nestled next to the fire were several animal bladders housing rendered buffalo fat and honey.

The area along the wall where her fair skinned daughter slept was vacant except for the few items of clothes that she had. That area was her little girl's space to use wisely to store whatever she chose to collect in the future.

She watched the smoke from the fire as it curled to the top of the lodge and escaped through the black, smoke-ringed hole at the highest peak where the lodge poles all came together. Soon the blazing fire would warm the lodge and she would have to shake her daughter to start the day.

Rosie again stretched the muscles of her entire body under her covers and explored her mouth, running her tongue around the new gap where her front tooth used to be. This was the third tooth she had lost. She already felt the new teeth coming in at the bottom where she lost her first two teeth back in the fall. Each time she felt her tooth get really wiggly, she told her grandfather, Laughing Crow. He then went to his medicine pouch along the wall of the lodge where he and Sharp Knife slept and retrieved his clam shells. (They were the same shells she'd seen him use to pull the few stiff hairs from his face.) He pulled her into his lap and told her stories and tickled her to get her to open her mouth, then very carefully but quickly he yanked out the barely-hanging-on tooth. It scared her each time it happened, but it didn't have time to hurt.

As she twisted her tongue between the two teeth on either

side of the gap, she thought about her family. Not the old, white family, she thought about them too, but her new Indian family.

She also thought about her friends. She had many friends to play with and she had learned so much from them. They all thought it a game to help her learn the language of The People and challenged her to learn new words every day. She thought about her girl-friend, Spotted Fawn, and smiled as she suppressed a giggle remembering when Spotted Fawn lost her first tooth and made a silly face to show off the new gap in her mouth. She and Spotted Fawn became friends soon after she arrived to live with The People and Rosie had learned much from her.

Last spring, soon after she came to live with The People, her father, Sharp Knife, asked her grandfather to name her. She didn't understand much of what was happening at the time, but now after learning the language, it all makes sense. Selecting names for people was serious business and only respected elders of the tribe were allowed to do so. For two weeks, she noticed Laughing Crow watching her more closely than normal. When she worked with Running Stream outside the lodge, grinding the seed from mesquite pods or scraping hides, she occasionally looked up to see Laughing Crow standing beside the lodge, leaning on his staff, just watching. He always smiled or made funny faces at her whenever she noticed him watching. Other times when she was playing with the other girls or running and chasing the boys, she occasionally found Laughing Crow passing by where she played.

One evening her mother told her to sit by the fire. "Tomorrow there will be a very special ceremony just for you," Running Stream said, smiling. "You will be given your name and welcomed into the tribe." Rosie didn't understand the words at the time but when her mother reached into a leather bag and pulled out a new, long shirt, skirt and moccasins made of soft, yellow doeskin and decorated with beautiful beadwork, and held them up to her to verify her size, she knew something special would be happening. The garments were beautiful. Rosie fingered the decoration on the moccasins and smiled at Running Stream. She held the jumper to her chest with one hand and reached out to hug Running Stream with her other arm. "Thank you," Rosie said, releasing Running Stream, stroking and admiring the beadwork along the neckline of the shirt.

"Someday we'll understand each other, my little one," Running Stream said as she gently rubbed Rosie's back. Her dark eyes glistened as a tear escaped down her cheek. "Some day soon."

The next afternoon Running Stream took Rosie to the river where they undressed and waded into the shallows. They sat in chest-deep water and Running Stream helped Rosie scrub herself with the fine sand from the river bottom until her skin glowed. She carefully cleaned under and around Rosie's fingernails with a broken twig and washed her hair with the suds generated from a yucca root. After their cold bath, they spread a trade blanket on the ground to lie on to let the summer sun and breeze warm and dry their bodies. As their hair and skin dried in the afternoon sun, Running Stream shaped Rosie's clean fingernails with a small piece of sandstone. She gently removed the tangles and smoothed Rosie's hair with a porcupine quill comb. Before they left the river, Running Stream gathered some fragrant wild mint from the river's edge. When they arrived back at the village, she crushed the mint into a pulp and mixed it with some rendered buffalo fat. She rubbed a small amount of the aromatic mixture between her hands and spread it sparingly through Rosie's hair, adding a delightful, minty fragrance and taming the unruly curls falling over her shoulders. She then helped Rosie dress in her new clothes.

Rosie waited outside the lodge, making sure she didn't get dirty, while Running Stream dressed for the evening. Sharp Knife and Laughing Crow dressed for the ceremony in their lodge. Soon, the men joined Rosie. Her eyes widened in surprise. Both had made a magnificent transition from their regular daily clothing. Their ceremonial clothes were adorned with glass beadwork much like Rosie's. They wore their hair parted in the middle with long braids hanging over their shoulders. Red, yellow, and green ribbons were plaited into their braids and extended well beyond the ends of their hair, hanging beyond their knees and fluttering in the wind as they walked. Round, silver conchos and several eagle feathers were braided into their hair along with the ribbons. Sharp Knife had small bells attached to the outside seams of his leggings from his waist all the way to the ground on both sides so that he made jingling sounds when he walked. Laughing Crow decorated his walking staff with colored ribbons and calico to flap in the breeze. Sharp Knife applied three-inch-long swatches of yellow and red paint on his arms, chest and stomach and painted the lower part of his face yellow. Laughing Crow carried a large, rawhide drum and a drumstick with a round, leather-covered head.

Laughing Crow teased and tickled her as Rosie played with the bells on Sharp Knife's leggings while they waited for Running Stream to join them for the celebration.

Soon Running Stream joined them outside her lodge. She wore a colorful outfit similar to Rosie's with red, yellow and green ribbons braided as a sash around her waist and extending to her knees.

Rosie held Running Stream's hand as they followed Sharp Knife and Laughing Crow through the village and into the council area. Most of the tribe had already arrived for the event and were gathered in small groups talking as Rosie and her family walked into the large meeting area.

Rosie realized that the eyes of the tribe were on her — the new girl with the strange, fire-red hair. She sidled closer to Running Stream and got a tighter grasp on her hand. She couldn't understand what the people were saying, but the way they looked at her, she knew they must be talking about her. She saw a girl about her age and later learned her name was Spotted Fawn, with some other children. Spotted Fawn gave her a wide grin and a wave. Rosie managed a smile and small, timid wave back.

Laughing Crow looked to the west, watching the layers of high clouds as they started to draw colors from the almost setting sun. He smiled, knowing his medicine would be very strong that evening. He waited a few minutes, occasionally glancing at the changing position of the sun while Sharp Knife greeted several men and Running Stream talked to a few women. Glancing at the sun once more, Laughing Crow asked Sharp Knife and Running Stream to sit on the ground behind him. He took Rosie gently by the hand, smiled at her to reassure her and showed her that he wanted her to stand directly in front of him, facing the sun. She looked back at Running Stream, and Running Stream nodded and smiled at her. Laughing Crow slowly bent and placed his walking stick on the ground and picked up his drum. He showed Rosie what he was going to do so she wouldn't be surprised by the noise. He banged the drum loudly and rapidly several times. Then he started tapping a regular rhythm. After several moments he started chanting in a high-pitched wail. Several other drummers picked up his rhythm and joined with their drums.

As he chanted and the drums played, the tribe members quickly began taking their places for the ceremony. Laughing Crow chanted to the gods to put the full power of the sun into the sky. He asked that the sky be filled with color as it drew the sun's power. He repeated his plea to the spirits, watching the setting sun while the entire tribe took their positions on the ground in a large multi-tiered semicircle behind him and his family, all facing the sun. The moment the large, red, fiery ball touched the flat horizon, the drumming stopped. The new silence after the loud drumming left their ears ringing. The entire tribe watched their powerful source of energy sink slowly into the ground, releasing behind it a majestically broadening palette of yellow, gold, orange, red, pink and purple across the sky.

Everyone — men, women and children watched the sun slip silently beneath the earth's surface. The moment the last of the top edge of the fire ball slipped out of sight, Laughing Crow led the entire tribe in a deafening cheer. Men banged drums and people yelled. The women trilled and the men yelped in excitement. Bells and rattles rang out to celebrate the beautiful display of the Spirit's power.

During the noisemaking, Laughing Crow and Rosie changed positions so they were both facing the tribe with Rosie standing directly in front of Laughing Crow. He placed his hands gently on her shoulders. The vivid colors of the western sky continued to spread behind them as Laughing Crow raised his arms for silence.

"The Spirits smile on us tonight," he said with a strong, loud voice, replacing his hands on Rosie's shoulder. "They, as we, are happy. The Spirits that give us life gave us a very good life this spring. The winter was hard. Then the warm power of the fire in the sky returned and with it came the rain. The rain refilled the streams and rivers and gave Mother Earth her strength to once again grow the grass that makes the horses and buffalo fat. The Spirits smile on us in many ways. They give our warriors the strength to defeat our enemies." Several of the young warriors hooted and yelped their affirmation. "They lead our hunters to the buffalo so we can be fed." Again the young warriors yelled their agreement. "They give our young mothers the milk to feed our babies. And when the spirits are especially happy with us, they give us our children. The spirits know that sometimes only a child can fill an empty heart. Hearts were empty in my family because Running Stream and Sharp Knife had no children. Now our hearts are full and happy. The Spirits brought us this child." He squeezed Rosie's shoulders, then gently stroked her hair.

"The Spirits love this child." He patted her shoulder gently. "They put the evening fire in her hair." The strength and volume in his voice increased as he continued. "Look again at the sky!" He raised both arms toward the heavens, now fully aglow in magnificent color. "That is your evening fire!" His hands returned to Rosie's shoulders. "This child's name dances about her head at all times. This is my granddaughter. This is *Evening Fire*. This is the daughter of Running Stream and Sharp Knife. She, like you, is of The People. She is your sister. Welcome your sister, Evening Fire, into your tribe and your heart."

Yells, trilling and yelping again erupted from the tribe as they got to their feet and came to Evening Fire and her family to hug them and formally welcome her into the tribe before the dancing and feasting commenced that would last far into the night.

Evening Fire didn't understand most of the words her new grandfather spoke that night or those of the smiling well-wishers who approached her after his speech, but she had a good, comfortable understanding that she was home and this was family.

Evening Fire continued to lie under her robe even though the lodge was beginning to warm from the fire. She watched her mother work. She loved her mother and knew her mother loved her too. During the months since she'd come to live with The People, her mother constantly talked to her. She patiently taught her the language along with the many jobs she must learn as she told her stories about life with The People. She also told of how much she'd wanted a little girl like Evening Fire to be her daughter. At first, Evening Fire didn't understand much of what was said, but over time, the words and phrases started coming together. Running Stream told her that she had prayed and chanted to the Great Spirit for a child to love, but the three that she had were all born dead. Then, as soon as she saw her husband bring Rosie into camp last spring, she'd immediately loved her. Her mother frequently told her how pretty she was while she combed and braided her long, curly red hair.

Besides the ceremonial clothes, Running Stream made her a set of leggings and a vest of soft doeskin, but during the long, hot days in the summer months, she just usually wore her soft, fringed loincloth and her vest to keep the sun off her tender shoulders and back while she helped her mother work or when she ran and played with the other children. Now, in the winter, she dressed in her everyday shirt and skirt along with her leggings and her high moccasins that reached up her calf.

As she lay there, putting off getting up and dressed, she thought about her father. Sharp Knife spent much of his time away from the family hunting or raiding. When he was in camp, he worked with his horses or sat, smoking and talking with his friends. But she knew her father loved her because when he was home at night in her lodge after eating, he pulled her close to him to tickle her. Then after her fits of giggles, he held her in his lap and stroked her hair while her grandfather told stories.

Laughing Crow told wonderful stories of long ago when the animals all talked and behaved like people. He stretched his wrinkled, old, toothless face into comical shapes and made funny voices as he told stories about coyotes, birds, rabbits, raccoons, rats, deer and buffalo. Usually the stories had a happy ending and solved a problem or taught a positive lesson of life.

Some of the other children had grandmothers living in their lodge with them and enjoyed the extra love of a grandmother as well as a mother. Evening Fire's family didn't have a grandmother, but Evening Fire got plenty of attention and love from the family she had.

Soon after she'd arrived at her new home, she noticed a peculiar trait of The People. The children were never punished or harshly reprimanded. After the treatment she'd received from the Indians who'd captured her, she was sensitive to such things. But with her new tribe, she never saw a child hit, spanked, talked harshly to, or scolded in any way. She did notice, though, that if a child behaved in an especially unacceptable manner, it was usually the grandfather or grandmother who helped the child learn in a patient, kind, and quiet way that there might be better options to their behavior.

As Evening Fire started reaching for her clothes to get

dressed, she thought about her old family. Her life was so different here. She had a full family that loved her here. During the last few months with her old family, she'd had only Andy because both her mother and father were too sick to notice her. And Andy was so worried about them and busy trying to feed them that he really didn't have much time for her either. She spent most of her time just tagging along behind him as he went about his tasks or staying at the cabin, playing by herself. She knew it wasn't her brother's fault that nobody paid her much attention; that's just the way it was.

Here in her new life, she spent hours every day with her mother, learning from her and helping her do the many jobs that women do. But what she really enjoyed was the happy hours when she played with the other children. She looked forward to the times when the mothers and children went to find firewood, berries, roots or seeds to process for food. The children made games of the work so they all had fun and got the job done at the same time.

Occasionally, while in her bed or outside working with her mother, if things got quiet, she found herself thinking about her brother.

She wondered what he was doing. *Was he traded away from the bad Indians to good Indians as I was? Does he have a nice family to live with? It seems like such a long time ago that we were together. And so far away.*

CHAPTER 11
Four years later

I lay curled under the buffalo robe listening to the howling, icy wind outside the lodge and the sleeping sounds of those inside lying around me. Since the weather was so severe and the snow getting deeper, I'd been allowed to sleep inside the lodge. Tonight I was waiting for the sounds of heavy breathing and snoring to finally put my plan in motion.

A stroke of luck had placed me with a small hunting party sixty miles south of the main village in the middle of a blizzard on the trail of buffalo. Coyote Den had refused to go with the dozen hunters and a handful of women to bring back a load of buffalo for the tribe. She'd sent me instead.

The passing years had toughened and matured me. Now eighteen years old, I was taller than Strings Bow Tight and more muscular. The hard work and harsh conditions had strengthened not only my body but my will to survive, escape and find my sister.

Every day I worked and learned the ways of the Comanche, whether I was doing the women's work or helping the men with the horses. I hoped that someday my will to escape would be underestimated and I would be given my opportunity. It had finally happened.

The small hunting party was traveling light, carrying only four lodges but eight extra horses for hauling back the meat and hides from the buffalo we were following.

One of my regular chores was to secure the horses in the evenings. Usually I just hobbled them and let them graze through the night, but with the severe storm getting fiercer, I tied them together with a series of hair ropes, strung between trees in a cedar break downwind from the lodges.

Earlier in the evening, I wrapped several strips of buffalo

meat in a leather bag along with a horse's mouth loop bridle I had stolen and hung it in a tree with the rest of the hides and meat to keep the wolves from taking them.

Sometime after midnight when I was sure everyone was asleep, I slowly rose from the lodge floor and pulled my buffalo robe around my shoulders. I grabbed my leather bag, containing the few tools I was allowed to have and tip-toed to the lodge opening flap. I pulled it aside and quickly stepped out, securing it behind me.

I braced myself against the first sting of icy wind, and trudged through the rapidly building snow, gathering the supplies I had so carefully positioned earlier. Pulling my robe tighter about me, I made my way to the cedars, fifty yards downwind from the quiet cluster of lodges.

The few snorts and neighs the horses gave upon my approach were muffled and carried away by the wind. I worked fast to untie the string of horses from the cedars and arranged three strings of eight horses on each lead rope. Then I fitted the bridle and mounted Strings Bow Tight's prized spotted stallion. I didn't attempt to steal a saddle, as they were all kept inside the lodges, close to the sleeping hunters. After adjusting the buffalo robe to try to block some of the frigid wind and driving snow from my ears and face, I quietly led the entire group of twenty four horses away from the camp. Keeping the north wind to my left, I rode eastward, first at a cautious walk, then a trot. Riding into the open prairie, well out of earshot from the lodges, I pushed the stallion into a gentle lope across the snow-covered flats being careful that I maintained firm control of the string of horses.

By the time daylight brought an overcast and still snowy day, I figured that I was no less than twenty miles from camp. I had a good head start, but by now the Indians knew I had escaped and taken all their horses. Fortunately the blowing snow erased any tracks I left. A smile crossed my face as I visualized the Indians splintering into groups, wading through heavy snow in different directions, trying to find some sign of my trail — and their horses.

I could imagine the rage Strings Bow Tight and the other warriors must feel toward me. A plains warrior considers a man inferior unless he is astride a good horse. They take great pride in stealing horses from their enemies, but to have their own stolen, leaving them afoot was the highest insult I could have given them. I also knew that I put the rest of the tribe in jeopardy because they were already hungry before the hunting party left them to look for buffalo. Now it would take, at best, two days for runners to return to the village through the snow and another day or two of hard riding with replacement horses back to the hunter's camp. By then, I had to distance myself as much as possible from them.

There was no way I could drop my guard or let up on the pace of my escape. I would do whatever it took, including driving my horse and myself to the ground if I had to, before I would allow myself to be captured again.

At mid-day, with at least forty miles separating the horses from their owners, I stopped next to a creek and released all the horses except the spotted stallion and a black gelding that had formerly belonged to a Texas settler. I had ridden both animals, switching back and forth every three or four hours since leaving the camp. Both were strong-muscled and thick-chested and weren't as winded as the others after hours of pushing their way through the snow.

Before I left the creek, I broke through the ice so the horses could drink.

After seeing that the two horses I was riding drank their fill, I mounted the spotted stallion and checked the wind direction. Getting my bearings, I turned my back to the icy wind and kicked the stallion into a lope, this time heading due south.

I rode all day, fighting the desire to ride a hard gallop, trying to be satisfied with a comfortable lope. I changed mounts at mid-afternoon, resting the stallion while I pushed the black gelding. I stopped for a few minutes every hour or so whenever I found a thin spot of snow to let the horses catch their breath and paw through the snow for whatever they could find to graze. I ate on the run, biting off small pieces of raw, frozen buffalo meat from the bag I carried strapped to my waist.

By late afternoon, the snowfall stopped. I allowed the horses to rest for a moment and took a long look behind me. There was a deep trail in the snow that stretched to the horizon — a trail that anyone could follow. Panic overcame me and I kicked my mount into a gallop, trying desperately to put more distance between me and the hell behind me. Soon my compassion for the horses brought me to rein again to a slower pace.

During most of the first night and day on the trail, I managed to ignore the cold. I'd become so used to the beatings inflicted for each minor infraction during my first few years as a slave, I'd learned to block out normal levels of pain. But as the sun went down at the end of my first full day on the trail and the wind picked up again, dry but even more cold, I started feeling the pain of the frigid air. I pulled the robe tighter around my ears and leaned forward along the horse's neck to make a smaller target for the unrelenting wind.

After dark, fatigue was showing on both me and the horses. I continued to push them over the snow-crusted prairie, guiding myself by the glow of the clear, star-studded night. About an hour before daylight I finally allowed myself to rest my head on the mane of the black gelding and close my eyes for a moment or two.

My subconscious took me to another time and place, the same place I had awakened from dozens of times, drenched in sweat, reaching but being held back, helpless to get to my little sister as she was taken away. I called her name over and over, but no sounds came out. They were muffled by her screams. *"Bub, you'd said you'd take care of me! Bubba!"*

I woke as my body flew into the snow. The gelding I had

been astride thrashed about on the ground, trying to rise to his feet. But his left foreleg didn't work anymore. When I ran my hands over his leg, I could tell that the bone had snapped when he stepped into a prairie dog hole. In a few seconds, I put him out of his misery with my skinning knife.

In a few seconds more, I was astride the paint stallion. As the sun came up and reflected off of the snow, I felt the force of the fatigue in my burning, red-rimmed eyes and tried to squint out its brightness.

I continued to rest the sturdy stallion every two hours to graze on the sparse prairie grass and stopped to allow him to drink alongside me at every creek and stream crossing, but every creature has its limits of endurance. That afternoon, three hours before dark, the stallion went to its knees, then toppled to its side and couldn't get up.

I lay on the ground next to the fallen stallion. Exhaustion had taken over every fiber of my being. I softly stroked the neck of the horse that had given everything he had to help me escape from my years of hell and whispered my thanks in his ear.

Out of my extreme desperation to survive and find my sister, I found the determination and strength to push beyond the physical limits I thought I had and somehow managed to pull myself to my feet. Gathering my robe once again around my shoulders, I set my course to the south and started walking.

A red tailed hawk circled in the fading light of dusk above the frozen buffalo grass on his last flight before roosting. He was seeking a careless rodent on its way back to its burrow. Instead he saw a lone figure, bent under a matted brown robe, slowly, mechanically putting one foot in front of the other in a straight, determined path across the darkening, frozen prairie. The hawk watched the figure from above, circling twice, silently gliding through the clear, cold evening air. The only sound across the vast prairie was the slow, rhythmic crunching as worn moccasins broke through the frozen grass with each step. The crunching was interrupted only by the distant echoing screech of the hawk as he lost interest in the human and dipped his wing to silently slide away to his evening perch.

CHAPTER 12

Tad hadn't kept up with Jake on this early morning's hunt as the dog darted, sniffing from one possible varmint hideout to another. Tad was enjoying the walk and found the crisp, mid-February air refreshing. Snow this late in the winter was unusual, but he knew it wouldn't last but a day or two under the clear blue sky and bright sun. He stopped for a minute as he approached the river, listening to the sounds of the fast moving water splashing over the rocks, echoing across the frozen bottom land. Taking in the winter beauty, he took a deep breath and surveyed the thin blanket of snow covering the familiar landscape. He hoped to come across deer tracks, but would be just as happy to bag a couple of rabbits.

He enjoyed being out early in the morning by himself in the late winter without the pressure of planting, harvesting or any of the hundreds of farm chores that couldn't wait in the other seasons. It gave him time to relax and think.

He never thought he would have to take over the farm five years ago at the young age of fifteen when his brother-in-law, Jeff, died fighting Comanches. But now he's comfortable in his role and looking forward to the busy planting season. Back in the old days, Jeff and Mister Will trained him well. Running the farm was hard work, but Jeff built confidence in him at a young age, and as promised, since Jeff's death, Mister Will was always there whenever needed.

His sister, Libby, picked up the pieces of her life after Jeff died and was seeing that their eight year old son, Billy, was challenged with his lessons every day. After her husband's death, she had dedicated herself to seeing that Jeff's dream of educating his family was being fulfilled.

Jake's barking brought Tad out of his thoughts when the

dog picked up a scent and raced away toward a heavy thicket next to the river. Tad followed at a trot and found Jake running back and forth next to the dense thicket, growling in a low voice with his hackles raised and a hesitation to go after something he couldn't identify.

"Calm down, boy," Tad whispered, stroking the dog's neck, "We'll find out what we've cornered soon enough."

He approached the thicket, circling the area carefully looking for tracks. The recent dusting of snow that fell shortly before daylight appeared to be undisturbed.

Cautiously he began to push the brush aside with his left hand. He cocked the hammer on his rifle and checked the load as he pushed deeper into the thicket.

It could be a cougar or maybe a bobcat waiting to lunge, Tad thought. *Might even be a sick or injured animal that crawled away to die.* Carefully he pushed another handful of brush aside, sucked in his breath and froze his finger next to his trigger. He'd uncovered a large, brown, furry lump.

Tad aimed his rifle at the object, thinking at first it was a dead or dying bear. Then he saw the toes of a pair of worn moccasins sticking from one end of what he finally recognized as a buffalo hide. *Could a wounded or dying Indian be in there?* Positioning the rifle tightly against his shoulder, he peered down its barrel to the figure. Slowly, he took several side steps around the dark lump to the end opposite the moccasins. A tangled tuft of curly red hair revealed itself from underneath the buffalo robe.

He carefully released the hammer of his rifle and shoved the barrel against the side of the head snuggled inside the hide. "Hey, Hey! You alive?" He took a half step back, waiting for a response.

There was a slight stirring under the hide.

Tad moved further back out of reach. He yelled again, louder this time, "All right, come out of there! Show your face! Come on! I'll shoot you right there if you don't show yourself!"

Tad took another step away from the object on the ground when it started moving. His finger eased away from the trigger as he watched the hide move. Grimy fingers closed around the edge of the hide and pulled it down to uncover the face of a filthy white youth, younger than himself, who looked more dead than alive. His skin was dirty beyond belief with bits of dried blood around his mouth and in his thin beard and caked on his hands. Although he was darkened and reddened by exposure to the sun, wind and weather, there was no doubt that he was a teen-aged, white boy when he revealed more of the dirty red hair and opened his red rimmed, blood-shot blue eyes.

Noise . . . What's that noise? Oh God! Why don't they just kill me? I tried to push the fleeting thought away and pulled myself farther into the warmth of the hide. *There . . . I hear it again.*

Exhausted, I started trying to make sense of the words from a language I hadn't heard in such a long time. *The words! I know those words!*

I slowly reached for the edge of the robe and pulled it away from my face and looked up at a young, dark skinned man pointing a rifle at me. I tried to untangle the cobwebs from my worn-out mind to speak. My mouth moved several times as I tried to form words that I hadn't spoken for so long. I finally got out a sound, barely above a whisper. "Pl . . . please . . . ." I moved my tongue over my cracked lips and tried to make the words again. I managed to pull my hand from under the hide and reached toward the man above me. A halting, scratchy sound came from my throat, "Please please help me."

"Libby! Libby, open the door!" Tad shouted, walking briskly, approaching the cabin, carrying the young man in his arms. As he stepped onto the porch, Libby flung the door open wide, her mouth gaping in surprise as Tad walked past her with the unconscious youth. He put him on her bed. "I'm afraid he's mighty dirty and smells rank, but he needs our help."

Libby blinked herself back to her senses. "Wh . . . Where did you find him? Who is he?"

"I don't know, Lib. I just found him out in the woods, just about like that, wrapped up in a buffalo hide! You think he'll die?"

Libby moved to the bed and took the young man's dirty, calloused hand in the soft skin of her own and stroked it for a moment as she looked into his dirty face. "Not if I have anything to do with it," she said quietly. Her voice then took on the tone of authority that Tad was used to when she had an important job to do. "Get some water going in the kettle, then get back here and take his clothes off. I'll get some soup going. We've gotta save this boy."

The Jefferson cabin came to life. Billy watched as his mother and uncle scurried around the strange young man on the bed.

Libby stayed close to her patient's bedside most of the time for two full days. She was away only to look after Billy and to take care of meals for her family. She spent the nights sitting in a straight-backed chair at the side of the fluffed up bed, watching her patient sleep, wondering who he was, where he'd come from and how he'd ended up barely alive, hiding in a thicket a quarter mile from her cabin. She sat for hours with the wick turned down in the lamp across the room, watching his face in the flickering light. She studied the line of his jaw as he gritted his teeth in his sleep and watched the wrinkle on his brow when he tossed about fitfully. She bathed his face and head while he sweated out the demons that were causing him so much anguish. Every few hours she managed to get a little more warm soup down him.

Libby woke with a start, feeling that she was being watched. Just as she realized that she must have dozed off a little before daylight, she saw him lying there quietly, looking at her. "Well, look at you," she said, sitting up straighter in her chair and blinking away sleep. "You're finally awake." She moved her chair next to the bed and smiled at seeing the boy responding to her care. "How do you feel?"

I had quietly watched the woman sitting next to me and studied her face before she awoke. *Who was this woman with thick eyelashes and soft, smooth, dark skin?* I looked around, trying to understand my surroundings. *A room. A real room with walls and a window.* Seeing her awake, I spoke, slowly and carefully forming the words.

"Wh . . . where am I?" I found myself struggling with the words, still bewildered as to my whereabouts.

"You're in the north end of Austin's colony in Texas. We're on the west side of the Brazos River. I'm Libby Jefferson. My brother, Tad, found you and brought you here. That was day before yesterday. You looked pretty far gone then. I don't know where you've come from or how long you've been there, but from the way you were dressed when Tad found you, I'd guess you were with the Indians." She smiled at me showing even, white teeth and sparkling dark eyes.

"You'll meet my boy Billy in a little while. He frequently drops in on you to see how you're doing. He and Tad are out taking care of morning chores." She stood. "I imagine you're getting hungry by now. All I've been able to get down you has been a little soup from time to time. Do you think you could eat some breakfast?"

I nodded and watched the attentive woman leave my bedside. I tried to collect my thoughts to understand why I was where I was. Slowly, it all started coming back.

First it was Rosie as I always saw her in my dreams, screaming for me, pleading with me to help her as she was being taken by the traders. Next I remembered begging Papa to run with Rosie and me from the Mexicans. Then it was Rosie again with the vacant look of shock after I buried Mama and Papa. One after the other, visions of the heartbreak, anguish, degradation and abuse of the last four years flashed through my mind.

I could no longer contain my emotions as I was overcome by the pain deep inside me. I muffled the sobs that shook my body with the pillow, unable to push the haunting memories away. The years of being racked with guilt for losing Rosie, enduring the physical abuse at the hands of my masters, losing Mama and Papa to the Mexicans, and surviving it all was more than I could handle. I cried for the relief of finding my way to the safety and comfort of civilization.

I sensed a presence in the room watching me, then felt the gentle touch of Libby, at first tentatively stroking my arm, then gathering me into her arms and holding me, comforting me as she would a child. She gently rocked back and forth shushing and whispering over and over that everything would be all right. After I exhausted all the pent-up feelings that I'd held inside for so long, I lay drained and breathless on the bed.

Libby sat next to me, now stroking my hand. "Maybe I know a little about how you feel. I've been through some heartache too. I don't know what you've been through or how bad it was." She looked into my eyes. "I guess I really don't know anything about you except that you're hurting and you need help and a couple of friends. I don't even know your name, but I'd like to offer myself and my family as friends."

I raised my face to look into her expressive, friendly eyes. "An . . . dy . . . Andy Bristow." I found myself struggling, saying my own name. "I just . . . c . . . came back from . . . from living in hell. Th . . . Thank you . . . Thank you, for giving me a . . . a piece of heaven."

CHAPTER 13

Under Libby's care and good food, I started regaining my strength. It took only another day before I was on my feet.

"Why look at you," she said the first time that I stood up from the bed. "It's about time you got up and stretched those muscles. We'll have you out and about in no time." She came closer and looked me up and down. She raised an eyebrow and said, "Now, we can't have you spending the rest of your life in Tad's old night shirt. You stay right there." She left the room and in a few minutes returned with a handful of Tad's clothes. First, she held a shirt up next to me. She stretched it across my shoulders and then measured the sleeves against my arms. "I believe that will do," she said, throwing it over a chair. "Now, let's see about the pants." She grabbed a pair of Tad's worn out work pants and measured them against me. "Uh huh," she muttered moving around, stretching the pants against my legs and waist. "A little shorter in the legs and a little smaller in the waist. Shouldn't be a problem."

While she was measuring me for clothes, Billy brought in a porcelain wash pan and a bucket of warm water.

"Tad cleaned you up as best he could shortly after you got here," Libby said, "but I suspect you may want to wash up, now that you're feeling better." She motioned toward the dressing table. "There's soap there by the pan and towels on the other side. There's also a fresh nightshirt in the bed-side table. I'll have your clothes ready for you tomorrow." She reached for my cheek and rubbed the back of her fingers against the thin growth of whiskers on my cheek and chin. "I'll be happy to give you a shave and a haircut, if you like."

I reached for one of the long braids of hair hanging over my shoulder. Looking at it, then throwing it back over my shoulder, I said, "I'd be happy to get rid of these, and I'd really like to have a shave."

By early afternoon of the next day, after an expert shave with a sharp razor and a skilled haircut and shampoo leaving my once long, braided, red hair now collar length and my curls more or less under control, I felt like a new person. Libby also presented me with a new pair of yellow deerskin pants and one of Tad's cotton shirts he had outgrown before it wore out. I don't know how she found time, but she also stitched together a new pair of moccasins during the hours that I slept.

As I regained my strength, I spent a few hours trying to remember how to read from books that Billy brought me until I learned how much he enjoyed reading out loud. His reading was not only entertaining to me, but hearing him read helped bring the language back to me that I had almost forgotten. He read from a small book of poetry and from a medical anatomy book with illustrations. He even enjoyed reading from a dictionary. What a bright boy he was. I was surprised at his advanced reading ability for his age and his appetite for learning. I especially enjoyed listening to him read from the Bible. It brought back memories of the Bible stories Mama told when I was a child. Also, after Libby finished her chores, she told me and Billy of the life of the Jeffersons and the Bowmans since the war for Independence.

"You know, Andy," she said, "just about everybody got burned out by the Mexican army after the fall of the Alamo. That army killing, looting and burning everything in sight started what some Texans call the Great Runaway." Her eyes took on a faraway look as her memory guided her words. "I heard later that there were almost thirty thousand of us, mostly women and children. Some old people too. Lots of sick folks. War refugees, I guess you'd call us. We were all trying to get out of Texas ahead of the Mexicans." She sighed, slowly shook her head and twisted a handkerchief in her fingers as she recalled the story. "Some had teams of horses or oxen and wagons. Some had their belongings in pushcarts, and some were just escaping for their lives on foot. Oh, the conditions were terrible. It rained hard for days and all the creeks and rivers were flooded. Mud — my God, I've never seen the likes of that mud. It was hub deep on the wagon wheels in some places. Lines of people and their belongings were miles long waiting to get on the ferries to get across the flooded rivers. There were more than a few —" her voice caught in her throat and her eyes misted for a moment before she continued, "graves dug in that mud for those young and old that just couldn't handle the terrible conditions. We were on the road two weeks and traveled over a hundred and fifty miles before we got to safety beyond the Sabine River, into the United States.

"Then after Jeff and Will Bowman helped Sam Houston and his army win the war, we came home to start over. We worked together with the Bowmans, as we always did, to rebuild."

She lifted her eyes to look around the room and a slight smile tilted the corner of her mouth at the sight of her comfortable surroundings. "This house was built first. Then, when ours was finished, we started on the Bowman's place once the new sawmill was installed down river."

Her eyes took on a sad, distant look. "It was while Will and Tad were away, hauling the first load of lumber from the saw mill that we lost Jeff in a Comanche raid. But we've never been able to find his body."

What an interesting group of people I've fallen into, I thought. *They're so different from me in some ways, but we're so much alike in many others. They've certainly had their hardships.* I couldn't help but feel a special bond with Libby and Tad because of slavery. Even though Libby told me that she'd had a good master who treated his people well, I understood her sadness that came through her voice and her eyes when she spoke of the slavery days. On the other hand, Libby could only have a small understanding of the physical pain and mental anguish that I had suffered as a slave at the hands of the Comanches. I was still unable to discuss my sister without fighting back tears, even after several days of talking with Libby, Tad and Billy about my life with the Comanches.

Regaining my strength was fueled not only by Libby's food,

care and attention, but also by the promise I'd made to Rosie and myself. That promise had carried me through the years of abuse, pain and misery while I was held captive and during my escape. The vow I'd made long ago was still as strong as ever. As long as I breathe in air, I'll never give up the idea of finding Rosie.

I knew it wouldn't be easy and I'd be starting with nothing. I'd have to outfit myself with everything I'd need to find her. I also knew I'd have to be better than the Indians at tracking, riding, and shooting.

I learned from the warriors when they returned from raids that some whites fought with a new handgun that fired several rounds without reloading. If I could get a weapon like that and learn how to use it well, I'll have a better-than-even chance of surviving an Indian fight. I also knew I'll have to find a good teacher to train me.

From everything Libby and Tad had told me, it appeared that Will Bowman might have the skills I needed to help me learn what I should know to be able to bring Rosie back. Libby told me about his military training as a young man in Virginia and how he and Jeff fought the Mexicans in the war. Then Tad related a couple of stories about fighting Indians with Bowman on the plains. Bowman seemed to be the best man in this part of the country to teach a young man how to fight anybody and survive to tell about it. I was looking forward to meeting this Mister Bowman.

About a week after Tad brought me home, the two of us sat on the edge of the porch after supper. Jake was stretched out between us and I started scratching his ears.

"You look like you're getting stronger," Tad said after we sat quietly for a few moments enjoying a warm, late winter evening.

"Thanks to you and Libby." I looked at the ground. "My talking is . . . is, uh, isn't too good. It's been a long time. I don't know how I can pay you . . . you and Libby for what you've done."

"Don't worry about your talking, you're doing fine and getting better every day. And no thanks necessary and certainly no pay for helping you. We just do what needs to be done out here. Anybody would have done the same. There's not very many of us around here, so we take care and look out for each other.

"Oh, there are some folks around that don't like the idea of free colored people living around them, working their own land." He glanced at me, "But for every one of them, there were several that went with me and Mister Will to try to find Jeff when the Comanches got him. For all they know, the next time we have an Indian raid, it might be one of their own who gets stolen or killed and they'll need my help."

"How did you and Miss Libby get free, anyhow?" I asked, not quite so conscious of my words. "I never knew free, uh, what's the word? C . . . colored folks. Fact is, hadn't known any colored folks till I met you. The farms along our river were about like yours, just folks struggling to get by. Nobody had field hands. No servants."

"Two reasons, I guess — we were owned by a good man, and he was influenced by Jeff.

You know, Mister Will freed Jeff before they got to Texas. I believe our old master was so impressed knowing Jeff and how he was educating himself and had the ability to make a good living, he decided to leave it in his will to set his slaves free when he died." Tad's teeth flashed in a smile. "That sure came as a surprise to all of us," he said. "Libby and Jeff were already married then. The old master knew Libby and I would have a good life with Jeff if we were free.

"He knew Jeff had the drive and ambition to make a success of himself and his family. Even though Jeff's gone, Libby, Billy and I aren't going to let them down. We're not going to let a war or some Indians or the weather or anything keep us from finishing what Jeff set out to do."

"And what's that?"

"Make a success of this farm and see that Billy gets the best education possible. Oh boy, I've never seen anyone as driven as Libby is to see that those two goals are met. Since Jeff's whole family was free and we owned our land because of the land grant laws, he did whatever it took for us to be educated. Jeff worked hard to educate himself after Mister Will gave him his freedom. He taught Libby and me to read and write and we've gone on to many other things since then, but he wanted so much more for his son."

"From what I've seen, looks like Billy's taken to his studies," I said.

"You're right. Billy, as young as he is, shows a real interest and lots of promise. Every time Mister Will goes to San Felipe or San Antonio, he brings back everything he can find to read that the boy hasn't already gone through."

"That Mister Will," Tad smiled, "he kind of likes to know that everything's all right with us. It's just how things were with him and Jeff. They looked after each other. We could handle things on our on I guess, but we all like it this way. We're all kind of like a big family here. I guess it's kind of hard for other white folks to understand the relationship we have with the Bowmans. We even work our fields together as a family and share alike."

Their conversation was interrupted by the sound of a rider approaching the cabin.

"Mister Will!" Tad called out as he recognized the tall, erect form of Will Bowman approaching in the fading light on his large, white gelding. "We were just talking about you."

"I hope there's some good to it," the man in his early thirties chuckled as he swung out of the saddle. He approached me and introduced himself. "Looks like Libby's cooking and good care has you on the mend," he said. "I knew you were in good hands with Libby so I haven't bothered you while you were getting well. I figured I'd let you get to feeling a little better before I asked whether there's anything I can do to help you find your family."

I paused a moment staring at the ground, then looked into Will's rugged face. "Don't really have no family 'cept my sister. Just don't know where she is. She's out there with the People, uh, Comanches, somewhere."

"You mean you don't have anybody? Uncles, aunts, grandparents?"

"None that I know of. Might be somebody back east, but I wouldn't know where. I was just a little kid when we came to Texas."

"I guess you aren't the first young man out on your own in a frontier like this. Jeff and I were only a few years older than you when we struck out toward Texas from Virginia. 'Course we had weapons, supplies and a plan."

"I've got a plan, Mister Bowman. I just need time to earn my way to get supplies."

"No need to call me Mister Bowman, Will is good enough for my friends. I just never have been able to get Tad to call me anything but Mister Will. I guess old habits die hard." Will smiled at a grinning Tad. Turning back to me, Will asked, "And what might that plan be?"

"Find my sister and bring her back."

Will looked at me for a moment, then reached down from the porch and broke off a dried twig from a weed. He stuck it in his mouth to chew before he answered. "Don't guess I need to tell you what a big job that'll be."

I shook my head. "No sir, I know what I'm up against. I lived with 'em for four years. I know their ways. I also know there's at least a whole tribe out there that would love to see me dead. I made a lot of trouble for them when I ran off. They were hungry in the dead of winter and I stole all their horses — their only means to get meat back to their tribe. I'm still surprised they didn't chase me to the end of the earth to see me dead."

"Andy," Will said, "if we had a trail to follow I'd round up some boys and take off looking for your sister right now, but from what Libby told me, the last time you saw her was right after you were captured. She could be anywhere now. I've been out several times during the last few years with neighbors, chasing down Comanche raiding parties. We tracked some down, and we killed a few, but we saw no signs of white children."

"I saw some Mexican kids with other tribes we met up with along the way," I said, remembering several instances of seeing other young slaves over the years, "but I never saw any other whites. I reckon there's more than just me and Rosie."

"There are," Will said. "We know there are white women and children who've been stolen by the Comanches scattered all over the Texas plains. The last time I talked with anybody about it down at San Felipe, I was told that there are documented cases of over forty-five white women and children that have been stolen from the settlements and not accounted for."

"At least," Tad commented.

Will continued, "And that doesn't even include the colored slaves and Mexicans that have been taken. Nobody knows what happened to them. I'm sure many of them ended up as slaves like you or became part of the tribe, if they're still alive.

"Andy, I'm afraid what it's going to take is a force stronger than a few neighbors searching to find them. I know you want to find your sister, but I'm afraid it's gonna take a while to get the means to do so."

I looked at the ground and ran my fingers through my hair. "I know you're right," I said "but I hate to think of Rosie being with them any longer than she has to. It's just hard to be . . . uh . . . patient when I know how she may be living — if she's still alive."

"I understand," Will said, taking his hat off and wiping the inside of his sweatband, "You're gonna need a good horse, a saddle, and a kit of supplies along with your bedroll. You'll need at least a couple of handguns, a good knife, and maybe even a rifle for Indian fighting. It's gonna take time and money to get everything together."

"Yeah, I know," I said, slowly shaking my head. "Right now I don't have anything — nothing to call my own."

"You know, Andy, maybe there's a way we can help each other. I'm sure that Tad will agree with me that it seems like we always need good help around here." Tad raised his eyebrows, nodding his agreement. Will continued. "The Bowmans and the Jeffersons work our places together. Have ever since Jeff and I settled here. If you want to stay awhile and help us with the work, we'll pay you a fair wage and promise you plenty of work, a clean, comfortable place to stay and plenty of good food. I'm sure you're welcome to stay here at the Jefferson place, or, you're just as welcome at our place. We have the next place to the north, up river. You'll meet my wife, Anna, and our children soon enough. Of course we wouldn't expect you to start working till you get your strength back. But I imagine from the way Libby sets a table, it won't take long for that."

Overwhelmed by the kindness around me, I was almost speechless. I thought I had just stumbled onto a couple of nice families that were taking care of me like they would an injured animal. I just kind of expected that I'd be on my way as soon as I was able.

I looked at Tad to make sure he agreed with Will. Tad's dark eyes met my gaze and he returned a smile and a nod and clutched my shoulder, squeezing it gently to seal the agreement.

"I'm a good hand," I said, looking earnestly at Will. "I ran our place by myself for the last year after papa got too sick to work, before the Mexicans came. I can do anything any other man can do."

"Does that mean you'll stay?" Will asked, grinning.

"If you'll have me," I said with a wide smile crossing my face. "I'll stay and work hard for you. I'm used to hard work. And if they'll put me up, I'll stay here with Tad and Libby." I paused, looking Will in the eyes and taking on a more serious expression. "I'd just like to ask for one other thing."

"What's that?" Will asked.

"Will you teach me everything you know about fighting Indians?"

"I'll be happy to," Will said, patting me on the back, "but I imagine Tad and I can learn a lot from you."

CHAPTER 14

Three days later, Will surprised me with another visit to the Jefferson home. He found me and Tad in the work shed behind the cabin, repairing harnesses. He reined up and slid off his saddle. "Morning boys," he said, tying his reins to a corner post. "Looks like you're getting the leathers and chains ready for plowing."

"Yeah," Tad said. "Andy sure knows his business with this leather. He ran his fingers along a repair of the harness leathers. Some of this old stuff wouldn't have lasted a week out in the fields. Thanks to Andy, we'll be ready for plantin'."

"I guess you could say I've had a little experience with leather the last few years," I said quietly, a little embarrassed by the compliment.

"Looks like we're all thinking about planting." Will said. "Just thought I'd stop by and let you know that I'm planning a trip to San Felipe tomorrow to pick up a load of cotton seed. Planting time is still a few weeks away but I want to have the seed available as soon as the ground's ready. Andy, I thought if you feel up to it, maybe you'd like to ride along with me."

"I'd really like that," I said, swelling with excitement. "Been a long time since I've seen a civilized town."

Will chuckled. "It's not much, but I reckon San Felipe could qualify as civilized, more or less. We could also get the word out about your sister. If anybody's sighted a red-headed captive girl with any of the Comanches, maybe they'd have some idea of where she is."

Turning to Tad, Will changed the subject, "How ambitious do you wanta get with planting cotton this year? You think we're ready to do more than the sixty acres we did last year?"

Tad stared off into space for a moment as if he was visualizing the un-worked grassland beyond their cotton fields. "I believe we could turn and break another ten or fifteen acres before plantin' time," Tad said thoughtfully. "You want to plan on seventy-five in cotton this year?"

"With the extra help from Andy and if we add some extra time to picking, I believe we can handle it. Last time I heard, the price is still up from last year. So, seventy-five acres it is. How about the corn? You want to stick with the same twenty-five acres that we did last year?"

"Yeah, with all the extra cotton, we'd better leave the corn the same."

"I agree," Will said. "I suspect we'll have our hands full with the cotton."

Will turned to lead his horse to the cabin. "I'll let Libby know that Anna and the children will be over in the morning. Andy, my wife won't be using her mare, so you can ride her. We'll bring her saddled up and ready to go. See you after breakfast tomorrow."

The next morning, I heard riders approaching and called Tad, Libby and Billy to greet the Bowmans as they reached the cabin porch. Will introduced his family to me before they dismounted. Anna, his pretty, dark haired wife shared the saddle on her mare with their five year old daughter, Texanna. Little three-year-old Jeff was riding in front of his father on Will's white gelding. Will led one of their mules harnessed with a pack frame.

After introductions and the Bowmans dismounted, Libby asked me, "Are you sure you're up to the trip?"

"As ready as I'll ever be." I smiled, anxious to be in a saddle.

"I think this boy's beginning to get cabin fever," Libby said with a smile.

"It feels good to be up and around, thanks to you."

Anna stroked her mare's mane and handed me the reins. I swung into the saddle. "She's an even-tempered mare," she said. "You shouldn't have any trouble with her."

"Thanks, Ma'am. I'll take good care of her." I tied a bag of food that Libby had prepared to the saddle horn.

"With everything you need to bring back, I'm surprised you aren't taking one of the wagons," Libby said to Will.

"I started to, but I realized how much it would slow us down. With just the two of us, we can make much better time on horse back. We can spread the load between the mule and the two saddle horses on the way back."

Will turned to Tad. "You have plenty of ball and powder, don't you?"

"Yes sir. That's something we keep plenty of. But better bring back an extra measure anyway. No need to worry. Everybody's gonna be just fine. We'll all stick close to the cabin."

Will smiled at Tad and squeezed his arm. "I know everything will be fine in your hands." He then squatted down in front of the children. "Now you three behave and mind your mothers and Tad. You understand?"

"Yes sir," They said in unison.

Will scooped all three into his arms and squeezed them. Then he slid his arms around Anna and smiled. "And you . . ." He looked her in the eyes and smiled. He held her close and kissed her on the cheek. He didn't need to tell her he loved her. It was in his eyes.

"We'll have plenty to do to keep us busy," Anna said.

Will hugged Libby. "Anything special you want while we're in town?"

"Bring back some heavy cotton fabric for trousers for this boy if they have any," she said, motioning to Tad. "I swear, I never can keep him in pants. I thought he'd stop growing by now."

"I'll see what I can do," Will said, winking at Tad.

Will stepped into the stirrup, swung his leg over and slid into the saddle. "We'll be back as soon as we can." He and I reined the horses away from the cabin and toward the trail.

I enjoyed the trip to San Felipe with Will after so many days cooped up in the Jefferson cabin. I felt fine for the last few days, but Libby insisted that I stay inside most of the time. When I did get out, I helped Tad with the chores around the place. Now on the trail heading south, the openness and freshness of the early spring air felt wonderful. During the hours alone with Will, I found him open and easy to talk to. His friendliness invited hundreds of questions from me. I was hungry for information about the world beyond the Comanche villages. I wanted to know what had happened with the Mexican army. What little I knew of the revolution, I had learned from Libby.

Will reminisced. "We lost some fine men there in San Antonio at the Alamo. Then the massacre at Goliad, another mission fortress south of San Antonio, was a terrible loss. Over three hundred unarmed men were killed there by the Mexican army when our boys honorably surrendered after they lost a fight. You can imagine how fired up we were with Houston's army when we finally got a chance to fight Santa Anna at San Jacinto. We won that battle and finished the war, but not before the Mexican army looted and burned much of our country."

I was quiet for a moment, remembering my own losses. "I guess that's when our troubles started — mine and Rosie's." I reflected a few moments and then went on to tell Will of the murder of Mama and Papa and the burning of our home by the Mexican army."

"Andy," Will said, sighing and slowly shaking his head, "it's a terrible thing that happened to your mama and papa. It's folks like that who are the real victims of war; the ones that can't help themselves. They were in the wrong place at the wrong time and didn't have the capability to get away. I lost some good friends and neighbors at the Alamo. That's the horrible side of war. The other side is that we won our independence from Mexico.

"After the war, almost every Texan returned to their land for a new start to rebuild their homes and their lives. Of course that included General Sam Houston. After he got his bullet wound from the final battle of the war patched up in New Orleans, he came back to a hero's welcome and was offered the presidency of the republic, which he accepted. His term lasted till 1838, and then President Lamar took office. He's still the president now."

"So what's this Lamar's attitude toward the Indians?" I asked. "Is he sending anybody out there looking for captives like my sister?"

"I wouldn't say they are specifically looking for captives, but I've heard that he's authorized the formation of these so called Ranger companies that go out beyond the settlements, looking for Indian raiding parties, protecting the farmers and fighting Indians where they find them."

We rode into San Felipe in the early afternoon the next day, and as I learned was Will's custom, we stopped at Sam Williams' land office. Mister Williams had been Stephen Austin's partner during the Mexican land grant period. Williams and Austin ran the land company that brought Will to Texas as a surveyor. Williams carried on the business after Austin's death shortly after the war. Whenever there was news from around the settlements, the courier always brought the news to the land office first.

"Well, look who's here," the balding, middle aged man said when Will pushed the door open to the unpainted wooden building. Williams greeted Will with a broad smile and a firm handshake. "Come on in Will and have a seat. Who's your friend?"

I shook Williams' hand as Will introduced us. After we sat down Will said, "Sam, Tad found Andy in the woods almost two weeks ago, more than half-dead after escaping from the Comanches. He got away during a snow storm way up north and made it to Tad's and Libby's place before he finally gave out. He probably traveled somewhere over two hundred and fifty miles. He was captured just after the fight at the Alamo."

"Good God, Son! How did you manage to stay alive so long?" Williams asked, now sitting on the edge of his chair.

"I just tried to give them what they wanted. I worked hard and managed to endure their beatings and abuse. I carried a load all day when we traveled — sometimes more than they'd load on a horse. They valued their horses more than their slaves. I learned not to antagonize them. I just tried to become invisible while I did my work and looked for an opportunity to escape."

"How many times did you try to escape before you actually succeeded?" Williams asked.

"None, I knew if I wasn't successful I'd be killed without question. I had to wait till I had a perfect plan before I was willing to try."

"You're a very lucky young man to be alive," Williams said.

"Yes sir, I know that, but I don't know if my sister has been so lucky. She was traded away from me right after we were captured. She was only seven years old then. I haven't seen her since. I was hoping somebody may have spotted her with the Comanches."

Williams hesitated a moment before he answered. "Son, I'm afraid there's very little word that ever comes back about white captives once they're gone unless on the rare occasion somebody like you escapes. Then we only hear about the captives of that particular tribe. We never can get a fix on them. As you know, they're always on the move."

"But she would be noticed, sir. She's got curly red hair, same as mine." I ran my fingers through my hair.

"I'd have to admit she'd stand out in a crowd of Indians with hair like yours," Williams said, staring at my unruly curls. "I'm sorry, Andy. I haven't heard of any sightings of your sister. I'll have to say, though, that your coming to town today couldn't have been at a better time from some news I got yesterday."

"Why's that?"

"A rider came through town yesterday afternoon telling about a council that's been set up between a bunch of the Comanche chiefs and some representatives from Lamar's government. As you know, Will, Houston tried to get some peace talks going back in '37, but it never came together. But for some reason, three Comanche chiefs rode into San Antonio, I guess it was about ten days ago and offered to parley. Colonel Karnes, he's the Texas government representative in San Antonio, agreed to talk with them on one condition — the Indians must return all white captives *before* any talks begin."

"Did they agree?" I asked, trying to control the excitement in my voice.

"Yeah, they did."

I could hardly contain myself. I wanted to jump for joy, but waited to hear the rest of the agreement.

Williams continued. "They agreed to return within twenty days, which should put it around March 19. That's less than a week away. Looks like you'd have time to make it there if you leave today."

My gaze darted to Will. "Will, I've got to go. Will you go with me?"

He thought a moment then answered, "Yes, yes we'll go, but we've got to get word back home that we're delayed." He hesitated a moment, trying to figure out how he would get his message back home. "We'll work it out . . . yes, we'll go."

I stood and reached across the desk to shake William's hand. Pumping his hand and trying to hold back fits of laughter mixed with tightness in my throat caused by a swelling of tears of joy, I managed to say, "Mister Williams, that's the best news I've heard in a long time. Thanks a lot."

"You're welcome, Andy. I hope they bring your sister in."

"It looks like we're ready to go," Will said, grinning, reacting to my excitement. He rose from his chair, put on his hat and shook hands with Williams. "Sam, thanks for the good news. We'll fill you in on the details of the council when we get back."

Will followed me out the door. Once outside, I almost exploded with joy: "Can you believe it, Will? Can you believe it? They're bringing in all the captives!"

"Now wait a minute, Andy. Just take it easy." Will stopped and faced me after we stepped off the porch into the street next to the hitching rail and the horses. "I don't mean to dash your hopes, but you haven't seen or heard from your sister for four years. I know you don't want to think of the possibility that she may not be living, but it exists. The point I'm making here is that I don't want to see you get too worked up over this. If we find your sister at San

Antonio, then that's wonderful. We can all go on with our lives. If we don't, then you can go on with your plans to find her. We'll just have to see what happens at San Antonio."

"I know . . . I, uh, know what you're saying." I nodded, still pumped up with hope, but trying to calm myself. "But Will, this may be the closest I've been to her. Maybe, just maybe . . . ."

I used the discipline that I'd learned to block out pain and fear inflicted by the Comanches to further calm myself as we walked across the street to the general store. Will helped me select a wide brim felt hat to control my curls and keep the sun off my face. When I put it on, I felt more like a white man and less like an Indian. We also got additional provisions that would see us through our trip to San Antonio. After we filled the list of supplies for the farm and put in our order for the cotton seed for the return trip to Virginia Point, Will asked about firearms.

"I can't keep that new Colt five-shooter in stock, the one they call the Patterson Texas," the shopkeeper said, shaking his head. "The factory only lets me order a dozen at a time, and I usually have 'em sold before I even receive 'em."

"When do you expect your next delivery?" Will asked.

"Any day now. Actually, they're over-due. Could be tomorrow; could be next week."

"Do you have three on that order that haven't been sold?"

"Let me check my paperwork here and see." The shopkeeper referred to a stack of papers behind the counter and in a few moments indicated that there were at least three that had not been spoken for.

"You just sold three of them when you get them," Will said and gave him cash to reserve the pistols. "We've got to take care of some business in San Antonio. We'll pick them up on our way back when we stop to get our seed."

"You goin' down there for the Comanche council?" The shopkeeper asked. "That's been the talk of the town the last couple of days. I've already talked to several fellers headin' thataway."

"They've got this boy's sister," Will answered, "and he was a captive himself till just recently. We're going to see if his sister is among the ones they bring in. By the way, you wouldn't know of anybody in town who might be headed north along the Brazos any time soon, would you?"

"Maybe, if they're still here." The shopkeeper rubbed the stubble on his chin. "There was a couple of brothers in here a little earlier from up river, somewhere below your place, I reckon. They said they're headin' back today after they get their mounts shod. They might still be over at the livery."

"Much obliged," Will said over his shoulder as he and I waved, hurrying out the door.

We found the Anderson bothers at the blacksmith's shed, next to the livery, just finishing their business before heading north. They readily agreed to pass the message of our delayed return to Anna, Libby and Tad. Even though the errand added almost another full day to their trip, they refused payment for their effort.

After making arrangements with the blacksmith to look after the pack mule, Will and I turned our horses to the San Antonio road and headed into the afternoon sun.

CHAPTER 15

We arrived in San Antonio just before sundown on the day before the Comanches were to arrive with their captives. There were no rooms available in town due to the recent influx of people from the settlements hoping to find their loved ones among the Indians. Clusters of people camped along the river just north of town. We selected a spot to camp next to a group of men who appeared to be traveling together. I counted eleven men lounging under the shade of a live oak tree. Some were playing cards on a blanket on the ground, and others appeared to be dozing in the cool breeze. They all appeared to be well armed.

"Would it be all right with you fellas if we throw in next to you?" Will asked.

"Make yourself at home," a young man answered from his reclining position leaning against the base of the tree. "We might even have a little coffee left in the pot there. Help yourselves." The man motioned to the pot balanced on some rocks over a small fire.

"Much obliged," Will said.

We dismounted and I took care of the horses. After watering them at the river and leading them a short distance from the camp into some grass for grazing, I hobbled them for the night. I returned to our packs for coffee cups and walked with Will over to our neighbor's camp to take them up on their offer of coffee and to get acquainted.

We helped ourselves to the coffee on the fire and approached the man who had welcomed us. Will knelt on one knee next to the man on his blanket, then introduced himself and extended his hand to shake. "And this is my friend, Andy Bristow." I knelt next to Will and shook the young man's hand. "Thanks for the coffee."

"You're welcome." He wore a heavy, drooping mustache and had friendly blue eyes. "Hays is the name," he said, "Jack Hays. I'm the captain of this Ranger Company here."

"So you're Rangers," I said, lowering myself the rest of the way to the ground. "Will was telling me about you and your men. Where have you been finding the Indians?"

"Mostly up in the hill country, just north and west of San Antonio. That's our ranging area."

"How far north do you go?" I asked, trying to keep the edge from my voice.

"Oh, a couple of times we've chased them pretty far north — well into the buffalo plains, but usually we try not to go out more than three or four days beyond the white settlements."

"Have you seen any white captives with the Comanches?"

"Maybe a couple, or they mighta been Mexicans — what was left of them anyhow."

Will interrupted to turn the conversation. "Andy and his sister were captured about four years ago. He just managed to escape within the last few weeks. He hasn't seen his sister since shortly after they were captured. We were hoping she might be one of the captives they bring in."

Hays looked at me. "I guess if you lived with them, you know how they are. It's probably a miracle that you're still alive. But a person's gotta keep hoping."

Will and I contributed some dried beef and potatoes that I had behind my saddle to the supper the Rangers were having and joined them around their fire for their evening meal. We spent the evening together as Captain Jack, as his men called him, and several of the other Rangers shared stories of a few of their recent encounters with the Comanches.

They explained that their job consisted of ranging through the countryside and beyond the settlements and farms looking for any evidence of Comanche raiding parties. Signs that they looked for, besides horse tracks, were smoke and buzzards. The smoke could be from a camp fire or it could be from a burned out settler's cabin. Buzzards could be enjoying the discards of a Comanche trail meal or feasting on the remains of the warrior's white victims.

"I'll tell you fellers," Hays said, removing his side arm from its holster, "Old Sam Colt sure changed our ability to walk away from an Indian scrape when he invented this here revolving pistol. It puts the contest very definitely in our favor when we have to go against the Comanches. Even though they are the best mounted fighting force anywhere in the world, they're still fighting with lances and bows and arrows for the most part, and now we have these." He slid the weapon back in its holster. "We each have two of them. Wouldn't go into a fight without them."

I watched as he put his pistol away. "We've got ours on order, back at San Felipe, soon as they come in from the factory," I said, hoping the envy didn't show in my voice.

"I guarantee you'll feel a lot better anywhere around the settlements with one of these Colts strapped on," Hays said, looking at his almost empty coffee cup, then throwing out the dregs and grinds.

The next morning, Will and I rode to town with the Ranger Company to wait for the Indians. Entering the town, we approached an old white, limestone building with an arched doorway and windows and four vertical columns that looked as if it may have once been a church. Portions of the roof were missing and many of the upper stones of the chapel appeared to be gone as well. Attached to the main building on either side was a tall rock wall that extended out and away from the main structure and then wrapped around to the back creating an enclosure that looked like a large fort. The walls were broken down in many places. Some areas in the walls seemed to even have been blasted apart. The whole place was in sad disrepair. My eyes seemed to be drawn to the old structure as we rode abreast of what I assumed had once been the main chapel. Will watched me looking at the structure.

"This is sacred ground, Andy," he said quietly, reining Barron to a stop in front of the old chapel. He nodded to Hays and told him we'd meet him in the plaza. The Ranger Company continued toward the center of town. I followed Will as he dismounted and removed his hat. I slid off my horse and pulled my hat off too, standing beside Will.

"Heroes died here," Will said, standing straight as the breeze wafted through his light brown hair. Neighbors and friends. Everyone — a hero. Some famous, others just simple farmers like me.

"Is this Fort Alamo?" I asked.

Will stood silently staring at the old building. Finally he simply nodded. "A hundred and eighty-three, Andy. A hundred and eighty-three men believed enough in freedom and independence that they became martyrs for their cause. So few patriots against six thousand Mexican soldiers. They led the way for the rest of us. They fought so valiantly. They gave us the strength to defeat Santa Anna. We must always make sure they, and the cause they fought for are never forgotten.

I nodded my agreement. We both said a silent prayer for the souls of the heroes and the welfare of their families.

CHAPTER 16

As we rode into the main plaza, we found that a crowd had already formed. Settlers from the edge of the frontier were bunching into small groups along the store fronts, as were the local citizens, both Anglo and Mexican. Although the town was filled with people, a quiet had settled about the plaza. The somberness of the day reflected the prayer of the settlers that the return of their loved ones would soon be fulfilled.

A sizable contingent of uniformed soldiers were scattered about the plaza and at the simple, one-room, stone building that served as a courthouse, which the parties would use as the Council House.

Will and I learned from the Rangers that President Lamar had appointed Colonel William G. Cook, the acting Secretary of War, Colonel Hugh McLeod, the Texas Adjutant General and Lieutenant Colonel William S. Fisher of the First Texas Regiment as Indian commissioners. They were all in the courthouse, had been given their instructions and were awaiting the Indians.

We followed Captain Jack and his Rangers to the courthouse where we dismounted and tied our horses to a rail. Will and I stood alongside the Rangers as they took up positions outside the court house while Captain Jack and another Ranger went inside the building to report for duty to the commissioners.

I could almost taste the tension in the air as I looked at the faces in the plaza. I suspected that many of the people wearing homespun and buckskin weren't residents of San Antonio. They looked much more like the Jeffersons and Bowmans and the other farmers we saw along the way from Virginia Point than San Antonio merchants and laborers.

I was caught up in my own thoughts and hopes when I was nudged by Jack Hays, returning from the Courthouse. "How long did you say you were with the Comanches?" Hays asked.

"Four years. Why?"

"I guess you talk Comanche then?"

I nodded. "Had to to stay alive."

"We need somebody who can talk to them so there'll be no misunderstandings. They must understand our terms crystal clear. Can you do that?"

"I guess I can as good as anybody else in town."

"Come on, I'll introduce you to the commissioners." Hays turned and headed toward the door of the courthouse.

"Wait a minute," Will said, catching me by the arm.

I turned to see that he was holding out one of his two pistols and his Bowie knife. "Here, take these. You shouldn't be that close to those savages without a weapon. Just hope you don't need to use them. We haven't had time to work on training."

"Thanks." I took the weapons and shoved them in my belt. "We'll cover the training later."

I turned to follow Hays inside the courthouse to meet the commissioners.

"They's comin'!" a shrill voice yelled, breaking the quiet of the plaza. A boy about eight years old rounded the corner of a building. Reaching the center of the plaza, he yelled, "The Injuns is comin'! They's jest up the road a piece."

He ran directly to the court house door where he was stopped by one of the Rangers; a tall, bearded man in leather pants stained black and shiny and a worn buckskin jacket guarding the door.

Looking up at the man blocking his way, the boy gasped to regain his breath from the running and excitement. "Tell them fellers inside there that them Injuns is gonna be in the plaza in a couple a minutes. I seen 'em comin' down the road. They's jest outside town."

"How many with them?" the Ranger asked.

"Must be somewheres maybe between sixty an' seventy," the boy panted. "They's kicking up a mess a dust."

"Thanks, son, I'll pass the word." The man opened the door

and disappeared behind it.

Within moments, a column of soldiers came from behind the court house and spaced themselves along both sides of the street.

Silence fell over the plaza with the anticipation of the first glimpse of the Indians and their captives.

The courthouse emptied of officials. Rangers and soldiers watched as the first of the Indians walked their horses into town.

The Chief leading the parade was a short, dark-skinned, grizzled-looking man. I later learned that this bald-headed, skinny old man wrapped in a tanned buffalo hide was called Mook-war-ruh, or Spirit Talker. Clustered about him were twelve other head men; chiefs over their own tribes. They were all wearing their finest ceremonial attire. Some of the men's faces were decorated with black paint. Their arms and legs were painted red and yellow. They were astride horses almost as colorful as themselves. Bright figures were painted on some of their horse's bodies. Others had their mane and tails plaited with red, yellow and green bits of cloth, ribbons and feathers. All of the chiefs were outfitted with their long bows and sets of arrows. Many also carried colorfully decorated fourteen-foot long lances. There was an abundance of knives evident, their handles extending from waistbands.

Behind them rode the women and children of the chiefs, also in their leather outfits trimmed with ribbons and beads. Many of the horses ridden by the women and children were pulling travois piled high with gear for setting up their buffalo-hide lodges.

I scanned the faces of each tribe member carefully, not only looking for Rosie, but to see if I could recognize any of those that held me captive, but Strings Bow Tight and his clan were not with the group. I knew the captives would be toward the rear of the tribe, as the lower members of the tribe and slaves always traveled at the rear, choking on the dust of those riding at the front. I could only make out obscure figures in the dust. Several children were riding in the midst of the group, but I couldn't make out their features.

The head chief stopped in front of the court house, some

twenty feet from the Texas officials. He waited quietly, staring at them while the rest of his tribe rode into a tight gathering behind him.

Chief Mook-war-ruh leaned toward a much younger warrior riding next to him and gave him some instructions. The warrior rode to the rear of the horde and stopped next to a figure dressed in women's clothes astride a sorrel mare. She held a hide over her head, concealing her hair and most of her face. Only her eyes were visible. She held the hide tightly over her nose and mouth for protection from the boiling dust. The young warrior barked some orders and she slid off her pony and stood next to him. He then gave orders to a smaller figure on a mule toward the rear. That figure also dismounted and stood next to the warrior.

I watched as the two followed the young warrior as he walked his horse to the front of the tribe. The rest of the tribe opened ranks as they moved through the maze of dusty horses and dark-skinned riders.

Watching the two figures follow the young brave, I tried to estimate what Rosie's size would be after all this time. In four years, she would have grown a lot, but the taller figure in the leather dress was the size of a grown woman. As they got closer to the front and the remainder of the Indians pulled their ponies aside, I realized the smaller figure was a Mexican boy, about nine years old. The two figures in dirty, leather clothing were captive slaves.

The captives stood in front of the Indians, between them and the officials.

Chief Mook-war-ruh straightened himself on his horse and spoke in a high-pitched, but strong voice.

Only the other Indians and I understood the words.

I translated for the commissioners. "He said that more people would be brought after you talk."

Colonel Cook approached the two figures standing by themselves between the Indians and the commissioners. I watched the taller figure as the colonel approached. She was a young woman with wisps of blond hair falling from under the deer skin she held over her head. She still held the skin over her nose and mouth. I saw her trembling as the colonel approached stopped beside her. Cook took a grandfatherly stance next to her and gently asked, "What's your name, Dear? How old are you?"

The girl stared at the ground as tears cascaded over her cheeks. After a long hesitation, she cleared her throat and haltingly answered in a muffled, slurred voice. "Matilda Lockhart. I'm sixteen."

I had to listen closely to understand her words. The delay in her speech was the same delay I'd experienced when I tried to speak in English after such a long time of neither hearing nor speaking the language. But there was another strange quality to the sounds she made behind the animal hide she held over her face. It was clear to me that she was struggling to make herself understood.

"How long have they had you?" Cook asked.

The girl continued to stare at the ground. After a few moments, she lifted her gaze to the Colonel. "They took me and my little sister two years ago."

"Wilson," the colonel called over his shoulder to an aid. "Take these children away from here. Take them somewhere safe and see that they are fed and made comfortable. Take six men with you and make sure they are well protected."

The soldier approached the girl and the small Mexican boy. With his escort of a half-dozen well-armed soldiers, he led the captives away from the crowd in the street.

The old chief carefully slid from his horse with the help of two teenaged boys and handed his horsehair reins to an old woman who approached from the rear. He stood in the street, leaning on his wooden staff, decorated with feathers and paint as the remainder of the warriors followed the bow-legged old man's lead and dismounted, turning over their mounts to women or children. They were careful to retain their weapons.

The mixture of people in the dusty plaza was as explosive as a keg of black powder. The white settlers held a hatred and fear of the Comanches that was stronger than any emotion they'd ever known. The native Mexican citizens; small ranchers and farmers from around San Antonio, who had endured the Indian raiding parties for a much longer time than the white settlers, could barely contain their seething contempt for the savages. The soldiers and Rangers each had his individual and personal reasons for their hatred. There were also the government representatives who had a rigid set of detailed instructions from President Lamar and his Secretary of War, Albert Sidney Johnston, neither of whom had any patience in bargaining with red savages. And finally, the Comanches had presented themselves. They added to the mix a most volatile and warlike culture with values on an opposite pole from that of the whites and Mexicans.

The Indians appeared in no hurry to commence the council. The young warrior announced that Mook-war-ruh was tired and that he must rest before the talk. I translated and awaited an answer.

"Who do they think they are?" An angry Colonel Fisher asked Cook. "Do they think we have nothing better to do than just wait around while they take a nap?"

"It's after mid-day anyway," Cook answered, pushing his hat brim back and squinting one eye toward the sun. "The counsel meeting could last awhile. We may as well eat first."

Cook turned to me. "Tell them to be back here two hours before sundown, we'll talk then." He addressed the other commissioners, tilting his head toward the building. "Come on back inside. I want to make sure we all understand where we're going with this."

I translated the message to the young Indian, slightly older than myself. The warrior responded with silence and cold, dark eyes that penetrated mine with the sharpness of a razor. I didn't drop my gaze as I had been conditioned to do from my years of servitude. I returned the young Comanche's silent challenge with a defiant, icy stare of my own. Our eyes locked in an unspoken agreement of understood hatred. After several moments of intense eye wrestling, I slightly curled one side of my mouth upward and *almost* imperceptibly shook my head in dismissal of someone of lesser status. Then with the silent challenge met and the pecking order between the two of us defined, I abruptly turned my ramrod-straight back on the Indian standing in the dust and followed the parade of officers back into the Council House.

Once inside, I listened as the commissioners reviewed the pre-set conditions that had been defined by President Lamar. Colonel Cook spoke as food was brought into the sparsely furnished room by several Mexican women and placed on the long table at one end of the room.

"Just so we all understand and agree, the President and Secretary Johnson made it very clear that there would be no ransoming of captives. We are also going to put an end to the so called, giving of presents. They came here offering all the captives in exchange for peace. That's what we'll give them, *if* they keep their bargain."

"They won't agree to that, sir." I spoke out and took a couple of steps toward the Colonel before I realized that I was out of turn. Captain Hays put his hand on my arm to silence me.

"Let him speak." Cook told the Ranger. Hays released my arm.

"And why won't they agree to it?" the Colonel asked.

"It's not their nature, sir. They believe there's some value to everything. They feel they have a lot to gain by bargaining for their captives, and they take great pride in their bargaining ability. They won't just turn 'em loose. No sir, they'll kill them first. I know their ways. I lived with them long enough to know that."

"They'll turn 'em loose this time," Cook answered with a cold edge to his voice that stated finality.

CHAPTER 17

The commissioners had just started serving their plates from the food on the long table when the lieutenant who had taken the captives away returned to the room.

"Colonel, I suggest you come with me," he said. "I think you'll want to visit with the girl they brought in before you meet with the Indians."

"We were just going to sit down to eat, Wilson. Can't it wait?"

"Beggin' your pardon, sir, but you might be lookin' at your lunch again if you wait till after you eat to see her."

Wrinkles formed between the colonel's eyes. He hesitated a moment, looking at the lieutenant, then slid his chair back from the table, stood up and strode toward the door.

I hurried across the room to meet him before he reached the door. "Sir, take me with you. She may be more comfortable talking with me than you. I'm closer to her age and I know what she's been through. She and I have both been slaves and have suffered at the hands of the Comanches. She'll talk to me."

"All right, Son, come on." Cook followed the messenger out the door.

I walked beside and slightly behind Colonel Cook as we briskly moved down the dusty street following the soldier. We passed a group of Indian boys playing with their scaled-down bows and arrows, firing their arrows toward coins that a patron from the saloon, who, with tainted judgment fueled by alcohol, was tossing in the air as a target. Some of the people on the boardwalks were watching the Indians with as much awe as fear and hatred.

The walk ended at a general merchandise store. Three soldiers were posted outside. As we turned into the store, the soldier escorting us said, "She's in the back, sir, in the living quarters. The woman said to have you go on in when you get here."

We stopped at a curtain at the back of the store. Cook drew it aside to find a door. He knocked softly.

The door opened and a red-eyed, pinch-faced, middle-aged woman ushered us into a parlor. It looked to me like she'd been crying.

"Oh, thank God you're here!" she said quietly, wiping her nose with a handkerchief. "That poor child, I can't believe she's still alive. She endured those . . . those . . . animals for so long. What ever you do, Colonel, you make those savages pay for what they did to that little girl."

"I understand your feelings, ma'am but we're not here for revenge. We're here to try to get the rest of the captives back and win some peace. Can we see the Lockhart girl?"

"I thought she ought to go straight to bed after we got her cleaned up," the woman said, "but she told me she wouldn't rest 'till she talked to the man in charge of the council talks. You wait here. I'll get her."

The woman left the room and returned in a few moments with the girl and another woman. The girl was clean and was wearing a dark-gray dress, much the same as the women wore. Her blond hair was still wet from the washing. Her nose and the lower part of her face were still covered, this time with a white, knitted shawl, draped over her shoulders and held to her face. She stood quietly in front of Colonel Cook for several moments, her eyes downcast. She then slowly lifted her gaze. She looked beyond the colonel's gray beard directly into his dark eyes.

Her eyes held his gaze on her face as she slowly slid the shawl away.

I steadied myself by clamping my jaws tight, swallowing hard, and locking my knees as I saw the girl's face. Hardened by being the victim of so many acts of brutality at the hands of the Comanches, even I was sickened to see the horrible disfiguration of what had been a beautiful young woman. The flesh of her nose was burned completely away, exposing bone and scarred tissue within a large gaping hole in the center of her face. The entire area around what had been her nose and mouth, including much of her lips and some of her jaw was nothing more than a mass of red and black wrinkled scar tissue. Several teeth were missing from her exposed, scarred gums and those that were left were broken and misshapen.

"I'm sorry to shock you this way," the girl struggled to speak clearly in her slurred sort of way, "but I wanted you to see what they did to me before you talk to them." She pulled a handkerchief from her sleeve and wiped at the flow of drool that was dribbling from between her teeth onto the ugly scarred mass on her chin. Her eyes were dry, but still red from crying earlier.

The colonel was visibly shaken. He grabbed the top of the chair next to him for support as the girl continued.

I strained to understand her barely discernible speech as her eyes moved to the floor in her recollection of the horrifying treatment she endured.

"When the men grew tired of me after forcing themselves on me for days, the women did this just for fun. Sometimes the men and boys restrained me while the women took turns holding torches to me . . . just to hear me . . . hear me scream." Tears welled in her eyes again. "They seemed to get enjoyment from watching me suffer. It's not just my face that they've ravaged. There are scars across my body — and deep into my soul.

"Sir, all in the world I have left is hope for others. My little sister is already dead. They beat her to death, but there are fourteen other white captives, mostly children being held at their camp. I can only pray that the rest of them will be freed."

I took a half-step forward and opened my mouth to speak, but the colonel stopped me, pressing against my arm and shooting me a harsh look. "Let her finish."

"I heard the chiefs making plans last night. I understand enough of the language to know what they were saying. I thought you should know." The girl seated herself on a green velvet upholstered chair, dabbed at her eyes and wiped again at her chin.

The woman who'd answered the door offered Colonel Cook a chair next to the girl. "Please sit, Colonel." He sat but tried not to stare at the girl's disfiguration as she spoke.

"They intend to bargain for each person one by one. They expect to win a prize for each captive. All the chiefs agreed that chief Mook-war-ruh is the best speaker and will speak for them. They also believe he's the best at trading for their advantage."

"I'll guarantee you this, young lady; they'll be no bargaining for captives." The colonel took Matilda's hand. "They came to us asking for peace and offered all the white captives as their part of the bargain. We intend to hold them to it."

Squeezing her hand gently, he asked, "Now, what can we do for you?"

She hesitated a moment before answering. She again looked him in the eyes as she pleaded, "Please sir, keep people away from me. Please hide me. I'm so ugly and . . . dirty. I'll never be clean again." She turned away from the colonel and buried her face again in the shawl.

Colonel Cooke stood and gently placed his hand on the young woman's shoulder. She softly sobbed into the knitted, woolen shawl.

The colonel opened his mouth briefly and closed it again, trying to find the right words to console Matilda. He started to speak, "Miss —" the words caught in his throat. He hesitated a long moment, cleared his throat, took a deep breath and started again, "Miss, I promise you, we'll stop those savages and get your friends back. You do everything you can to get well."

He made eye contact with me and nodded toward the door and walked out of the room. I saw the colonel's gesture, hesitated briefly, looked back at the girl and reluctantly followed him through the store and onto the street.

I found him on the boardwalk, leaning on a post, his head thrown back, filling his lungs with fresh air. Neither of us spoke all the way back to the council house.

I was disappointed that I still knew nothing of Rosie's fate, but hoped that before the day was over, I would find someone who did.

The colonel immediately called a private meeting with the

other commissioners. I waited outside with Will, the Rangers and soldiers.

In less than an hour, word was sent to the Indian leaders for them to assemble at the council house for their meeting.

After telling Will of our visit with the girl, I had to leave him outside with the Rangers while I went back into the small stone building and positioned myself next to the delegation of commissioners and local officials.

The grim-faced commissioners and the local San Antonio officials were seated in chairs behind the long table that had been cleared of food and placed in a prominent location in the room. A dozen or so other men stood along the walls, behind and beside the commissioners.

Chief Mook-war-ruh, leaning on his staff, led the group of thirteen chiefs, all in their finest feathers and beads as they filed into the room. Once they were all inside, they stood briefly then sat on the floor across the room from the Texas officials.

I watched as the well armed Indians filled the room. Most showed knife handles at their waistband and carried their bows with a quiver of arrows slung over their shoulder. Several carried war clubs. I also observed earlier, before the meeting, that the white citizens were heavily armed as well, especially those standing behind and beside the commissioners. Single shot and revolving pistols and knives extended from belts and pockets. Several long rifles were held, cradled in the arms of their owners. Tension, fear, hatred and distrust hung in the stuffy room like an evil vapor, ready to explode.

Outside in the courtyard, soldiers, Rangers, settlers, Mexican farmers, merchants, women and children milled about. The rest of the Comanche delegation, mostly women, children and a few young warriors squatted and sat on the ground waiting for the talks to conclude.

CHAPTER 18

After all the chiefs took their position, the door was closed and a deadly quiet filled the room. Each side glared at the other for several long seconds. Colonel Cook rose from his chair, cleared his throat and addressed the chiefs. He spoke slowly, selecting his words carefully, pausing after each phrase to allow me to translate accurately. I listened and spoke loudly and with authority, hesitating at times, choosing the right words to ensure the translation reflected exactly the meaning intended:

"President Lamar has authorized me to respond to your offer of returning the captives you hold in exchange for a treaty of peace. I am authorized to make a peace treaty with you only when you have returned *all* the captives in your possession.

"There will be no payment of any kind for the captives. Your payment will be your peace treaty. You will release all of the captives to us; *then* we will discuss the terms of the peace treaty. Your initial communication indicated that you had many more captives than the two you brought with you today. I demand to know how many captives you have and where they are."

Colonel Cook sat, folded his hands in front of him and stared at the head chief.

First, there was silence, and then several of the chiefs responded loudly to each other and the head chief, gesturing in anger toward the whites. I didn't attempt to translate the angry words of the under-chiefs since Chief Mook-war-ruh had been selected to speak for the group.

Rivulets of sweat trickled down my sides from my armpits as I glanced at the men standing beside and behind me. I could read the stress in their eyes and saw it in their hands when I noticed several of them tense their fingers toward their weapons.

Many of the chiefs were angrily talking and shouting at once when Chief Mook-war-ruh lifted a hand for quiet. When the others fell silent he turned and spoke, gesturing with his hands to his group of chiefs. Turning back toward the commissioners and with the aid of a couple of the other chiefs closest to him, he slowly stood. Standing straight but bowlegged, his fringe of long, gray hair under his bald pate flowed over his narrow shoulders as he leaned on his colorful staff. He looked around the room at the table of commissioners, the local officials and the group of men standing behind and beside the table for several moments before he spoke. He then started his oration.

I listened carefully and translated: "We have traveled many days to make peace with our white neighbors. We are a peace-loving people. We have only taken a few children to help with our work because the white people have taken our hunting land and our people are hungry. Some of our people are unable to work because they have no food. We bring you that clumsy girl who fell in the fire and the Mexican boy as tokens of our good will and ask nothing in return for their release. But we have many other children that we have cared for and loved like our own. They are safe and we are protecting them."

I watched the other Indian leaders as their eyes scanned the white men to gauge their level of belief in what the old chief was saying.

"We are a poor people and have little. You are a rich and have much. You scar our sacred earth with pointed metal sticks and make your grain grow on our hunting ground. Now the buffalo don't come. Our people are hungry. We demand payment for the children so we can feed our people. We will trade. Those children help gather food for our people who are too sick to work. You bring us many horses and spotted buffalo. You bring weapons. You bring gold. We bring children."

Chief Mook-War-Ruh completed his demands and stared at Colonel Cook for a few seconds before making further comments. When he completed his speech, he puffed out his chest, postured with a stubborn frown and placed his fist on his hip, waiting for me to complete the translation.

I know I heard the last comment correctly, but hesitated before translating. My gaze darted to Colonel Cook and the rest of the Anglo delegation. I had been watching the faces of the white men in the room as I'd translated the Chief's words and saw their anger grow, along with my own, with each word spoken by the old Chief.

As I translated his last words: "So how do you like my answer?" I watched the old man, who was now slightly nodding with a look of smug satisfaction that his counter-offer would be accepted.

Colonel Cook spoke quickly, but softly as he turned toward the rest of the delegation, trying to defuse the situation. "All right, everybody just stay calm. Andy, don't translate this." He then addressed the soldier at the door. "Wilson, bring in your troops."

The chiefs watched as the officer left the room, then return with ten more soldiers who stationed themselves in front of the Anglo delegation, positioning themselves at the ready with their weapons across their chest. Two of the soldiers stood defiantly in front of the door.

"Now, Andy," the colonel said, "listen carefully, because I don't want any misunderstanding about what I've got to say. You tell them that we will not talk peace until we have our people back from them. You tell them that until we get our people back, they are all being made our captives. They will be held here until every white prisoner is returned to us. Furthermore, they will all be killed in ten days if the white captives are not returned safely. Is that clear?"

I looked at the colonel, my mouth agape, feeling the color drain from my face. "I understand you, Colonel," I sputtered, "but they won't stand for it. No sir, they'll die right here before they'll be locked up."

"Son, you've got your orders." Cook stood, his back rigid, his face stone cold and expressionless. "Tell 'em!"

I looked at the chiefs, then at the soldiers, then at Cook who motioned to me with a stern nod to get on with it. I screwed up my courage, took a deep breath and started translating the message.

The chiefs listened intently. As soon as the meaning of my words struck them, their faces twisted in disbelief. Suddenly several chiefs jumped from their positions screaming for help from the outside, and scrambling for the door swinging knives and war clubs at anyone in the way.

Pandemonium broke out. Everyone was shouting, shooting, slashing and struggling as the Indians threw themselves on us. War clubs flailed, rifles and pistols billowed smoke as lead balls flew for their mark and arrows left their bows as the pent-up rage exploded.

I lurched backward, reaching for my weapons. I produced Will's handgun in my right hand and fired into the face of a chief who was attempting to gut me. I managed to sidestep another in mid-swing with his war club who had just been shot in the chest by a white man at close quarters.

It was over as fast as it had started. All the Comanche chiefs were dead or dying. Three white men were dying and several had severe injuries. One white man, whom I learned later was the father of kidnapped children, had to be pulled off a dead Indian as he continued to drive his fists onto the body, working through his rage.

I staggered out the door of the council house and hung my body over a hitching rail. I gasped, coughing and gagging from the dense black powder smoke and the stench of death that had filled the room. I soon found myself on my knees, retching the ghastliness of the slaughter from my body.

The plaza and streets were as chaotic as inside the small, bloody room. Indian women and children screamed and ran in all directions as soldiers, Rangers and armed townspeople tried to corral or kill them. Indian women fought as viciously as the men when they were caught or cornered, slashing out with knives or biting and kicking. Even the children turned deadly with their scaled-down bows and arrows. A judge fell dead in the street with a small arrow protruding from his chest. Women and children of the town were running along the streets taking cover from flying arrows and bullets wherever they could. Several young braves ran for their horses, mounted in one leap and galloped through the streets, firing arrows at townspeople as they made their getaway.

Captain Hays saw the Indians whipping their ponies out of town, heading north.

"Come on boys!" he yelled to the Rangers within earshot. "We've got to stop them before they get back to their camp." Word passed within seconds among the Rangers, soldiers and civilians clustered around the courthouse and twenty men, including Will and I were punishing our mounts toward the Indian riders.

I pushed Anna's mare for all the speed she had. I knew the fate of the captives at the camp if we couldn't stop the warriors.

I saw the cloud of dust floating above the prairie ahead of us, but I couldn't see the figures causing it. Although I drove the mare as hard as she could run, Will and several others who rode stronger geldings and stallions pulled ahead of me, gaining on the Indians. After a hard run of not more than fifteen minutes, the dust cloud dissipated as we galloped through prairie grass. We were approaching a large stand of cottonwood trees along a creek. Two dozen buffalo hide lodges were nestled among the trees. The four warriors were no more than 100 yards ahead of the militia.

Fifty yards out from the camp two of the Indians jumped from their ponies and took defensive positions beside cottonwood trees, firing arrows at the militia. Several riders including Will and Hays raced past the two Comanches firing arrows, heading straight into the camp behind the two leading warriors. The two Indians firing arrows at the approach to the camp got off two or three arrows each, bringing down one rider before Rangers riding at the head of the militia dropped them. Will and Hays and a couple of other Rangers caught up with the other two braves as they galloped into camp. Hays shot one of the Indians as he jumped from his pony, heading for the main lodge structure. Another Ranger took down the other as he reached for the flap to the lodge. Rushing past the fallen warrior, Will threw open the lodge flap and found the round room full of white children and several old Indian women, one of whom was holding a scared and trembling little girl in front of her, preparing to pull a butcher knife blade across the child's throat. Will stopped the arc of the knife before it started by putting a hole in the middle of the old woman's forehead.

Hays burst into the lodge behind Will in time to stop any further acts of murder by the other women.

I heard gunfire from within the lodge and raced through the opening to see that Will and Hays had matters under control except for calming nine terrified children. I made a circuit of the lodge, searching each child's face for Rosie's features and found that she wasn't there.

I searched the camp and the surrounding area with several men for other white children and Indians and brought in eight more old women and men and a few teen aged boys who had been left to guard the captives, but no more white children.

When the Indians were secured with their hands bound behind their backs and tied to each other, Will and I and a few other men tried to comfort the former captive children. They were examined for injuries and, although some had scars and signs of abuse, none were as severe as Matilda Lockhart's.

Some of the men started gathering supplies and horses for the trip to take the children and the new Indian prisoners back to town, but I needed some time alone.

Will found me sitting on a large rock along the edge of the creek, pitching stones in the water. He approached me, leading our horses. "You all right?"

"Yeah, I guess."

"Been through a lot today."

"I've had worse."

"Any of the children seen Rosie?"

"Nobody. Nobody's seen her, Will!" I spat out the words, unable to keep my emotions inside. "I was hoping that somebody at least could just tell me if she's alive." I threw the last rock in my hand as hard as I could across the creek.

"I know, Andy. But we're just now starting to look. We'll keep looking. We'll find her."

CHAPTER 19

It was almost dark when the Rangers, civilian militia, white and Mexican children and Indian prisoners approached the river outside of San Antonio. More people joined the procession as we passed each scattered group that had come to town for the council meeting and were camped along the river. People cheered as they first saw the tired and dirty children astride the horses.

Feelings were still so strong after the events of the day that several times the Rangers and militia had to step between the civilians and the Indian prisoners.

Parents of lost children ran to us when they learned that children had been found, calling the names of their loved ones and racing from one horse to the other looking for their children. Three children were joyously reunited with their families from the groups camping along the river. Most of the time, however, the mothers and fathers left the procession empty handed and in tears. The children were also looking anxiously for their parents. Many of them did not know that at least one parent, if not both, had been killed when the children were captured by the Indians.

Word of our arrival had preceded us as we rode into the plaza. A throng gathered almost as large as earlier in the day for the council meeting to welcome the children and hail the Rangers and militia as heroes.

Outside the courthouse Colonel Cook and the other members of the delegation met what was now a large assembly of jubilant Texans, the rescued children, a rag-tag band of Indian women, a few old men and some Indian children.

"Thank you, gentlemen, for bringing our children home," Cook said. "You have the gratitude of all of us here and President Lamar. You have earned your rest. Turn your prisoners over to the army. Those ladies over there have volunteered to take care of the children until we can find their families." Cook motioned toward a small group of women clustered on the boardwalk.

Will and I took our leave from our comrades with the promise that we would camp with Captain Jack and his Rangers again later that evening.

"There's one other thing I've got to do before we leave town," I told Will as we turned our horses away from the plaza.

"What's that?"

"I've got to talk to Matilda Lockhart."

We were soon back at the general store. Inside we found the woman I had met earlier in the day.

"Begging your pardon, ma'am —"

"You're the young man who was here with the Colonel," the woman said, recognizing me.

"Yes ma'am, I was. I really wanted to talk to Miss Lockhart then, but I just didn't get a chance."

"I'm sorry, young man, but she really doesn't want to see anyone."

"I understand. I heard her say she just wanted to be left alone this morning, but I'm sure she'll see me. You see ma'am, I was a Comanche captive myself. I just recently escaped. My baby sister was captured with me, but I haven't seen her since the Indians traded her away right after we were captured. All I want to do is just ask Miss Lockhart is if she's seen my sister."

The woman hesitated, staring at me, biting her lower lip, then said, "Wait here a moment."

A few minutes later I was shown into the parlor while Will stayed in the store.

Matilda Lockhart was waiting for me as I entered the room. "Please sit," she said, motioning to a chair on the other side of a small, round table from where she sat. She had once again covered her face with the shawl.

"I really do appreciate you agreeing to see me." I looked earnestly into her eyes. "I just couldn't leave town without talking to you." I explained my reason for asking to speak with her and concluded, "Even though none of the children that we brought in tonight had seen her, I knew you'd been with the Indians longer than most of them. I thought that maybe you might know something the rest of them didn't."

"How old was she?"

"She was seven years old when they took her. That would make her almost twelve now."

"And her hair, was it like yours?"

"Same color, but a little curlier than mine. Her eyes were like mine too — blue."

Matilda stared at the table top, focusing on what I told her. Then she lifted her eyes to meet mine. I listened carefully as she slowly spoke, doing the best she could to make herself understood.

"Andy, about two years ago, shortly after I was taken, the tribe I was with traveled north for many days. I guess maybe four or five weeks, following the buffalo. We met a few other tribes along the way, but I remember this one tribe we met at a big flint quarry where we were collecting flint before we started back south again. They had a white girl with them. Andy, she had long, curly red hair. She was about ten years old. When I saw you earlier today, I knew there was something familiar about you. Now I know what it was. She looked a lot like you!"

I bit my lip with excitement and leaned forward on the edge of my chair. "Did you talk to her?"

"No, they wouldn't let me get close enough. But she smiled and waved at me."

"How did she look? Did she look healthy?" There was so much I wanted to know, I could hardly wait for her answers.

"As far as I remember, she looked good. But I was pretty far away. I couldn't really tell much about her. But I do remember her hair. From what you've told me and what I remember about her hair, I don't think there's any mistake — I saw your sister!"

"Matilda, you don't know how happy you've made me." I rose from my chair and squeezed her hand. "Thank you! Thank you so much!" I was almost out of breath with excitement. "If there is anything, and I mean *anything*, I can ever do for you, please let me know. Just send word to the Bowman farm on the Brazos in the Austin colony."

Matilda looked at me with sad eyes. "I don't think there is anything anyone can do for me, but you can help your sister. I just hope you aren't too late. Go find her, Andy."

CHAPTER 20

I filled Will in on the details of my conversation with Matilda Lockhart while we rode to the Ranger camp. My excitement hadn't worn off during the ride.

"I just can't believe that now I have some hope of finding her."

"I know you're ready to start looking, but it still may take a while. There's a lot to do before you're ready."

"I know, and I appreciate your help. At least I have reason to believe she may be alive."

I shared my good news with the Rangers that night after dinner around the campfire. This led to a discussion as to how far north Rosie's tribe may be. An older man with long hair and gray streaks in his beard puffed on his briar pipe thoughtfully and said, "If they make their home territory to the far north, they couldn't be much farther than a hundred miles or so north of the Canadian River, somewhere between the Canadian and the Arkansas."

"Why's that?" I asked.

"You get much farther north than that and you'll run into the Sioux and Ute. There's Kiowa and Cheyenne up there too. I reckon the Kiowa and the Cheyenne get along with the Comanches alright, but the Sioux and Ute hate the Comanches almost as much as the Comanches hate white folks. But it ain't unusual to find Comanche tribes up along the Canadian River. There's a huge flint outcropping right along the Canadian, just north of that big canyon up there they call the Palo Duro."

I interrupted the Ranger. "Flint outcropping! She mentioned a flint quarry. That's where she thinks she saw my sister. Are there many flint areas up there?"

"That's the only one I know of in that area and it's a big one. Indians come from all over to use it. Been doing it that way for hundreds of years. They follow the buffalo in the summer and bring back a good sized load of flint to make their arrow heads. If the southern tribes don't make it far enough north to get flint, they'll trade for it with the northern tribes."

"That's what the tribe I was with did." I said. "We never went to a flint quarry. Just how far is that place from here?"

"Oh, let's see." He blew a low whistle through his teeth as he thought. "Must be at least three hundred miles or so. Maybe more. But you know that whole area up there ain't never been mapped very well. Here's another thing to consider: just because your sister may have been spotted way up north don't necessarily mean she's still there. Them tribes sometimes travel a thousand miles or more in a year. I'm sure you know that."

"Yeah, I do," I said, "and I walked every mile of it."

The Ranger continued. "They're always on the move. Who knows? Your little sister might be within a hundred miles of here by now, or maybe even farther south, down beyond the Rio Grande."

The talk turned to recounting the events of the day. When asked what the final count of the fights had been, Captain Jack summarized the statistics.

"I was told that there were thirty-three Indian men, women and children killed. Another thirty-two ended up in the jail. Many of those were injured.

"On our side, there were seven killed, including the sheriff, a judge and an army officer. Ten others were seriously wounded and many more suffered less serious injuries. While we were chasing those warriors back to their camp, there was a big ruckus in town. Indians were running all over; up and down the streets, trying to get into houses, even climbing down chimneys. Women and children were fighting like wild animals. Some white women had to fight them off with axes."

Hays spit a stream of tobacco juice into the fire. The reflection of the fading fire light flickered off his face as he poked at the dying coals with a mesquite stick, stirring up new flames. He stared into the fire as if the crackling flames were whispering to him. "Boys," he said, eyeing each of the men surrounding the fire, "once word about what happened today gets out to the tribes scattered out there," he nodded toward the darkness away from the fire, "all hell's gonna break loose."

CHAPTER 21

Will and I filled the long hours on our ride home talking war and battle strategies. He was educated and trained at a military academy in Virginia before he came to Texas twelve years earlier and had fought both Mexicans and Indians. I needed to learn everything from him that I could.

"You have to understand, Andy, what they taught us back in the academy has very little to do with fighting Comanches. Back there, they taught us the way the European armies fought. The Indians don't follow any rules of war like that. They don't draw and fight from battle lines. More often than not, as you know, their battle lines are moving at the speed of a galloping pony. The Comanches don't have artillery and they don't have infantry. But what they do have is the best fighting cavalry the world has ever known, bar none. If we remember that and train to be better horsemen than them, or at least just as good, we might just stay alive. I'm sure you've seen what they can do on horseback while you lived with them."

"They wouldn't let me practice with them, shooting the bow and arrow in battle practice, but I know how they ride. They used me to help them break the rankest wild horses. I got thrown hundreds of times wearing the horses down before the braves finished their training, but I also learned better ways to train horses. You don't have to break a horse's spirit to train him."

"Speaking of horses, you'll need a well-trained stallion or gelding to keep you out of trouble when you're fighting Indians," Will said. "And you need to feed him grain along with the grass. Those grass-fed Indian ponies are fast, but they can't out run or stay up with a well-conditioned grain-fed horse in a long race."

"What about weapons?" I asked.

"You need to be well armed and know your weapons like they're an extension of your hands. You need to have as much modern firepower as you can carry. You don't ever want to be in a position where you don't have reliable weapons ready for use. You were lucky in that Council House fight. You could have just as easily missed. You might not always be that lucky. You want to replace luck with skill, so that every time you pull a trigger, you hit your mark — every time.

"We'll start our training when we get home. You can repay me for that new Colt pistol we're gonna pick up at San Felipe out of your wages and we'll blow a lot of powder and ball, but by the time we get done, you'll be an Indian fighter."

I listened to Will's advice and thought about it for a moment. "So, how long do you think it will take? I mean, to get really good."

"It depends on lots of things. It could be just a few months, maybe longer. It depends on how much time we can invest in the training. I know you're anxious to find Rosie, but the best advice I can give you is don't go out to try find her before you're ready. Look at it this way, Andy, the worst thing you can do for your sister is rush things and go out there before you're ready and get yourself killed.

"We'll focus on your training, but there're other things to consider too. We've got farming to do. We've must get our seed in before the spring gets away from us. And we've got to get some work out of you so you can earn your keep." Will smiled and winked at me, then clicked his tongue and gently spurred his white gelding to pick up the pace toward home.

The next morning we rode into San Felipe and brought Williams at the land office up to date on the news at San Antonio. Then we stopped by the general store to pick up the cotton seed and see whether the weapons we'd ordered had arrived.

"Just got them in a couple of days after you left for San Antonio," the shop keeper said walking toward his counter. He pulled out three .36 caliber five-shooters.

"Got some extra cylinders, too. They're designed for easy change out of the complete cylinder. You can have up to ten shots before you have to totally reload."

"Let's see how they work," Will said, picking up one of the weapons.

The shopkeeper demonstrated the process of changing out the cylinders.

"You just punch out this wedge pin here and the barrel and cylinder come right out. Then you take your spare cylinder that you've already loaded up with ball, powder and cap and slide it into the pistol and put her back together the same way she came apart."

We watched him carefully as he took the pistol apart into four pieces; the handle, the cylinder, the barrel and the locking wedge, laid them all on the counter, changed out the cylinder, then reassembled.

Will shrugged, "Whoo! Looks a little awkward to have your weapon in all those pieces if you're trying to reload on the run."

"Look at it this way, Bowman," the shopkeeper said, handing Will the weapon, "how many times have you had to reload your muzzle loading flintlock rifle in a hurry?"

"Plenty of times."

"And how many pieces of hardware did you have to handle while you were reloading?"

"Well, let's see. The rifle itself, the powder horn, the ball, the patch and the ramrod."

"Don't forget having to prime the pan and adjust the flint," added the shopkeeper. "What would you say your average time was for the reloading process?"

"Somewhere around a minute, I'd guess."

"All right, during that minute, you're on the ground. You're not on the move and you're a sittin' target, messing with your powder, your ball and your patch. You're pouring powder, loading the ball and patch, jamming your ramrod several times to seat the ball and patch and then you're loading up your pan while one of those Comanches out there would be able to get off maybe twelve to fifteen arrows. Any one of 'em would have enough force behind it to go all the way through a full grown bull buffalo at thirty feet. Then, after your reload, how many shots would you have before you had to reload again?"

"Whew," Will whistled air between his teeth. "I see your point," You've sold us. We'll take three of those extra cylinders, and go ahead and give us thirty pounds of lead, a .36 caliber lead ball mold, ten pounds of powder and three hundred caps and patches. A powder flask with a measuring tip on it would be good too. We'll take three of those if you have them. If you have some secure leather holsters we can carry the pistols in, we'll take three of them, too."

"Actually, I have some pistol belts with the holsters on them. There's a loop that goes over the hammer to lock your piece in the holster till you need it. They even have a built-in pouch to carry your extra cylinder. They're made special for this particular weapon." He showed one to us.

Will nodded. "We'll take three of those too." Then Will turned to me and handed me some money. "Andy, go on over settle up with the blacksmith for looking after the mule, and get him harnessed up. We should have everything together by the time you get back."

The pack mule and horses were soon loaded with seed, weapons, staple goods and gifts and we turned our backs on San Felipe and headed north to Virginia Point and what I now considered my home.

Late in the afternoon on our second day on the road from San Felipe, we were approaching the familiar view of the Jefferson's expanded log cabin. Shouts of greeting came from the vegetable garden next to the cabin as Libby, Tad, Anna and the children left their work to meet us.

"Looks like you've been busy," Will said, admiring the garden after the hugs and kisses.

"We already have the garden in over at your place and we'll be done by mid-day tomorrow on this plot," Tad announced, proudly.

"With a little rain every now and then and this hot sun, looks like we'll be eatin' well again this winter," Will said.

"It seems we timed our return perfectly too," I said, joining in the conversation. "We can start planting cotton right away."

"Maybe we can work out some of these saddle sores behind a plow," Will said, grinning and massaging his backside.

I made a point of not asking about my training after we started the planting. I knew the Bowman's and Jefferson's livelihood depended on a good crop, so I pitched in and gave my all to long days behind a plow.

After several days of plowing and planting, Will, Tad, and I were sitting under a shade tree at the edge of the cotton field, eating our mid-day meal. Will broke the silence.

"Tad, you know we brought a lot of powder and ball home with us along with those new revolving pistols. I've agreed to work with Andy to help him learn how to shoot so that every shot hits its mark. I want you to work with us too. Even though you and I have been out a few times and had our share of Indian fights, we've been lucky we didn't get hurt or worse. I want to make sure nothing ever happens to you like happened to Jeff. I want all of us to be the best we can be defending ourselves in a fight."

"Sounds good to me," Tad replied with a grin. "I've been itching for a chance to try out that new revolver anyway."

Will made a plan with Tad and me that we would stop work one hour early three days a week and learn the skill of soldiering on the frontier. We stayed true to our plan through the rest of the spring and on through the summer. By early July, with the planting over with only harvesting the vegetables in the gardens and hoeing the weeds from the cotton, we increased the training.

As it turned out, I was as much an instructor to Tad and Will as I was a student. After we all became proficient with our accuracy, doing stationary shooting at the range we set up, I brought up the Comanche style of fighting.

"But, fellas, they're always moving. They aren't going to stand still like these targets."

"I know," Tad said, "We've seen what they can do on horseback. It's amazing."

"Sounds like we need a little horseback battle practice," I said.

"I'd say the more tools we have in our pockets, the better off we'll be," Will answered. "Can you train us to ride the Comanche way?"

"I'll do what I can," I said, "but the rider is only half of the fighting unit. Luckily enough, though, I believe we have good partners for you two with Barron and Buck." I walked over to the two geldings, hobbled and grazing a dozen yards or so down the slope from where we were practicing shooting. We were getting them used to the sound of pistol fire. Barron was the stately looking white that Will had been given as a gift from his father before he'd left Virginia. Buck was the lively buckskin that Jeff had ridden cross-country with Will. The horse had been Tad's friend and companion since Jeff's death. They both were mature, well-trained and dependable mounts.

"One of these days, I hope to get a strong stallion for myself," I said, stroking Barron's long, white mane.

"We'll make that happen when we find the right opportunity," Will said, patting me on the back.

CHAPTER 22

The next morning, a Sunday, I was up early. I brought Buck up to the Jefferson cabin and was braiding a strong, woven leather loop into the buckskin's black mane when Tad stepped off the porch to watch.

Tad grinned as he walked up and stroked the horse's forelock. "Looks like we're getting ready for our first riding lesson."

"Just thought I'd get Buck ready. We'll get Barron fixed up when we go over to Will's place."

After breakfast, Tad and I rode double to the Bowman farm and gathered Barron from his corral and led him up the rise to the wide veranda of the large, two storied, white painted house.

When we arrived at the front porch, I started braiding the strong strap I'd brought with me into a loop in Barron's mane.

Will, Anna and the children came onto the porch as I was finishing the loop.

"Looks like you're ready to get some riding training done this morning," Will said.

"We thought we'd give it a try," I answered.

"Why don't you go ahead and show us what we need to do?" Will asked. "Tad, can he take Buck, since he's already warmed up?"

Tad handed me Buck's reins with a grin. "Be my guest." They all sat on the edge of the wide veranda as I prepared to ride.

All right, I thought. *Since I'm going to be teaching 'em, I might as well show 'em what I've got.* I handed my hat to Tad, grabbed the saddle horn and easily swung into the saddle in one leap. I nudged Buck in the ribs with my heels. Within seconds, he was in a full gallop, the loose reins in my mouth, the strap slung over my shoulders. I rode in a wide circle, fifty yards out in front of the Bowman's veranda, stretching against the strap around my shoulders, testing it. At the far end of the circle, I fell away to the far side of the horse and disappeared from view from the house for a few seconds. Then my head and right arm appeared, extending beyond Buck's neck and under his head, with the rest of my body still shielded from view. I extended my right arm, grinning and pointing my forefinger at my audience and made motions like I was firing my revolver. Then as the galloping horse approached the group, completing the circle, I flipped myself to the opposite side of the horse, but this time I positioned myself upside down so that my head, shoulders and arms were extended below the racing horse's belly. Drawing alongside my friends, no more than fifteen feet from them and hanging upside down, I pretended that I was drawing a bow and releasing arrows toward the shocked group on the porch. Then I made another full circuit, still at a gallop, demonstrating the use of the loop braided into the horse's mane, flipping my body from one side to the other and then concealing myself totally again as I rode past the onlookers. After my second pass, I pulled up and trotted back to the front of the house.

Tad, Will, Anna, Texanna, and little Jeff all cheered and clapped their encouragement and appreciation of my riding skills.

I brought the horse to a stop, slid off and handed the reins back to Tad. "He did well for the first time as an Indian pony," I said with a wide grin, patting the buckskin on the neck.

"Do it again! Do it again!" Texanna screamed in delight.

I chuckled. "Maybe a little later,"

"I've never seen such riding in my life!" Anna's hands were still clasped tightly under her chin. "How in the world do you keep from cracking your head or breaking your neck doing such stunts?"

"I've never seen anybody break their neck,' I said, "but I have seen a few boys who got a little too brave before they've had enough practice crack their heads either by falling or getting too close to the hooves."

"If this is what it will take to be able to walk away from an Indian fight, I'm all for it," Tad said, smiling. "Besides, it looks like fun."

"I don't know if I can watch you doing this," Anna said, shaking her head almost in a shiver. "Y'all go on down by the corral or someplace where I can't see you."

"I wanna watch," Texanna said, tugging at her father's hand. "Come on, Papa,"

"Me too," said little Jeff. "Go on, Mama. You go back in the house. We're gonna watch Andy ride upside down."

"All right," Will chuckled, but you both are gonna stay way back out of the way. I want you to sit on the corral fence while we learn to ride like Andy."

We took the children to the corral and lifted them onto the top rail, then started the training.

Still holding Buck's reins, I said, "I'm sure you've seen that they attack in waves. They never send all of the warriors to the enemy at the same time." I grabbed a stick from the ground and drew lines in the dirt as I explained. "They'll send a few within striking distance to fire their arrows, then retreat. Then the next group will do the same. If they manage to draw you out toward them, like this," I drew another line, "they'll bring out another group to outflank you." I drew a line representing the Indians surrounding us and marked a heavy x through it. "Don't let that happen. Anytime they're riding toward you, they'll use their shields to protect themselves, so don't waste your powder then. Those shields are made of layer after layer of tough, thick buffalo hide with stout glue between each layer. I've seen them come in after raids with lead balls imbedded in the leather. Save your shot till they turn to ride away. Hit them then. Aim for the middle of their back.

"If you ever find yourself in a running battle with them, that's where these loops come in handy." I fingered the leather woven into the horse's mane. "They don't have to stay in all the time, but if you're in a situation where it's likely that you could run into a raiding party, it would be a good idea to put it in and keep it there for awhile."

I unbraided a few straps and then took a few minutes to show Tad and Will how to securely braid the straps into the horse's mane and how to make the right-sized loop to do the job. "A lot of warriors have survived a battle by using this loop to make himself invisible to his enemy."

I mounted Buck and slowly showed Will and Tad how to use the strap effectively to swing from one side of the horse to the other, and then extended my body forward to shoot under the horse's head, then downward to shoot under its belly.

After a few hours, both Will and Tad were able to swing back and forth and then appear under the horse's neck while at a moderate canter. They both saved learning the under-the-belly technique until they became more proficient with the under-the-neck technique.

Every time Will or Tad rode past the corral fence, riding along their mount's side, the children let out a loud cheer and clapped their hands.

We continued our training two days a week, along with our normal chores. As the summer progressed, we chopped weeds in the cotton and harvested vegetables from the garden. We had already picked the corn for fresh roasting ears in the earlier part of the season. Then, as the hot, dry summer progressed, we started pulling the dried corn from the parched stalks.

By late August, most of the corn had been stripped from the stalks and the cotton rows were, for the most part, free of the moisture-sucking weeds. Our feed storage bins were packed full of corn and there was enough left to take two wagonloads to San Felipe to the market. It was still at least a month until the cotton would be ready to pick.

We honed our shooting and riding skills through the summer with many hours of practice. The three of us had all become experts with our five-shooters. Seldom did we miss a stationary target larger than eight inches within fifty paces. The pistol training on horseback took dedicated practice, but toward the end of the summer, we were all three becoming good marksmen from the back of a galloping horse, from either atop the saddle or hanging off to the side, shooting under the horse's neck.

Every night, as I fell into bed, tired, but satisfied with a good day's work and fighting practice, I thought of Rosie. *Rosie, I haven't forgotten you. Every day brings me closer to you. You'll see.*

CHAPTER 23

After finishing a training session one afternoon, we were all three walking Buck from the barn up the rise to the Bowman's wide front porch before heading back to the Jefferson place when a lone rider approached the house from the north, across the pasture. He met us at the porch. There was a freshly killed deer tied behind his saddle.

"Good evenin'," the stranger waved as he approached us in the Bowman front yard. The ruddy-faced, middle-aged man with a large, brown mustache was dressed in buckskins and moccasins and he wore a friendly smile under his sweat-stained, well worn, felt hat. From the looks of him, he had been traveling for some time. "Southerland's the name . . . Scotch Southerland." He slid off his bay gelding and extended his hand to shake with Will.

"Will Bowman," Will said. "This is my place and these are my friends, Tad Jefferson and Andy Bristow."

"Howdy, boys. Pleased to meet you." He shook hands with me, but didn't offer to shake with Tad. "I had a good idea I was into the north end of the Austin grant, but just hadn't run into any houses or cabins yet. We crossed the river from the east a ways up stream and I've been out hunting for a little dinner for me and the boys. This sure is a nice place you have here, Mister Bowman." He was eyeing the wide porch with the tall pillars around three sides of the front of the house and the white-painted siding. "Not used to seeing such fine homes this far north."

"We got a sawmill put in down-river a few years ago, and there have been several of us who've built with milled lumber in the area now," Will said. "But there are still a lot of log homes around too."

'We don't get many visitors coming in from the north, not white ones, anyway."

"We've been huntin' some horses," Southerland said. "Spending most of our time to the east, north of the settlements, kinda working our way west. Been picking up a few wild horses here and there. We're getting a little too close to Comanche country to be running horses through parts farther west now. So unless I want to lose my investment along with my hair, we're heading south, working our way down toward San Antonio and on through the towns closer to the coast, selling horses as we go."

"How many in your outfit?" I asked.

"Horses or wranglers?"

"Both."

"We've got something between five and six hundred head now, and only eight wranglers besides me. Got way too many horses for the help I have. By the time I split up the boys to do the night watches, I'm in trouble. Guess we're lucky we haven't had any thunder storms lately to spook 'em and get a stampede going. You know anything about horses?" He directed the question to me.

Tad and I looked at each other and grinned. "A little," I said. "Why?"

"I really need some more help. I'll pay you forty dollars, and you can have your pick of any two of the horses that ain't broke yet if you'll stick with me till we get to the coast."

"How long will the job take?" I asked.

"No more than a month on the outside."

"Excuse me, Mister Southerland," Tad said. "How many men you need?"

"A good handful, I reckon. Any more men on the place here?" Again, he addressed me and then looked toward the barn and the house.

"I might be interested," Tad said.

Southerland looked scornfully at Tad, then glanced at Will.

"That's between you and your master, boy."

Will and I looked at Tad for his response. Tad hesitated briefly. Will started to speak, but Tad cut him off.

"Sir," he said, straightening himself to his full height and looking Southerland in the eyes, "I'm a free man. Have been for seven years. I *am* my master."

Southerland stared at Tad a moment. "Well, ain't that somethin'. I ain't never seen none of your kind before. I reckon in that case, I could use you, if you wanta work."

"I'll think about it." Tad said, tilting his hat more to shade his eyes and looking away toward the cotton field.

"We'd both have to think it over," I said.

"Y'all think about it real hard. I could use all of you. We'll be bringing the herd through this way about a mile or so to the west tomorrow, sometime around mid-morning, I reckon. We'll stay plenty out of the way of your cotton out there." Southerland spat a stream of tobacco as he looked over the cotton field. "If you boys can get away from the farm for a little while till it's time to pick that cotton out yonder, come on over in the morning. I'll show you the job and we'll talk about the details.

"Would you be happenin' to need some good horses, Mister Bowman?"

"No, not for me right now," he answered. Will had talked to me and Tad about needing a couple of older gentle mares for Texanna and Jeff soon, but I imagine he didn't want to take on wild, unbroken prairie horses for that. He'd wait and find what he needed from the settlements.

"Reckon I'd best be headin' on back to the herd then." Southerland reached for his saddle horn and eased back into the saddle. "Them boys back there gonna be gettin' hungry in a little while."

He glanced at Tad and me before turning his horse. "You boys think it over. If you decide to join up with us, you'll need a saddle and bridle. I've got a good-sized remuda that you'll be able to work from. You'll also need your kit and bedroll and a weapon with some fixins." He looked at the holstered revolvers we all wore. "Them five-shooters there, they'll do fine. Hope to see you tomorrow." He turned his bay and cantered away across the prairie to the north.

Will looked at Tad and me. "So what do you think?"

"I guess the question we have for you is what do *you* think?" I answered.

Will thought a moment before he responded. "Well, on the positive side, the work around here's under control, thanks to you two. The corn's about all in. And he's right, the cotton won't be ready to pick for a while and you'd be back by then. I guess we could afford to be without you for awhile. Andy, you need a good saddle horse, and Tad, you're going to have to replace Buck some day. Also, Tad, you haven't been off your place and mine except to San Felipe and chasing Indians since we came back after the war. I know you can both handle the job. You're both grown men and you can certainly handle yourselves away from home."

Tad and I looked at each other and grinned.

"But then," Will continued, "on the other side, you need to understand the work's hard and dirty. You'll be in the saddle all day, every day for long hours, sometimes choking on dust. And you know you'll have your share of night watches. You'll be sleeping on the ground every night in all kinds of weather. You won't go hungry, but you won't be eating Libby's or Anna's cooking either." Tad looked at me and knitted his eyebrows.

Will went on describing the down side, as he saw it. "You could run into trouble along the way from outlaws or Indians. We haven't had a Comanche raid anywhere in the settlements that I know of since the Council House fight last March. I don't know how long that will last after what happened there. The women and I can take care of ourselves here, but that many horses would be awful tempting for a band of redskins.

"So after looking at the good and the bad, what do you think?"

Tad and I looked at each other. Tad began shaking his head. "I won't leave Libby and Billy alone for that long."

"Now Tad," Will said, putting his hand on Tad's shoulder, "you know we don't leave each other alone like that if were gonna be gone for awhile. Anna and I will love to have Libby and Billy here with us for awhile. You know how much Libby and Anna enjoy their time together. So don't let that get in your way." He shifted his gaze to me. "Andy, how about you?"

"From the picture you paint, it sounds a lot easier than what I did while I was with the Comanches. Of course, I was just a slave to them, so my work was always hard. When several of the tribes came together for hunts or councils and then traveled together, there could be up to fifteen hundred horses that we herded for days, sometimes weeks at time. Since I wasn't a member of any family, months went by when I didn't have the shelter of a lodge to sleep in, and sometimes all I got to eat were the scraps that they didn't want, same as the dogs. I had to steal much of what I ate to survive. So I guess living on the trail with Mister Southerland would be easy for me. I sure would like to have a couple of good horses. We'll talk with Libby tonight and decide then."

The next morning, Tad, Libby, Billy, Jake the dog, and I rolled up to the front of the Bowman house in a wagon pulled by two mules, leading two other mules and Buck behind us. Tad and Libby sat on the bench as Billy and I swung our legs from the tailgate, holding on to the dog between us. The wagon was loaded with gear for Tad's and my trip and several bags of clothes and things for Libby's and Billy's stay with the Bowmans.

Will, Anna and the children were finishing breakfast when they heard the wagon and met us on the porch.

"Oh good!" Anna exclaimed. "So I guess this means you'll be staying with us a while." Anna ran down the steps and took Libby's hand as she stepped down from the wagon.

"After the boys told me what they wanted to do, I agreed that they needed a little adventure away from home," Libby said, hugging Anna.

"But they won't let me go," a dejected Billy complained as he stomped past Libby and Anna and into the house, carrying an armful of books.

Will chuckled. "You'll get your chance for adventure. Just wait and see."

Will walked with Tad and me as we led the extra mules and Buck to the corral to turn them in with Barron.

"Andy," Will said, "when we get back to the house, I want to pay you the wages I owe you. You might find something along the way that you can't live without, like another one of those Colt revolvers."

"I *would* feel a lot more comfortable if I had another one with an extra cylinder, but what I really need now is a saddle and bridle."

"Oh, that's right." Will said. "Just go ahead and take mine. I'm not planning on going anywhere, but if I need to, I'll just use Anna's." We went in the barn after putting the livestock in the corral and picked up Will's saddle and bridle, a blanket and a forty-foot lariat. Once back at the house, Tad and I put the tack in the wagon while Will retrieved my pay from the house.

After Will gave me the money, he handed a folded piece of paper to both Tad and me. "I don't know if either of you will need it, but that's a letter of introduction from me for both of you. I've gotten acquainted with lots of people throughout the settlements since way before the war. Some may even stretch the truth a bit to say I have a little influence. Perhaps these letters will be of some help to you on your travels.

"Tad, your letter also explains your status as a free man, an honest man, a property owner and a citizen of Texas. I know you understand what it's like away from our little community of Virginia Point. Most white people in Texas are probably a lot like Southerland and have never known a free black man. Many, if not most, will resent your status. If we were farther east in Louisiana or Mississippi, I'd be concerned about slave catchers going after you, but I doubt that you'll have that problem here. We can't change other people's attitudes, but I know that you know how to handle yourself. Just be careful. You two just watch each other's back."

"We will," I said. "Thanks for everything. I don't know how I can ever repay you for your kindness."

"You can do that by being here when it's time to pick cotton. There's gonna be plenty to do then." Will laughed, slapping both of us on our backs. "Come on, let's say goodbye to the women and kids. You have a herd of horses to catch."

CHAPTER 24

After hugs and a few tears shed by Libby for Tad's departure, Will drove the wagon across the prairie to meet Southerland and his herd. It didn't take long before we saw evidence of something stirring up dust north of us, heading our way. Within a half-hour we saw the leading edge of the herd of horses. Southerland was waving a red blanket in the air to help control the movement of the horses.

"Morning, men," Southerland called as he approached the wagon. "I was hoping I'd find y'all out here this morning."

"We thought we would come on out and see what this is all about," Tad said.

"See you brought your gear." Southerland looked over the contents in the wagon bed.

"Step on down here and I'll fill you in," Southerland swung his leg over his saddle and dismounted.

Will sat in the wagon and tied a bandana around his face to block some of the dust. Tad and I watched the horses slowly move past while we listened to Southerland explain the duties and expectations of the job.

"If you're used to bein' in the saddle, this ain't too hard. Old Beanie usually gets us up with the smell of his coffee about sun up. We'll get a good breakfast and we're on the trail before the dew dries on the prickly pear. It's a long day, but it has its rewards."

I watched some of the stallions the wranglers were driving to keep the remainder of the herd in control while Southerland explained the daily routine to us. After a few minutes, Tad and I sealed our deal with Southerland with handshakes. Then Southerland whistled loudly and waved his blanket toward one of the wranglers. A young man rode up.

Southerland said, "Josh, go pull out a couple of mounts

from the remuda for these boys. They just threw in with us."

After another round of handshakes with Will and promises to be back at Virginia Point in time to pick cotton, Will turned the wagon and headed back toward his farm. Tad and I were soon mounted on green-broke mares and joined Southerland at the edge of the traveling dust storm, slowly moving south.

We were assigned to work with two other wranglers the first day to learn the ropes. The young wrangler, Josh Ewell, who'd brought us our mounts, was assigned to train me. Another wrangler named Albert Wilson was given Tad to train. It didn't take Josh long to figure out that I knew what I was doing and after the first hour or so, he just casually rode close enough to nod or wave to satisfy his assignment from Southerland. Tad was shown that as long as you kept the stallions in line and at the desired pace, the rest of the herd would follow. I worked close enough to Tad to see that he soon determined that there really wasn't much to herding horses other than keeping them corralled in a tight group and moving at a slow enough pace so they could graze along the way. I was glad to see that Southerland's company had established a good pace for the horses to move and graze. A herd like we were working could travel no more than fifteen miles a day without the horses losing weight.

Southerland maintained a southerly route, usually around a mile or two west of the Brazos. He knew that most of the farmers had settled close to the water and felt confident he could sell a good number of horses to them along the way. He never missed an opportunity when passing a farm house or cabin to meet the owner and offer horses for sale as the herd moved slowly in the distance. The natural landscape provided the occasional creek or stream that allowed the stock to water as they made their slow progress south.

By early afternoon, Tad and I were glad Libby had loaded two large biscuits with several strips of bacon and wrapped them in a kerchief and tucked them in each of our saddle bags. We learned that the cook provided a hearty breakfast every morning and the wranglers usually took an extra biscuit or two and some bacon for a mid-day snack on the trail while the herd kept moving. Then the cook took his wagon ahead of the herd to find a place to camp for the night and start setting up for supper.

Two or three times a day each wrangler pulled a fresh horse from the remuda of broken and trained horses that were mixed with the herd. The practice kept each rider on a fresh horse throughout the day and avoided excessively tiring the working horses.

The afternoon went almost like the morning except mid-afternoon when we passed beside a farmer's cotton fields. Southerland broke away from the herd and rode to the farmer's house. In a little while he came back with the farmer beside him, riding a mule. Southerland sold the farmer two horses: a yearling colt and a filly. As the farmer picked his choice, two of the wranglers threw loops over their heads with their lariats and led them back to the farmer's corral. The slow pace of the herd never changed during the sale and delivery of the two horses.

About two hours before sundown, Southerland told my trainer, Josh, to break away from the herd and take me with him to go hunting for supper. A creek was off to the right, about two miles from the herd that eventually angled back east toward the river. I figured we'd probably camp close to the creek for the night. Trees and underbrush lined either side of the water. It looked to be an ideal place to find game.

We tied our horses at the edge of the thicket. The wind was calm so I reached down and pulled a handful of buffalo grass, held it up to eye level and dropped it. The grass fell with the very slight breeze, indicating which direction we should hunt, in order to be downwind from the game. We walked quietly into the thicket and crouched behind a growth of small cedars looking toward the creek, upwind from our position. We worked our way through the thicket toward the creek, stopping every few minutes to listen and look through the shadowed brush. I soon heard something that Josh didn't hear. I quietly raised my finger to my lips and pointed to my ear to signal Josh to listen closely. Then Josh heard it. It was the sound of turkeys pecking and scratching in the ground and occasionally gobbling. We continued to watch from our concealment as a flock of no fewer then ten turkeys slowly scratched and pecked their way toward us. A large tom and an adult hen were approaching first, ahead of the others. Again with hand signals, Josh and I agreed on who would take which bird and slowly took aim. I sighted with my pistol and Josh drew a bead with his single shot rifle. I whispered "One, two, now!"

The two shots rang out simultaneously. Feathers and birds flew, but two of the largest lay on the ground.

We collected our birds, remounted and rode south, beside and then ahead of the herd to catch up with the cook. The camp cook, a pleasant, grey-haired Mexican man named Benito whom they called Beanie, drove a long-bed wagon pulled by a pair of mules. Wooden boxes in the bed carried his coffee, flour, beans, salt, jerked beef, and other odds and ends that he used to somehow put meals together on the trail. Behind the wagon seat were stacked several of the wranglers' bed rolls. Tied to the rear of the wagon was a longhorn heifer with a calf beside her. Beanie had driven his team of mules steadily all day to get ahead of the herd and find a good place by water to camp for the night. Josh and I found him beyond the creek, out of the way of an easy crossing, near several large cottonwood trees. A fire crackled and steam was wafting from two large coffee pots, ready for the thirsty wranglers when they got the horses settled down for the night. We dropped the turkeys off with the cook. He thanked us with a wave and flashed a smile reflecting several missing teeth under his full mustache. We then returned to the herd to help get the horses across the creek and settled onto a meadow.

That night Tad and I got acquainted with the rest of the company. Most of the wranglers, except Southerland and Beanie, appeared to be under twenty-three years old. There were two young Mexican men, Raul and Pablo, who spoke a combination of English and Spanish. I could understand most of what they said because I had learned some Spanish from another captive, a young Mexican boy who was taken from his family on a raid below the Rio Grande about a year after I was captured by the Indians. There were two teen-aged brothers; sixteen-year old David Walberg and his eighteen-year old brother Aaron. Tad and I learned the Walberg brothers were orphans after losing their parents and a younger sister to smallpox several years earlier. Tad had gotten acquainted with his trainer, the friendly and talkative fifteen year old Albert Wilson during the day. I didn't know much about my trainer, Josh, because he appeared to be more serious and quieter than the rest of the boys. At fourteen years old, Alexander Whitworth was the youngest of the group. He wore a pair of fragile-looking spectacles under an old, oversized, floppy felt hat.

As we gathered around the campfire for supper, Southerland introduced us to the oldest-looking man in the group besides himself. "Boys, this here is Augustus Matthews. We just call him August. He's number two in charge here. He's been with me for over five years now. Whenever I'm not around and you need to know something, you ask him."

The bearded Matthews shook our hands and handed us both tin plates and cups. "You boys better dig in." He motioned toward the two large pots simmering over the fire. "You never know if those eating machines will leave anything for the real working men." He grinned and nodded toward the rest of the hungry wranglers, some of whom were tossing friendly insults back at him as they gathered around the fire with their plates, spoons and cups.

"Don't let him worry you," Beanie called in his Spanish accent from the back of the wagon. "These boys never go hungry."

As twilight faded to black and the stars overtook the evening sky, Tad and I joined the other men for our first supper on the trail. Beanie had put together a tasty meal of turkey and dumplings, beans, cornbread, honey and coffee. Some of the men were sitting cross-legged around the fire or leaning against their saddles; others were leaning back against the closest cottonwood trees. Listening to the lively banter around the campfire, I had my first real opportunity to observe my new companions. Although most had taken time to splash water from the creek on their faces and hands before supper, they all had an unwashed look. Dust from the trail caked their clothes and lay in a thin layer on their hats. Several wore scuffed and worn knee-high boots. A couple had on high-top shoes and the rest wore plain, undecorated moccasins. Their clothing was a mixture of leather shirts and pants, homespun cotton or wool pants and shirts or clothes made from store-bought yardage. All of their attire looked worn and in need of repair beyond the benefits of a good washing. If any of them owned a kit of needle and thread, it wasn't apparent. I determined that there must be a razor somewhere in the group, because several appeared to have scraped whatever whiskers they could grow from their faces within the last several weeks. However August Matthews and Scotch Southerland and the cook were the exception to whatever shaving conventions were common to the group. Matthews wore a full, trimmed beard, and Southerland left his moustache long and flowing beyond the corners of his lips and extending to his chin. Beanie's beard looked as if it received a shave every few weeks, except the moustache which flowed on either side of his mouth to his chin.

I only saw three other modern revolvers besides mine and Tad's. The rest of the men were armed with an assortment of single shot handguns and Tennessee-style long rifles.

The young men were spirited and enjoyed needling each other and telling stories at each other's expense. They all seemed to enjoy a good laugh around the campfire at the end of a hard day's work.

Southerland issued the night watch schedule and Tad and I

had our watches at twelve o'clock and two o'clock, respectfully. I drew my watch with Pablo, one of the young Mexicans. Tad shared his with Aaron Walberg. The night watch consisted of saddling up and slowly circling the herd, keeping any of the horses from straying outside the perimeter and maintaining vigilance for rustlers or Indians. Within the first half-hour or so, the night watch became as routine as driving the herd during the day, just much quieter and a lot less dusty.

Tad and I adapted well on the trail with Southerland's company. We were both accepted by the other men and pulled our own weight. Each day was much like the previous one, with Southerland making side trips, sometimes several times a day, to sell horses along the route. On the fifth day on the trail, I asked Southerland when I could select my horses from the herd.

"I'd hate to have my heart set on a couple and a farmer beat me to them for cash somewhere along the road. So I thought I'd ask if I could go ahead and claim mine."

"I don't see any reason why not. A couple of the boys have already put a claim on some. You might as well too. Have you made a choice?"

"I believe so. There's a young sorrel stallion with a flaxen mane and tail with a white blaze between his eyes and two white stockings that I've been watching. He can't be over about three years old. Looks pretty strong. Then there's a buckskin filly that I like too."

"Show me the stallion."

We rode into the slow-moving herd looking for the sorrel stallion. After a couple of minutes of searching, I spotted him. "That's the one," I said, admiring the stallion through the dust.

"I was afraid that might be the one you wanted when you described him to me."

"What do you mean, you were afraid?"

"That horse is mighty rank, Andy. August got a mind to try to claim him about three weeks ago, right after we caught him.

He tried the better part of an afternoon to break him, but he could barely get on him, much less ride him. All he got out of it was a couple of broken ribs. Have you ever had to ride every day with broken ribs?"

"No sir, but I had to walk every day, carrying heavy loads after the Comanches broke mine when I was a little kid. Hurts a lot. Do you think August is still interested in him?"

"Don't know." Southerland looked strangely at me, apparently not understanding my comment about the Indians. "You better ask him. He did have first claim."

I looked through the dust cloud to find August but didn't see him right away and assumed he was on the other side of the herd. "I'll talk to him about it tonight," I called over my shoulder to Southerland as he rode back to his position on the edge of the herd.

I approached August that evening as we unsaddled our mounts and carried our tack to camp and asked about the sorrel stallion.

"Aw, that one," August said, unconsciously rubbing his side. "He's a tough one for sure. I thought I was pretty good at breaking horses, but he got the best of me. He'd be an excellent mount if anybody could ever break him."

"I'd like to give him a try, if that's all right with you."

"I believe my body would thank me if I decided on a different one. You go ahead and take him. Most of the others will be a whole lot easier to break and train than that one. He's just got way too much spirit."

"That's exactly what I'm looking for. Thanks a lot." I shared a smile with August and shook his hand. "I'll start working with him right away."

I placed my saddle where I would be sleeping for the night and removed my lariat from the saddle horn. I called to Tad who was just dropping his saddle. "You want to help me for a little while?"

"Sure, what's goin' on?"

I explained my plan to Tad as we walked into the herd to find the stallion. "After I get the rope on him, I want to get him outside the herd so there'll be less distraction. Then you just keep the rope taut. I'll do the rest."

The horses had settled down from their long walk and were quietly grazing. I tried to throw my loop around the stallion's neck without spooking him or the other horses. I hit my mark on the third try. I let out about twenty-five feet of rope and slowly led the horse away from the rest of the herd into a shaded area next to a stand of live oak trees. He was reluctant to follow at first, but finally agreed to come with me.

I handed the rope to Tad, and then just watched the horse. After a few nervous minutes of twitching, trying to pull away and looking around, the horse started watching me. I stood very still, looking the stallion in the eyes. Then I raised my left hand, palm upward toward him. I stood like that for several minutes, just quietly looking him in the eyes. I took a small step toward the stallion, still quietly watching him. Then another step, all the time looking him in the eyes. Any time he looked away or tried to pull away from the rope, I waited where I was, still with my left arm outstretched until he made eye contact with me again.

Once I got close enough, I slowly touched the sorrel on the forehead and started whispering to him in a calm, gentle way. I very lightly brushed my fingers up and down his forehead, gradually increasing the pressure as I stroked him. Then I slowly expanded the area of my strokes to just above the nose and around the ears, all the time whispering and talking gently to him. Next I moved my hand to the right side of his neck and stroked his mane and scratched and stroked his neck with my fingers, then my whole hand. I then started reversing the process, back to the mane, then the ears, then to the forehead and top of the nose, still talking quietly. Then ever so slowly, I started backing away along the rope toward Tad. As I felt Tad's presence behind me, I stood still for another five minutes, just quietly talking to the horse and looking into his eyes. I finally took the coil of rope from Tad, led the stallion back into the herd and released the rope.

Once we were out of the herd and walking toward the camp, Tad said, "I've never seen anyone try to break a horse like that. Usually, they just jump on and try to wear them down."

"I've done it that way too, but I plan on this fella being my friend for a long time, and we've just met. I want him to trust that I won't hurt him. Eventually, he'll look forward to working with me. This process takes a lot of patience and time, but I hope that if I can work with him a little every day between now and the time we get to the coast, I'll have a really good friend who's willing to do anything I ask."

"Have you thought of a name for him yet?"

"Yeah, several, but I kind of think Prince fits him."

"Prince," Tad nodded and smiled. "Hey, Prince, come here, Prince. Whoa, Prince. Prince sounds pretty good to me." The smile gave way to a wide grin.

"Guess its Prince then." I laughed. Come on. Looks like Beanie has supper ready."

We followed the Brazos south to San Felipe with the slow-moving herd, then headed west toward San Antonio. I worked with Prince every evening before supper after getting the herd settled down for the night. Every day at the start of the taming, I repeated the same steps I had established our first day together, then with each passing day I was able to add new steps. After the first four days, I could run my hands all over the horse's body without any rejection or shying away.

The next step was to introduce him to the saddle blanket by first showing it to him, letting him smell it, then gently rubbing it over his body. When Prince got used to the saddle blanket, I placed it softly on his back and removed it several times. The next day, I borrowed a wooden box about two feet high from the cook and led Prince beside it. After I welcomed him for his training session by talking to him gently, slowly running my hands over his body, and putting the blanket on his back, I placed one foot on the box and slowly, very slowly, lifted myself to my full height while standing on the box, again continuing to gently talk to and stroke the horse. This got Prince comfortable seeing me at the same height I would be in the saddle.

The next day, after repeating all the previous steps, I stood on the box and leaned some of my own weight onto the horse, then pulled away. I repeated the process, adding more of my weight each time, leaning over the horse's back on my stomach until the horse accepted all of my weight without complaint. The next day, I brought the saddle and repeated the processes until I slowly and carefully placed the saddle on his back without tightening the cinch. At the end of the tenth day of training, I got the horse to take the bridle and bit. Finally, at the end of two weeks of painstakingly repeating each step of the taming process every day, I gently lifted myself into the saddle and walked away on Prince without any resistance.

About the third day of my training process with Prince, we started attracting an audience of interested onlookers. By the end of the first week of our work, there were five other wranglers using my technique with their chosen mounts on the outskirts of the camp each evening before supper. Tad chose a young grey stallion and a white filly to train for himself and was only two or three days behind me training his stallion.

After two and a half weeks of training, I was working the herd with Prince for about three hours each day. The stallion proved to be everything I thought he would be. He was fast, agile and responded well to commands. Although he hadn't been tested yet, I knew Prince would have the stamina to withstand being driven hard for long periods of time. I felt confident that if any horse could take me to find my sister, this new stallion would be the one.

CHAPTER 25

Southerland's horse sales along the trail were successful. By the time the herd reached San Antonio and camped north of town along the river, the herd had dwindled to about four hundred head.

In order to secure more sales from the town's residents and merchants, Southerland decided to maintain camp outside of town for three days before moving south toward the coast. Only two wranglers at a time were needed to control the herd while we were stationary for several days. So Tad and I took advantage of having a little time to ourselves by visiting the town.

As we rode toward the river, we saw the old mission compound ruins. Like Will and I had done earlier that spring, Tad and I stopped beside the Alamo to offer prayers for the fallen heroes.

When we reached the center of town, I pointed out the old stone court house, which now bore the name, The Council House, since the Indian fight. "I almost met my maker there," I told Tad.

"Were you scared?"

"Didn't have time to be. It all happened so fast, I was just glad I had Will's pistol. That's why I want another one of these," I patted the five-shooter on my hip. You never know when you'll need it."

When we reached the general store, we dismounted and tied our horses to the hitching rail. Once inside, we removed our hats and started looking for firearms.

A middle-aged woman with her hair tied in up in a bun approached us. "May I help you?"

"We're looking for handguns, ma'am." I answered, looking beyond her shoulder at some rifles hanging on the wall.

"My husband can help you better with those than I can. Let

me get him for you." The woman started to turn toward the back of the shop, but looked back at me. "I know you." She studied my face and hair for a moment. "Oh, yes, I remember now. You're the young man who visited with that poor little Lockhart girl last spring, bless her soul."

"Yes, ma'am, I am. How is she?"

"That poor child. I can't tell you how many nights sleep I've lost thinking about her. She stayed with us here until her family came to take her home. I don't see how she can ever overcome her ordeal."

"Yes ma'am, I know."

"She told me that your little sister was taken by the Indians. Is that right?"

"Yes, ma'am, over five years ago."

"Well, I'll pray that you find her some day."

"Thank you, ma'am."

"Let me find my husband for you now. He'll be right out."

In a few moments, we were greeted by a gray haired gentleman, wearing a white apron. "My wife tells me you're looking for handguns."

"Yes sir. Do you have any of those new Colt five-shooters?"

"I do as a matter of fact. I think I have three or four left." He reached to a shelf under the counter and pulled out what looked like a duplicate of the weapon I wore on my hip.

"That's exactly what we're looking for," I reached for the revolver to inspect it.

"Tad, what do you think?"

Tad, who was looking at merchandise across the store, turned to face the shopkeeper and me.

"I hope we'll never need them, but it sure will be good to have an extra one, just in case. We'll take two of them, mister, and extra cylinders, too."

"I don't think so," the store owner said, his eyes narrowing. He looked at the pistol on Tad's hip. "I don't know how you got that," he nodded toward the revolver at Tad's side, but I don't sell firearms to slaves."

I looked at Tad, confident that he would handle himself well, but not sure which tact he would take.

Tad stood in the middle of the store facing the store owner. He was dressed much like me, in buckskin pants and machine woven, home stitched cotton shirt in good condition, a leather vest, felt hat and moccasins; groomed as well as two wranglers off the trail could be in working clothes.

He put a big smile on his face to the store owner and said, "Sir, it appears I have forgotten my manners by not introducing myself upon entering your store. I'm Tad Jefferson. I've been a free man in Texas longer than Texans have had their freedom from Mexico. I carry a letter signed by Stephen Austin certifying my status as a freed man and a citizen of Texas. I own a league and a labor of land on the Brazos River that I farm and hold the land grant title to, also signed by Stephen Austin. I am the brother-in law of Jeff Jefferson and neighbor and friend of William Bowman, both of whom hold letters of commendation from President Sam Houston for their service to him, personally at and after the battle of San Jacinto and I carry a letter of introduction and recommendation from Mister William Bowman of Virginia Point in the Austin Colony."

'Now, I understand that you wouldn't be willing to sell firearms to a colored slave, but sir, I believe you may have me mistaken with someone else."

"Well . . . maybe so," the storekeeper said, turning to his counter to retrieve another pistol and two cylinders.

"Oh, we'll also take 20 pounds of lead, seven pounds of powder and 300 caps and patches," Tad said, ticking off the items on his fingers.

Back out on the street after paying for our new weapons and supplies, we tucked our purchases into our saddle bags. It had been hard for me to contain my smile through paying for our goods and getting out of the store.

"Well, Mister Jefferson, very impressive credentials," I said, grinning.

"Sometimes, you just gotta do what you just gotta do," he answered, a small smile creeping across his face.

CHAPTER 26

I spent part of my idle time while at the San Antonio camp starting the taming process with the buckskin filly. I learned she was more accepting to my training than Prince, but I had no intention of training her to the saddle yet because of her age. She was still too young to ride but showed great promise when she matured a little more. I just wanted her to be comfortable with me and to follow well on a lead rope.

I was also ready to go into the next phase of training with Prince while Southerland was making his sales deals. I challenged August Matthews to a shooting contest, and sweetened the challenge by offering Matthews the use the new Colt revolver I bought in town. I tied Prince to a tree about forty paces from the river's edge, then Matthews and I walked to the water and started shooting at rocks and other targets across the river. We made a shot each and then moved two or three steps back away from the river toward Prince and repeated the process.

Prince appeared nervous and jumpy at first with each shot, but all the while I spoke to him in my quiet, calming voice. After we emptied both revolvers and the extra cylinders, we were within just a few feet of where Prince stood. After reloading, I mounted up and trotted Prince along the riverside, shooting into the water. When I emptied my first pistol, I returned it to my holster and pulled the second from my belt. I turned the horse up-river and kicked him into a full gallop, firing off all five shots as he raced along the river's edge. Prince acted as if he had been listening to gunfire all his life.

"I wouldn't believe it if I hadn't see it with my own eyes," Matthews said as I trotted into camp and pulled Prince to a stop. "He's behaving like a totally different animal. I take my hat off to you, sir." Matthews removed his wide brimmed felt hat and with a large sweeping motion, bowed to me.

I grinned. "Just try the gentle taming method the next time you get a wild or contrary horse to work with. It might save you a couple of broken ribs."

"That's good advice, Andy. I'll take it."

There was one other thing I wanted to train Prince to do while we had the time, before we started moving the remainder of the herd to the coast. On the day before we left San Antonio, after my morning watch, I brought Prince into the shade of a hackberry tree and carefully braided the woven leather strap into a loop in his mane. I asked Tad to go with me and we rode down river, out of sight of the camp.

"What do you want to ride way down here for anyway?" Tad asked, as we descended a knoll that separated us from our camp.

"Oh, I just didn't want the boys to think I'm showing off."

"I don't think doing something that might save your life is showing off." Tad said. "I'm just anxious to get my horse to this point."

I tugged on the loop, testing its security. "All right, here goes." I nudged Prince into a gentle canter downstream along the edge of the river and started talking to him in the gentle voice and leaned far to the right in the saddle. Then I leaned far to the left. I strung the loop around my shoulders, pulled my foot from the left stirrup and leaned far to the right alongside the horse's neck. I was almost talking into his ear. I repeated the process on his left side. Then I went farther down along his neck, extending my head and shoulders below his head. We rode like that for a few moments, and then repeated the process on the other side. Prince was responding splendidly to my instructions. I pulled the revolver from its holster and reached under the horse's neck and fired off two shots. Prince didn't waver. He kept loping straight ahead, apparently without any concern for what I was doing on his back. I fired the other three in quick succession. There was still no negative response from Prince. I returned to the saddle and came to a stop, praising my horse for his performance while exchanging the pistol's cylinders. I turned the horse around, this time heading toward Tad, and pushed him into a hard gallop. At top speed, I swung to the animal's side and fired off five shots at targets on the other side of the river from under the horse's neck. I then righted myself in the saddle and rode to Tad.

"Whoa! Whoa, boy!" I called, bringing Prince to a stop next to Tad. I laughed, patting my new partner on the neck. "I think I'll keep him. I don't believe anything can rattle him."

As we rode back to camp, we made plans to finish training our horses before we reached the coast and were discharged by Southerland.

"I just need a few more days with my stallion before I'll be riding him," Tad said.

"While you're finishing with him, I can work with your filly and get her to where she can follow a lead rope. That's all I've done with mine. Then we'll be able to head right back to Virginia Point without any training delays."

Southerland had a successful sale at San Antonio and the horse company left town the next morning with slightly less than three hundred head. We were traveling toward Victoria, and then on over to Linnville on the coast.

Tad finished his taming process for his gray stallion, during the next several days as we headed south to the coast. He worked the horse a few hours every day to get him used to long hours in the saddle.

We pulled into Linnville on the twenty-seventh day since joining the company at the Bowman farm. Linnville was a small commercial port on the Gulf coast. Its primary business was receiving goods for shipment into the interior of the country, especially to towns like Victoria, San Antonio, Goliad, Gonzales and the new capital at Austin. Once the imported goods were unloaded, the ships were then reloaded with Texas export goods like cotton, corn, furs and hides bound for the United States and

Europe. There were several warehouses in the town for shipping and receiving goods and I counted three seagoing vessels at anchor in the bay.

That evening, after settling the herd for the night and setting up camp, Scotch Southerland paid Tad and me for our work.

"Sure do appreciate everything you boys have done." Southerland said. "You've both been really good hands. You've got a place in my outfit any time."

"We'll keep that in mind," I said. "But we've got some farm work to do and some good people depending on us to help harvest. Maybe we can hook up with you another time."

"I'll look forward to it. Now you boys stay and have supper with us tonight and sleep here. You won't even have to do a night watch. That'll be a nice relief for you. You can head out first thing in the morning."

After bidding goodbye to our friends the next morning, we outfitted ourselves in town with supplies for the trip home. As we rode out of Linnville that morning, I had a good feeling that I was taking care of the things that I needed to do to move on with my life. I had a good, modern weapon on my hip and another in my belt and the confidence that I could use them well. I had a well-trained, strong horse that would take me into — and more importantly deliver me safely from any battle. I had the fighting skills and desire to take on any obstacle in the way of finding my sister.

CHAPTER 27

Tad and I were enjoying our quiet ride without the dust of a large herd of horses and at a faster, more comfortable pace astride our stallions with the fillies trailing behind us through the south Texas countryside. On the morning of the third day after leaving the Southerland Company we had just broken camp and were riding through the pleasant little town of La Grange. A few people were outside the stores and nodded at us as we rode by. One shopkeeper was in the process of opening his store and the liveryman was filling a watering trough along the street with buckets from a barrel in the back of his wagon.

I suddenly heard the growing sound of approaching horsemen riding hard on the road behind us. I turned and saw a group of no fewer than fifteen riders loping toward us. One of the riders at the front of the group shouted as they reached the center of town, "Indians have raided Victoria and Linnville!"

"Hello the town!" another man yelled. "Indians killed over twenty people in Victoria and Linnville and have taken women and children. We need volunteers to fight!"

People spilled from the buildings and surrounded the riders in the streets to hear the news.

"We need people to spread the word to others in the countryside. We need militia men to join us," one of the riders told the gathering knot of locals.

"Where are the Indians now?" I asked.

"Last we heard, they was goin' back the way they came," one of the riders said. He wore a bushy, blond beard and buckskins. "They're probably somewhere south of Gonzales by now. Looks like they're following a trail north, heading toward the hills west of Austin. They've swept the whole country clean of horses and mules between Cuero and Linnville."

"How many are they?" asked the liveryman.

"I didn't believe it at first," said another rider, an older man with a full, drooping, white moustache, "but I heard from several different people that there was somewhere around a thousand Comanches, including five hundred warriors. The rest of them were women, children and old men. They sacked and burned the warehouses at Linnville and they're moving all that loot plus somewhere around fifteen hundred horses with them. In addition to all the horses and mules they stole from the farms in the area, there was a horse trader around Linnville that lost his whole herd to 'em."

Tad's jaw dropped as he and I looked at each other.

"Those were Scotch Southerland's horses!" I said. "He's the horse trader. We just left his company three days ago. Tad and I been working for him for the last month. Was any of the horse company hurt?"

"Don't know any of those particulars. All we know was somewhere around twenty people were killed from Victoria and Linnville and some women and children were taken. You must'a left Linnville just a few hours ahead of the attack."

"First thing in the morning, three days ago."

"We were told they struck late morning, and spent the rest of the day and night tearing the place apart. We helped bury some folks yesterday. Now we're gathering men and looking for Colonel Burleson. His place is up the road aways, just outside of Bastrop. He'll be able to raise his militia from Bastrop and Austin. Then we need to meet with General Huston and his troops and several other militia groups that are gathering at Plum Creek, just southwest of Austin."

"You mean Sam Houston is leading the army again? Tad asked, surprised that the hero of San Jacinto would be leading the army again after being president.

"Naw, this is General Felix Huston, General of the Texas army. He'll be leadin' the fight.

"It looks like the Comanches will be moving through there sometime tomorrow. They're traveling really slow with all those stolen horses and hundreds of pack animals loaded up with plunder."

Tad and I looked at each other again. I opened my mouth to speak, but Tad interrupted me. "Of course we're going. With that many Indians, your sister may be with 'em."

Tad and I dismounted and approached the liveryman. Within a few minutes we'd made arrangements to leave our fillies with him and promised to retrieve them in a few days. Several men from the town had ridden to nearby farms to collect militia. Others in town were outfitting themselves and saddling their horses to ride with us while we waited in the street.

Soon the growing group of volunteers, now numbering thirty-four, rode out of town, heading north to Bastrop.

Along the way, we got more details of the raid at Linnville from one of the other riders, a skinny, bearded man named Lucas.

"From what we was told, they was several ships that had just unloaded their cargo. Them warehouses was all loaded. Them redskins just took over the whole town and busted into ever warehouse and stripped 'em clean. There was everthang in them warehouses from furniture and house goods to clothes, food and whiskey; everthang you could imagine. The only way most the folks in town escaped with their hair was by runnin' for boats and rowin' out to the merchant ships in the bay."

By mid-day our company reached Bastrop and Colonel Edward Burleson's home. He immediately sent riders to the surrounding farms to gather his militia. He also sent two men with fresh horses to Austin to collect volunteers there and have them meet us on our way to Plum Creek.

While we waited for the Bastrop militia to assemble at Burleson's home, Mrs. Burleson and her daughters fed us all under the shade of three large pecan trees next to the house. She provided several hams from her smoke house, canned squash from her garden and cornbread fresh from her oven.

Tad and I also had an opportunity to get better acquainted with some of the men in our company. I learned that the man with the brushy blond beard wearing buckskins who had helped spread the news in La Grange was Jacob Robson. When Robson learned of Rosie's and my capture by the Indians, he placed a beefy arm around my shoulder and squeezed. "Thank God you finally got loose," he said, staring into my eyes. "I know how bad you want to find your sister. I lost my whole family — my wife and two little girls and my younger brother three years ago to them savages at my place, up the Colorado River a ways. We hadn't no more than put the new cabin up after the Mexicans burned us out during the war when a raidin' party attacked my place. I was out huntin' when they come. Must'a surprised my brother, Jonathan, out in the field. Looked like he didn't have no chance at all. Filled him full of arrows, scalped him and cut him up real bad." I watched Robson as he talked. His eyes had a downcast, far-away look, but remained dry. "When I got there, the cabin was still burnin'. Found my wife and the girls, what was left of 'em anyway, in the burned-out cabin. They burned 'em up, Andy." Robson raised his gaze to me, the pain showing through his pale, gray eyes. "But I guess I don't have to tell you how they are. I'm sure you know first-hand. Guess the only reason I'm still in Texas is to kill as many of 'em as I can. I go after 'em ever' chance I get. Ain't got much else to do."

"You don't go by yourself, do you?" I asked.

"Sometimes I do, sometimes a few other boys go with me. There's lots of folks scattered about that lost kin to them Comanches."

"Sounds like you're the kind of man I need to have along when I go after my sister if we don't find her with this bunch we're going after now."

"You just let me know, Andy. I'll be happy to go with you, and I know a bunch of others who'll come along too. Several of 'em are ridin' with us now."

Soon riders were joining our troop in groups of twos and

threes from the surrounding farms. By mid afternoon, a company of over fifty volunteers left Burleson's yard to gather one more group of fighters before merging with the other Texas forces at Plum Creek.

We learned that Burleson was taking us to recruit a group of Tonkawa Indians, lead by Chief Placido, who was a friend of Burleson and whom Burleson knew would agree to any opportunity to fight and kill their age-old enemy, the Comanche.

Several of the riders around Tad and me were discussing Indians as we rode toward their camp.

"You know them Tonkawa," an older man said addressing Tad, "they get great delight in eating people."

Tad looked doubtfully at me. "Is that true?"

"Yes, I'm afraid it is. I heard plenty of stories about that while I was captured by the Comanches. The Comanches believe that the greatest way to die and to please the Great Spirit is to die in battle. But if you're mutilated and cut up with parts missing after you're killed in battle, there's no way to find your way to their idea of heaven. The Tonkawa make sure the hated Comanche has no way to their heaven. They not only mutilate them after killing them in battle, but they eat their flesh."

Burleson was recognized as he rode into the Tonkawa Indian camp at the head of the column of volunteers and was taken immediately to the chief's lodge. Upon being told of the widespread raiding by the large group of multiple tribes of Comanches and their location only thirty miles distant, a wide smile creased Chief Placido's face as he nodded his agreement to join in the fight.

While the chief gathered his warriors, I noticed the differences between the Tonkawa camp and the Comanche way of life I was used to. The Tonkawa appeared to live stationary in their mud and stick huts rather than the nomadic life the plains Indians, with their horse culture and their very portable buffalo hide covered "tee-pees" as the white men called them. The most noteworthy difference between the two was the absence of horses among the Tonkawa. But the lack of horses had no bearing on Placido and his men's eagerness to fight Comanches. As Colonel Burleson turned his horse from the Tonkawa camp and spurred to a trot, Chief Placido placed his hand on Burleson's horse's rump and he and his thirteen warriors trotted on foot as our company rode for thirty miles without rest.

Along the way, we were joined by twelve more volunteers from Austin, which brought our total to seventy-eight volunteers.

As we rode, I watched my fellow volunteers and noted the differences between the fighters. Most were white men who had established themselves in Texas from the United States in the last several years. Some were recent immigrants from different European countries. A few were native Mexicans whose families had owned their Texas land for generations. Many were farmers. Some of the men wore thick cotton pants and others wore leather pants and wool or cotton homespun shirts. Some were merchants, wearing store-bought clothes. There were a couple of teamsters, astride their mules. A preacher was among the group, wearing his black, swallow-tailed frock coat. Several men appeared to be successful land owners, dressed smartly and mounted well. Others looked to be backwoods types in buckskins and moccasins. There were several boys, still in their teens but old enough to fight, and there were also a few old men with white beards riding with the group. The headgear they wore was as varied in appearance as the volunteers with everything from neatly blocked, wide brimmed felt hats to floppy, sweat-stained hats. Some wore wide straw hats and others wore cotton caps. Some even wore caps made from animal skins. The Tonkawa Indians were dressed very simply, with little more than a loincloth, leggings and moccasins. A few wore leather vests. They carried their bows and arrows in their hands.

As the sun set, leaving an orange and red tinted sky, we rode into the camping areas already occupied by General Huston and his small force of regular soldiers and several other militia groups near Plum Creek. The Comanches were still miles south of us, slowly making their way north. Huston had scouts posted along the Indian's path, providing regular reports advising of the enemy's progress.

After hobbling our horses close to our campsite, Tad and I visited with some of the volunteers from the other companies. We approached several young men relaxing under a cottonwood tree, next to the creek.

"Has any of your group engaged the enemy yet?" I asked.

"Naw, we jest come over from Seguin this afternoon," a shaggy haired young man about my age answered. "I 'magine we'll get a chance to fight tomorrow though."

I removed my hat so they could see my curly red hair. "If you see a girl about eleven or twelve years old with hair like mine, it could be my sister. She was taken by the Comanches about five years ago and I haven't seen her since, but I have reason to believe that maybe they adopted her. Anyway, I'd appreciate it if you'd look out for her tomorrow, and help me spread the word about her." After getting assurance from the group that they would help, we moved from camp to camp asking support looking for Rosie. We also started asking whether anyone had seen or heard of Scotch Southerland or any from his company.

"We heard about a horse trader losin' his entire herd down at Linnville," a settler wearing leather pants and a homespun shirt said. "You may want to talk to Captain Caldwell's boys, down yonder." He pointed over his shoulder to another set of small campfires. "I heared he picked up some men that had follered them red-skins from down around the coast."

We followed the fire glow to the next set of campfires. Upon walking into the light from the campfire, I saw Southerland and August Matthews leaning against their saddles.

"Well, look what the cat done drug up!" August said, breaking into a grin.

"We were hoping to see you here somewhere," I said as Tad and I walked around the fire to shake hands with our friends.

"Sorry to hear about the herd, but glad to see you two alive. Were any of the other boys hurt?"

"No, thank God. We all got out all right," Southerland said. "I learned a long time ago that our lives are worth a lot more than a few horses. When I saw how many Indians we were up against, I told the boys to high-tail it away from the herd and let 'em have 'em. Losing horses is just an occupational hazard sometimes when you do what I do. But it'll give me some satisfaction if I can drop a few of them thieves tomorrow. I made good money on this trip after paying off the boys."

I said, "We were just visiting around with the troops and volunteers telling them about my sister and asking them to look out for her. If you'd do the same and help spread the word to the rest of your company, I'd appreciate it."

"We'll do it, and you two look out for yourselves tomorrow," Southerland said, again shaking hands with both of us.

CHAPTER 28

That night we busied ourselves at the campfire melting lead bars and molding additional balls for our pistols and insuring all our gear was in excellent order before we crawled into our bedrolls. After a short, fitful sleep, Tad and I shared an uneventful two hour watch before daylight.

After a quick breakfast of jerky and coffee, I approached Colonel Burleson. "Sir, Tad and I just finished our morning watch, and we're wide awake and ready to go. If it's all right with you, we could ride south aways and relieve the pickets there and watch for the Indian's approach."

"That'll be fine. Just stay far back in the brush and out of sight. We've got information that the Comanches camped about five miles south of here and are probably moving this way already. Whenever you see the first of them, come on back here and let us know."

We found the pickets almost a mile south of the main Texans' camp. The two men we relieved were grateful for the opportunity to return to camp to get breakfast before the fight. We positioned ourselves well in the brush next to the creek, but in such a way that we had a clear view of the prairie for miles to the south and west. The land in front of us was rolling, open prairie with large areas of dry grass waving two feet high. The only way the Indians could evade us would be to try to outrun us on the prairie or dash into the woods along the creek. The woods were not a good escape option because of the dense berry patches growing so thickly in places. Penetration, especially by horseback, would be impossible.

We passed our time waiting for the Indians by braiding leather loops into our horse's manes. Shortly after we finished carefully attaching the woven straps, we saw the leading edge of the Indian tribes approaching in the distance. There was an arc of people and animals almost a half-mile wide leading the massive parade that stretched behind them farther than we could see. I couldn't make out details of individuals yet, but I could see, even at a distance, that among the hundreds of Indians on horseback, many were driving large herds of horses.

"You seen enough?" I asked Tad.

"I've seen enough to know we're really outnumbered. I only counted about two hundred volunteers and soldiers last night to fight these savages. We can't even see all of them right now, but of what I can see, I'd guess there's five or six hundred, and that's only part of them. We can't even see how far back they stretch."

"Yeah, but remember, the people who've seen them said there are about five hundred or so *warriors*. Those are the ones we need to be concerned with now."

"We'd better get back and let the colonel know they're here."

We slipped out of our hiding place and rode the mile back to the Texans' camp unobserved by the Indians.

We found Colonel Burleson with General Huston and the other leaders standing in a circle, discussing their battle plan.

I got the colonel's attention.

"Colonel, they're about a mile and a half south of us, heading this way. They'll be coming over that rise out there in a little while. They're spread out about a half-mile wide and stretch back farther than we can see."

"All right, gentlemen," General Huston said, stepping back from the circle of men, "We've got our plan. Now let's go execute it."

The leaders collected their horses and rode to their troops. Tad and I fell in behind Burleson as he rode to his company. We noticed that the Tonkawa Indians had all tied a white strip of cloth around their head so they wouldn't be mistaken for Comanche during the battle.

"All right, boys," Burleson called. "We're going to form a line to the west; out there about a half-mile from here. General

Huston and his troops are forming a line on the east side, out aways from the woods. There's another group in reserve in the woods. After we get into position we'll draw some of the warriors out to us, and then send skirmish lines in. Everybody understand?" He hesitated a moment looking over the troops, and then yelled, "Forward!"

As we rode to our position, closer to the now visible approaching Indians, we saw an amazing sight. Instead of preparing for battle, the warriors and their families were struggling to maintain their looted goods and horses and keep them moving. Scores of horses and mules were fashioned with travois, heavily loaded with everything from furniture to bed linens and bolts of colorful cloth. Some of the horses had strings of pots and pans dangling from them and clanging noisily. Others had spittoons and chamber pots tied to their backs and hanging off their sides. More had bulging bundles of blankets and quilts tied to them. One old woman close to the front of the procession wore several felt hats, stacked one on top of the other. Most of the warriors tied yards of colorful streaming calico and silk ribbons of red, green, yellow and blue to their painted horses' manes and tails and into their own hair, allowing the long ribbons to flow far behind them in the wind. They also draped colorful yard goods over their horse's necks and behind their saddles, much of which was dragging in the dirt behind them.

Warriors, women and children alike were working to maintain control over the large herds of horses scattered among the slow-moving procession. Many of the men were dressed in ready to wear clothes they'd stolen from Linnville. One warrior toward the front of the procession was wearing a tall, black stovepipe hat, a pair of thigh-high black patent boots and soft, brown calfskin gloves. He wore a green swallow-tailed coat backwards, buttoned up in the back with the tails resting on his knees. He was also carrying a red parasol and was singing at the top of his lungs while we took our positions.

As Burleson's men, including Tad and I, approached our

position, a small group of warriors moved forward of the others as if they were preparing to engage us.

Once in position, Burleson gave the order for us to dismount. He walked his horse along our line, making sure each fighter was ready. Tad and I removed our hats and tied them to the back of our saddles by their chin straps so they wouldn't interfere with the fighting. "All right, men," Burleson looked over his shoulder at the Indians. "they'll make their move any time now. Don't waste your powder till they're in range. Make every shot count." He then walked his horse behind the line of men waiting for the Indians to attack.

Each man twisted his horse's reins around his wrist. Most knelt to make a smaller target of themselves and to be able to steady their aim.

It didn't take long before several braves rode toward the line of volunteers, yelling, whooping and shaking their lances, all the time with their shields up in front of them. Then as they approached firing range, they spun around and raced away beyond range to taunt us.

"Hold on, boys," Burleson said calmly. "They're just trying to draw your fire."

The Indian with the stovepipe hat and the parasol soon joined the knot of braves taunting the line of Texans. He spun his horse in circles, hooting and yelping, then raced ahead of the others toward our line while flapping his parasol up and down. He skidded to a stop about ninety yards from the Texans to spin his horse back and forth, pointing the parasol out in front of him toward us, hooting, laughing and pointing at us. He repeated this process several times while the other warriors watched from a safe distance. Each time the warrior in the tall hat rode toward our line, he rode closer and became more brazen in the way he challenged us. He charged to within seventy yards of our line and threw both his arms out to his sides, parallel to his shoulders, one hand holding his shield and the other holding the parasol, to show how invincible he believed he was against his enemy's bullets.

Keller, the white mustached man, was kneeling next to me with his left elbow propped on his knee, squinting through his rifle sight at the obnoxious Indian making a spectacle of himself. Just loud enough for me to hear, he said, "I believe I've had *jest* about enough of that ole boy." He squeezed the trigger.

The rifle ball imbedded itself deep in the center of the Indian's chest, knocking the stovepipe hat off his head as he tumbled off the back of his horse. Several of the surprised warriors behind him fired arrows at us, but they all fell short. After retrieving the dying Indian from the ground, they retreated, screaming and wailing their outrage at their loss.

It became apparent to us that there was little, if any, coordinated effort on the part of the Indians to attack or to prepare to defend themselves. Most seemed to be much more interested in maintaining their loot from the Linnville warehouses and keeping their horse herds moving than being bothered with fighting.

Burleson watched the warriors retreating toward the main body of people and horses and shook his head. "Boys, looks like we're going to have to take the fight to them. Break into smaller groups and advance, then retreat. Then repeat the process. Always watch your position and don't get surrounded. Keep in mind where you'll reload. All right, get in there and take 'em down!"

Tad and I had previously made a point of getting acquainted with the other members of our troop who were armed with repeating pistols. We quickly formed a squad of fighters armed like ourselves and within moments were galloping after a group of warriors who were attempting to slip past us to the west, driving horses and heavily loaded pack animals.

Although the Tonkawas came to the fight without horses, it took them only a few minutes into the fight to become mounted. On several occasions, I saw Tonkawa warriors run to a mounted Comanche, and after the swift use of a tomahawk or war club, throw the injured Comanche to the ground, take ownership of his horse and ride away to kill more Comanches.

There appeared to be conflicting orders and confusion among the different tribes, as if they were only traveling together but had no central leadership or battle plan. Occasionally, a small group of braves attempted to position themselves parallel to the galloping Texans to fire arrows at us, but my squad picked them off easily with our five-shooters. Several times during the fighting, Tad and I protected ourselves from approaching groups of warriors, and surprised both the Indians and the other members of our squad, by swinging into our loops, riding alongside our horse's necks and shooting Indians from beneath our mount's heads.

The Indians were soon scattering across the prairie, stretching the moving caravan up to two miles wide and six miles long. Our squad ranged throughout the masses of people and horses, targeting pockets of warriors traveling together. We frequently engaged in horse races to shoot them and then spin away after nearly emptying our pistols to find a safe place to reload.

During one break in the fighting, we retreated to the safety of the brush next to the creek to rest, reload and refresh ourselves with a few sips of water from the creek. I finished reloading before the others and while I waited, I watched the continued progression of the Indians beyond the woods, paying particular attention to the women and children, looking for Rosie. Suddenly I recognized a face. I looked closer through the swirling dust. It was the ugly, hateful face I had seen every day for years. It was Coyote Den.

The old woman was riding a horse and leading another, pulling a travois loaded high with bundles of loot including bed linens, three chamber pots and several bolts of brightly printed cotton fabric. I looked at the cluster of people around her and recognized several of the other old crones that I'd worked so hard for and from whom I'd received only punishment in return.

But the one I'd hoped someday to meet in battle was her son, Strings Bow Tight. I suspected he wouldn't be far away from his mother and the rest of his tribe, so I began looking for him from my place of concealment. It didn't take but a moment to find him and several of the other young warriors who had humiliated me and treated me so harshly. They were driving a tightly packed herd of no less than 150 horses and mules, trying to keep up with the cowardly old women and hurrying to get away from the attacking Texans.

I called quietly to the others behind me who were finishing with their loading. "Boys, this war just got personal for me. There's a score I need to settle out there. That bunch hates me as much as I hate them and they'll do whatever they can to kill me. This is my fight with them. You don't have to stay with me if you don't want to."

"They's just Injuns, ain't they?" one of the volunteers said. "I come here to kill Injuns."

The rest of the men voiced their support.

"All right then, I appreciate it. The ones I'm after are right in front of us." I pointed through the brush. "There's one in particular that I want. That's him with the crooked nose and the red and yellow paint on his chest. He's mine." I looked around. "Is everybody ready?" After an affirmative response, I called, "let's go," and led the group out of the thicket and back to the fight.

As our small party emerged from an opening in the thicket, I rode directly into the horse herd, to within twenty yards and slightly behind Strings Bow Tight.

"Strings Bow Tight!" I shouted in the Comanche language. He didn't hear me. Again I yelled, "Strings Bow Tight," to get his attention over the din of the herd of horses and the other noises of hundreds of Indians and horses moving across the prairie. As he turned, I ran my fingers through my curly hair with my left hand and finally got the attention of the young warrior.

His eyes widened in shock and disbelief as he recognized

me.

I grinned and shouted in Comanche, "Did you like your long, cold walk last winter?"

The surprise on the Indian's face turned to rage. Strings Bow Tight quickly strung an arrow and raised his bow to fire just as I cocked the hammer on my Colt and put a hole in the middle of his face. Other shots rang out around me as men in my squad took out the other warriors in the immediate area who recognized me at the same time as Strings Bow Tight. I turned and leveled my pistol at the old woman, now no longer interested in her loot. She screamed. Her face filled with shock and anguish as she fell off her horse to run to her dead son. I held my bead on her for several seconds as she gathered him in her arms, wailing her grief. My horse held his position among the frightened, tightly packed animals crowding around him. I watched the old woman on the ground, engulfed in swirling dust with sharp hooves all around her and the lifeless figure she held as she looked up at me. I saw her expression change along with a glint of recognition in her eyes just before she was kicked in the head and trampled by the horses that were terrified by the shooting. I lowered my arm and released the hammer on my pistol. *Would I have shot her? I'll never know now.*

As the running fight stretched into the afternoon, the Comanches and the horse herds spread farther apart, resulting in a battleground extending up to eight miles wide and twelve to thirteen miles in length.

The long morning stretched into an even longer afternoon, and it was clear to everyone involved that there was no fight left in the Indians. By mid-afternoon, they'd abandoned most of the heavily laden horses and mules. Loot that had been too hard to maintain on the run was littered over the expansive battlefield. Hundreds of abandoned horses grazed contentedly on the prairie in groups of twenty to thirty, left by the retreating throng of Indians, now much more concerned with getting away from the punishing bullets of the white men than maintaining their plunder.

With my need for revenge satisfied, Tad and I spent less time as the afternoon passed chasing warriors and more time looking for Rosie. We sought out the clusters of women and children traveling together and at a distance called her name. Anytime I saw a figure that looked about twelve years old, I called, "Rosie? Rosie? It's Bubba!"

Tad hollered, "Rosie! It's your brother, Andy!"

We rode from one group of women and children to another, avoiding further skirmishing trying to find Rosie. As I yelled her name, most of the women and children looked curiously at me, especially when I called in their language. But no one responded and we were finally convinced Rosie wasn't there.

As twilight settled over a prairie littered with piles of discarded goods, grazing horses and dead Indians' bodies that hadn't been retrieved by their families, Tad and I turned our horses to the Texans' camp.

"Andy," Tad said as we headed for camp, "those Comanches have to be from the southern tribes. This whole raid was to take revenge for their losses at the Council House fight. I'd be willing to bet that the northern tribes had nothing to do with the Council House fight. They may not even know about it. And I'd also be willing to bet that Rosie's with one of those tribes, way up around the Canadian and Arkansas rivers. That's where that Lockhart girl said she saw her, way up north, by the Canadian. Right?"

"Yeah, that's what she said."

"Did you ever go that far north with the tribe you were with?"

"Not really. We seldom went that far north. There are lots of different Comanche tribes up farther north than I was. Besides the Comanches, there's Kiowa and Cheyenne up in that area."

"Do you think it's possible that the Kiowa or Cheyennes have her?"

I hesitated a moment. "I've never considered that, but I guess it's possible. When she was taken I just assumed it was another tribe of Comanches. I didn't know one tribe from another back then. I guess she could have been traded to any tribe."

When we reached camp, we gave our count of verified kill to Colonel Burleson and later learned that there had been over forty Comanches killed and left on the prairie and only one Texan killed and eight wounded in the battle. We also learned that all of the captives that had been taken at Victoria and Linnville were accounted for. Unfortunately, most of them, women, children and slaves, had been killed by the Comanches rather than released unharmed. Only two were found uninjured.

We also learned that the goods left on the prairie, including the horses, would be divided among the men who'd fought in the battle rather than returned to their rightful owners. Several men around the campfire were excited about the opportunity of receiving the goods.

"This here's war, and we won it," one of the men lounging around the fire said. Another man grinned and added, "To the victor go the spoils."

"Speaking of victory," Tad said, nodding toward the Tonkawa camp about fifty yards downstream, "sounds like the Tonkawa are taking theirs seriously." The Tonkawas had just started their celebration of their victory over the Comanches and were beating their drums, singing and dancing.

"Thank the Lord I'm hard of hearing," Keller said through his flowing, white moustache. He was leaning on his saddle across the fire from me, puffing on his pipe. "They ain't gonna get no quieter. It only gets louder and lasts all night. I can take the racket they's makin' all right. It's when they start cookin' up them Comanches, now that kinda puts a knot in my gullet. I'm glad I already et my supper 'cause it stinks like hell when they go to roastin' them greasy Injuns over that big ole bonfire. And it looks like we're down-wind of 'em. That ain't good. That smoke'll come rollin' down this way 'fore long."

Tad and I looked at each other. Tad tilted his head to the south and raised his eyebrows while we listened to the singing and hollering getting louder.

"Not that we don't appreciate your company, gentlemen," I said, starting to gather my belongings. "But before we get too settled in here, I think Tad and I have agreed to move downstream aways. With the breeze from the south, that'll put us upwind from our noisy neighbors."

"Boys, that sounds like a reasonable suggestion," one of the men said, starting to pick up his things.

"Mind if I join you?" another one asked.

Soon the whole camp was gathering their belongings. After kicking dirt on the fire and collecting our horses, we all moved seven hundred yards south to a quieter, more peaceful camp.

CHAPTER 29

Tad and I had no interest in the spoils of war, understanding that the rightful owners had probably lost everything. We knew how hard we had worked with Southerland's Company and could imagine the effects of the Linnville business owners' losses.

The next morning, we told our leaders to not include us in portioning the goods left on the prairie. We had a long way to travel and had our own livestock to pick up at La Grange before proceeding back to Virginia Point.

After learning how to find Jacob Robson and several others who had offered to help find my sister, we bid our new friends goodbye and headed east to pick up our fillies. It took us almost a full day before we turned to the hitching post in front of the livery stable at La Grange. After filling the livery owner in on the details of the Plum Creek fight, we picked up our horses and headed northeast toward Virginia Point.

In San Felipe we made the customary stop at the Williams Land Company office to tell Sam Williams about the Plum Creek fight so the news would get out to the rest of the eastern settlements.

After walking out of Williams' office, instead of mounting my horse, I led him across the street to the general store.

"Tad, the last time we were in that store, something struck my fancy."

"What's that?" Tad said as he fell in beside me.

"He had some well-made saddles. I can't borrow Will's saddle and bridle forever." We tied our horses outside and entered the store.

I had been thinking about buying a saddle ever since we left the La Grange Livery. I'd looked at a couple of saddles there and could afford to pay for one then, but had no way of carrying it at the time. The filly wasn't yet trained to carry a saddle. Along the way between La Grange and San Felipe, Tad and I both had taken time to train our fillies to the saddle.

When we emerged from the store, I carried a new saddle over my shoulder. I didn't have enough money to pay for the bridle and blanket so Tad loaned me enough to cover those. Tad held the filly still and calmed her while I gently placed the blanket and saddle on the nervous young horse.

My mind drifted to my priorities while we worked with the filly. When the saddle was secure, I said, "Tad, I believe I'm almost ready now."

"Ready for what?"

"Ready to get serious about finding Rosie."

"I thought you were serious all along."

"I was, but I wasn't ready. Now I've got everything I need."

"That's true," Tad said, swinging into his saddle when we finished with the filly. I noticed him watching me as I readied my stallion to ride.

"You're not the same skinny kid I found in that thicket last winter."

"I guess not, thanks to all of you." I chuckled, sliding into Will's saddle on Prince. "I imagine I've put on fifteen pounds or so and grown a couple of inches since then."

Tad glanced at me and grinned. "I'd say at least that much." We kicked our horses into a trot away from the store's hitching post. Turning serious again, Tad said, "I know I always want to be on your side in a fight, but you're still not ready for the fight you're after."

"Why not?"

"You know you can't go it alone. You need a company of men, as many as you can get. You need good men you can depend on who know how to fight. You need men with a good reason to be out there, willing to be away from their families for weeks and risk their lives fighting Indians."

"I know." I said, staring at Prince's mane. "I've got a good idea of what I need to do, but the timing's not good. I've got other obligations. But the right time will come and I'll be ready."

CHAPTER 30

We had only a few days to rest and enjoy our reunion with Libby and Billy and the Bowmans after our weeks in the saddle before the cotton was ready for harvesting.

We soon found ourselves in the fields, bending over our long sacks, dragging them between the rows, pricking our hands on the sharp, dry husks, filling our fingers with endless handfuls of cotton. Days blurred into weeks as the sacks filled and were emptied into wagons, then driven to the market at San Felipe. Everyone worked, even the children who pulled their small sacks behind them, sometimes complaining, sometimes daydreaming, but eventually filling and emptying their sacks, only to start over again.

As the days passed and our work progressed, the daytime temperature started providing some relief. When we first started picking, we were soaked in sweat by mid-morning. Later, after almost a month of back-aching work, the October morning air was crisp and mid-day was comfortable.

A celebration erupted one afternoon in late October as we completed stripping the last rows and emptied our sacks into the wagon. Tad and I climbed into the last of the three loaded wagons, then pulled the children in behind us to help tamp down the load. Soon, we were all jumping up and down in the cotton. The children were giggling and throwing cotton at each other. Then Will, Anna and Libby all climbed up to join the fun. Amid the laughter, cotton and children were flying through the air, and then bouncing back onto the soft bed. We played until we were all out of breath.

After a few minutes of catching our breath and with the children still giggling and poking at each other, Will said, "As much fun as this is, it's not getting these wagons to market. We still have some work to do so we'll be ready to leave for San

Felipe first thing tomorrow." Tad and I had already made several trips to San Felipe, transporting two wagons of cotton at a time to the cotton dealer. For this trip, we planned for everyone, including the women and children, to go to town so the women could shop before winter.

That evening while Anna and Libby made their shopping lists in the Bowman kitchen, Will, Tad and I were in Will's barn preparing for the trip. After loading Will's old surveying tent and a few other supplies on top of the cotton in one wagon, I was laying out the mule's harness.

"Will, Tad, we need to talk," I said in a serious tone.

"What?" Will asked, stopping his work.

"I need your help."

"What kind of help?" Tad asked.

"I want to try to find Rosie this winter. She's been gone too long. I just can't wait much longer."

"You know we'll help you," Will said, placing his hand on my shoulder. "We told you that last spring. The women have known for a long time that we'd be going out with you whenever you thought you were ready. Looks like that time is here."

"Thanks to all of you, I feel like I am ready now. But like you've told me, we need a good plan. I think I've got it now.

"Will, do you remember when we were in San Antonio, we learned from those government men there was somewhere between thirty-five to forty-five white captives believed to be alive, living with the Comanches?"

"Yeah, I remember."

"We found nine at San Antonio, so that leaves a whole lot more that may still be out there, including Rosie. That doesn't even count some Negro and Mexican captives they might have. I don't know how many people they've killed in the settlements here in the last fifteen years or so, but I know there are more than a few folks who have lost kin to them, and they live for the day when they can get their children back. I believe if we time it right I could raise a good number of men who're willing to go with us to rescue as many captives as we can find."

"So why do you feel winter is the best time?" Tad asked.

"Two reasons. First, most everybody in the settlements are farmers like us and are doing about what we're doing now, getting their crops in and getting ready for next year's planting. When we get back from San Felipe, we still have to burn off the stalks and clean the fields for next year, and we'll be done with that by about the first of December, right?"

"Yeah," Will said, "we should be done *before* then."

I continued. "After that there's not a whole lot to do around here until it's time to plant again in mid-March or so. I believe most everybody else is on the same schedule. Winter is the one time when they can get away from their farms for up to a couple of months or so."

"The second reason has to do with the Indians. Winter is when they hunker down. They don't move as much. They'll be easier to track and find, and many times a good portion of their warriors will be far away on hunting trips. The women and children will be in the camp because there won't be any food to gather at that time of year.

"I believe if I knock on enough cabin doors and travel far enough to spread the word, I could get a good number of men to join us."

"Sounds like a good plan, Andy." Will said. "What do you think, Tad?"

"I'm in," Tad said with a grin, "as long as Libby and Billy are safe."

"There's one other thing," I said, looking at Will. "I want you to lead the group. Everybody in this part of the country knows and respects you, and many fought with you at San Jacinto. I know that if I just mention your name as the leader, I'll get more men to join. Will you do it?"

"As long as Anna and the children aren't left here by themselves, how can I refuse?" Will grinned, slapping me on the back.

CHAPTER 31

Libby, Anna and the children had been looking forward to and enjoyed their rare opportunity to shop in town. Libby and Anna had as much fun selecting yard goods for sewing as the children did getting some hard candy. Along with the staples of flour, sugar, salt and coffee, they found treats like oranges and apples. Tad, Will and I re-supplied ourselves with extra measures of lead and powder, planning to spend several nights after our arrival back home melting lead and molding thirty-six caliber balls for our pistols. Upon our return to Virginia Point, it took less than two weeks to prepare the fields for planting. By late November I was ready to start my recruiting process. The evening before I planned to leave, Tad and I were outside the Jefferson cabin quietly arguing.

"You know you don't have to do any of this." I said. "I can do the recruiting myself and Libby's been through enough, losing her husband to Indians. She doesn't need the possibility of losing her only brother to them too."

"I know I don't have to do any of it, but you'd do the same for me wouldn't you? Besides I've been out there before when Will and I and some neighbors went looking for Indians. Now I'm older, better trained and armed. I was just a kid then. I know what I'm doing now."

We both turned toward the porch as we heard the door to the cabin open. Libby stepped onto the porch and put her fist on her hip.

"I heard you two. There'll be no arguing over what I need or don't need . . . *I'll* tell you what I need." She pointed her finger at us. "I need to have you two do what you believe is the right thing for you and your friend. Now I'll tell you what *I'm* doing. Tomorrow morning, Billy and I are taking one of the wagons and we're heading south past San Felipe on down to the old Bell place to spend a few months with my friends down there. Andy, those are the folks who got their freedom when we did after our old master died. They've been good friends for years and it's been too long since we've had a nice, long visit. If you two want to ride along with me for a ways, you're certainly welcome. You'd better get up early." She turned and went back into the cabin.

Tad and I looked at each other and broke into laughter. I reached out to shake Tad's hand. "Looks like we're going to get more saddle time together, partner."

Tad and I stopped at every cabin within a mile's ride of the road between Virginia Point and San Felipe and camped with Libby and Billy along the way. Most farmers we encountered knew Will, and Tad through Jeff, as Jeff had surveyed the land with Will for the settlers. The people we visited were supportive of our plan and all responded favorably. A few said they would join Will's company and asked for details of when and where to meet and how long we would be gone. Others said they were in favor of what we were doing, but couldn't leave their families for such a long time. Some others couldn't join us in our mission, but offered to help supply us with food. At each place we stopped, we asked the settlers to pass the word to other neighbors who might not hear our message.

In San Felipe, we hugged Libby and Billy goodbye and asked Libby to help pass our message farther south. We met travelers in San Felipe who were going east toward Nacogdoches and agreed to carry our message. Sam Williams also said he would pass our plan on to others passing through.

On leaving San Felipe, we headed west on the San Antonio road to continue our mission. We were encouraged by the positive responses we received as we visited with the settlers along the way. For every farmer who promised to join us, ten more gave us encouragement and promised to pass the word to their neighbors. We never had to make camp or sleep on the ground along the way as someone always offered us the hospitality of a hot meal and a comfortable place to sleep.

By mid-December we had taken our message beyond San Antonio, south to Goliad, then back northeast once again through the countryside and small villages to the San Antonio road. Satisfied that our plan and request for help had reached hundreds of families and had been carried by others to hundreds more, we pulled our coat collars up against the chilly north wind and headed once again toward the Brazos River and Virginia Point.

On the evening of the twenty-third of December we rode past the dark Jefferson cabin and straight on to the Bowman house. "Hello in the house!" Tad called toward the lamp light beyond the windows as we crossed the yard to the wide front porch.

We slid from our saddles and tied our reins to the rail as Will opened the front door. "Sure glad to see you two," he said, walking down the steps, his hand outstretched to shake. "Come on in. We're just finishing supper. There's plenty more for you. I want to hear all about your trip."

I smiled. "One of Anna's meals sounds really good right now, but we'd better take care of the horses first. I'm afraid we got a little anxious to get home, and it's been a while since we stopped to feed and water 'em."

"Ya'll go on down to the barn then," Will said. "I'll meet you there directly. I just need to ask Anna to set a couple of extra plates."

Will soon caught up with Tad and I as we walked down the gentle slope to the barn. "So how did it go?"

"We talked to a lot of people," I said. "Everybody seemed to be in support of what we want to do. Lots of folks have been affected by Indian raids one way or the other over the years. A lot of men said they'd join us, but I guess we'll just have to wait to see who shows up."

We were invited to stay at the Bowman house until we left

on our campaign. It was still almost a week before we expected the men to start arriving. We spent our time helping Will finish some jobs around his place before we left. One of the projects was building toys.

While Anna kept the children occupied in the house, Tad and I helped Will put finishing touches on toys he had made for the children. We helped him sand and paint a little wooden wagon for Jeff and a doll cradle for Texanna.

On the morning before Christmas day, Tad and I collected cedar greenery from the pastures north of the house and helped Anna arrange them with some red ribbon and colorful calico strips to make wreaths and strips of greenery for decorating both outside and inside the house.

The sounds of children squealing woke everyone early on Christmas morning. Texanna and Jeff found the new toys when they bounded down the stairs from their bedrooms. Soon everyone was up and enjoying the children's excitement. I watched Texanna play with the cuddly rag doll that Libby had sewn for her.

I thought of Rosie, years ago, when she was a carefree little girl, playing with her doll that Mama made for her. I remembered Christmases when Mama and Papa sat in the floor with me and Rosie, playing with us and with whatever gifts we had for Christmas. I remembered one year when Papa bought me a shiny red top from the store at the Smith settlement and gave it to me for Christmas. Another year, Papa made me a flute from a hollow reed he cut from beside the river. Rosie was always thrilled with the gifts she received. Once it was a pair of stockings Mama knitted for her. Another time it was a little book Mama made from pieces of white cotton cloth she had painted pictures on and sewn together. One year we both were given oranges for Christmas. We had never seen oranges before. I remembered the tangy mist that tickled my nose when I sank my fingernails into the peeling. Then, after separating the first wedge from the others, I experienced the sweet and juicy taste of my first bite.

Surrounded by so much happiness in the Bowman living room and watching the children play, I again felt guilty about what I had let happen to Rosie. *She had so few years to have a happy childhood,* I thought. *It had been so long, even before we were captured, that I'd seen her happy.* With Mama and Papa both being so sick and me as preoccupied as I was with my adult responsibilities there was little for her to be happy about. I realized she must now be almost thirteen years old. I shook my head in thought. *Same age I was when we were first captured . . . God, I've got to find her.*

I was currying Prince outside the Bowman barn, mid-afternoon on the twenty-ninth of December when I looked up and saw three men riding toward me from the south. One of them, riding a sorrel, was leading a mule packed heavy with supplies. Another, riding a black, was well armed with a rifle protruding from a scabbard on each side of his saddle and a revolving pistol in his belt.

The third, a tall man wearing buckskins with a grey blanket draped over his shoulders and a wide-brimmed hat pushed back on his head, spurred his bay gelding ahead of the others. "Is this the Bowman place?" he asked.

"Sure is," I said, grinning. "My name's Andy Bristow. Will Bowman is up at the house." I tilted my head over my shoulder.

"I reckon we're at the right place, then," the tall man said, swinging a leg over his horse's rump and stepping down. The other two men slid out of their saddles. "Name's Freeman Dillard," the tall man said, reaching to shake my hand. He motioned toward the man leading the mule. "This here's Isaac Ballentine, and that feller over there scratchin' his backside is Jesse Damon."

"It's been a long ride," Damon said, grinning at me. "Didn't know how long it would take us to get here, so we gave ourselves plenty of time."

"Where you from?"

"Down around Refugio," Dillard said.

"You *have* traveled far."

"So you must be the young feller who's organizing the campaign," Damon said.

"That's me. I sure appreciate you fellas coming to give us a hand."

"When we heard about your plan from a couple of men traveling down our way from Goliad, we decided we had to come and help out if we could. Jesse lost some kin to the Comanches a few years ago, and my brother was killed by them shortly after he got here right after the war with Mexico. If they've got your sister or any other kids or women, we'll help you get 'em back."

"That's what we're going to try to do." I said. "I wish we had better accommodations for you while we wait for the rest of the men, but you're welcome to camp out here around the barn anywhere." I waved my arm toward the live oaks surrounding the barn and corral. "Looks like the good weather's gonna hold for a few days. There's plenty of firewood scattered around on the ground, and I'll take a wagon later over to the river to bring back more."

"How many men will be joining us?" Dillard asked.

"Guess I don't really know," I said, pushing hair from my eyes. "We talked to lots of people for three weeks while we were out recruiting. A good many said they'd join us. A whole lot more said they'd pass our plan on to others. We'll know for sure on the morning of the first of January. That's when we plan to leave. Anyway, you men just make yourselves at home here. I'll bring Captain Bowman over later."

Anna Bowman received several invitations from neighbors around the Bowman farm, asking her and the children to stay with them while we were on our campaign. She decided to rotate her visits among three friends' homes until Will returned.

On the morning of the thirtieth, Will packed his wagon with Anna's, Texanna's, and Jeff's things, tied his saddle horse along with Tad's and my young fillies, still too young to ride, to the rear of the wagon and drove away toward the neighbor's farm. Two hours later he rode back to his barn to find eight more men camped under the trees. He welcomed them and shared coffee with them while getting acquainted.

Men continued arriving at the Bowman farm in groups of two to five the rest of that day and all of the next.

CHAPTER 32

As dawn cracked to a chilly but clear morning on the first of January, 1841, Will, Tad and I were in Will's barn preparing our livestock. Barron, Buck and Prince were already saddled and we were almost finished with the pack animals. We were using Will's team of mules to pack our supplies. Will packed the old canvas tent that he and Jeff had used when they'd surveyed land for the new settlers coming into Stephen Austin's and Sam Williams' land grant. Will also included his surveying instruments so he could take readings to be able to determine our exact location on an old map of Texas that he carried. Stephen Austin had given him the outdated map in 1835. It didn't reflect up-to-date settler's locations, but known rivers, streams and geographical features of the areas we would be traveling were included. Will expected the map to be a great help during our campaign.

I filled bags on the pack racks with smaller sacks of flour, sugar, beans, cornmeal, coffee and cooking gear while Tad loaded extra blankets, black powder, lead bars and bullet molds. We each put a ten-pound sack of pre-molded bullets in our saddlebags and then added our personal gear, including extra clothes and a rain slicker on the pack animals. Finally we led our horses outside.

The brightness of the sun peeking over the horizon and burning off the ground-hugging fog caused me to squint as I looked over the barn lot. I counted the clusters of men and found no fewer than fifteen campfires scattered about west of the barn under the hackberry and live oak trees. Horses and mules were staked and hobbled beyond the campfires. Most of the men had finished their breakfasts of jerky and coffee or johnnycakes and were moving about, getting their gear packed and ready to saddle up.

Will, Tad and I visited with groups of men for a few minutes and in several cases renewed old friendships. Will recognized a wrinkled face and a toothless grin under an old weather-beaten hat. It belonged to his sergeant major from the San Jacinto fight. "Jenkins, is that you?" A big smile developed as he strode toward the man, standing with a group saddling their horses.

Jenkins stuck out his hand to shake as Will approached.

"When I heered you was goin' to lead an Injun campaign, I figgered I'd just ride up here and see if you could use an old soldier."

"There's always a place for you in my outfit. Really glad to see you," Will said, pumping Jenkins' hand. "We've got some catching up to do. We'll have more time to talk later."

Tad and I saw and visited with some of the men we'd met at the Plum Creek fight, including Jacob Robson and a handful of his friends.

Soon Will called out, "All right, men, finish your morning business and assemble here in front of the barn, mounted and ready to ride in fifteen minutes."

When the men started gathering in front of the barn Will walked his horse among them, guiding them into a military formation.

"All right men, form up in columns of twos — two straight lines side by side. That's right. Come on, tighten it up a bit." He counted the men as they formed their columns. Satisfied that everyone was in place, he walked his horse to the front of the troop and looked them over before he spoke.

"First, I want to thank you. I want to thank you all for being here, and I want to thank Andy Bristow for asking you to come. But most of all, I want to thank you for those people that you are going to rescue from the Comanches. We believe that *right now* there may be as many as thirty or so white children and women living with the Comanches. Some have managed to survive as slaves like Andy over there." He nodded toward me. "And some others may have been adopted into the tribes. Very few ever escape as Andy has.

"In order for this campaign to be a success, it must function as a military operation. Now we all know that as much as our republic's leaders would like to send an army out there to bring those captives back, the truth is that the funds just aren't there to raise the army and outfit it to do that. And the Rangers who are operating down south don't have the resources to take the search to the northwestern reaches of Texas. So thanks to you and the sacrifices you've made to be here, we're going to do that ourselves. That's what living on the frontier is all about, helping your neighbors with whatever they need.

"I want to be very clear about the purpose of the mission and how we will carry it out. This will not be a mission to exterminate Indians." Will hesitated and looked over the men. "This is a *rescue* mission! I'm going to say that again so everyone thoroughly understands. This is a *rescue* mission! Our goal is to safely bring back as many captives as possible. We are going to leave this morning with ninety-two men. And gentlemen, I will do everything I can to return right here to this spot in fifty or sixty days with ninety-two healthy men and as many freed captives as possible. I believe that can be done with a minimum of bloodshed on either side.

"With that said, if any of you came here with the express purpose of going out to kill as many Indians as possible, I invite you to modify your goals to align with those of this mission or return home." He hesitated a moment to let his words sink in. Several of the men cut their eyes at each other, looking to see if any would challenge Bowman. None did.

"Of course, I expect you to defend yourself if necessary, but I believe the fewer of them we injure or kill, the fewer causalities we will suffer. And we may just manage to keep the captives alive. The Indians will also have less motivation for revenge if they have few or no casualties." He looked at the company, scanning their faces. "Are we still all together on this?" He hesitated again. Most of the men remained silent with the exception of a few, scattered "Yes sirs."

"The next thing we must do is select the leaders of our company. When Andy first told me of his plan, he asked me to command the operation. He knew I had formal military training at a military academy in Virginia, and was commissioned as a captain by Stephen Austin and led a company of cavalry with Sam Houston at the Battle of San Jacinto. Also over the years I've been involved in Indian fights after their raids on the settlements. Those are my credentials. Does anyone have a problem with my background or authority to lead this campaign?" He again hesitated, waiting for a response, but heard none. He nodded. "So let's get on with it. How many of you have any kind of military background? Indian fighting, Mexican war, whatever? Let me see your hands." Almost half of the company raised their hands. Will went through a quick process of questioning each one about their fighting experience.

When he came to Jacob Robson, Robson told him of losing his entire family and of his multiple trips into Indian country to kill as many Comanches as possible. "I've killed more than my share, just working the hate out of my system. But Cap'n, if fightin' by your rules means we can bring back just one child to their family, then I'm with you."

"I appreciate that, Robson."

Will finished interviewing the veterans, and asked another question. "How many of you have repeating pistols?" About thirty men raised their hands. Some had their pistols in their hands. "All you men with repeating pistols, fall out and form up to my left. Form two squads over there. Your squad leaders are Andy Bristow and Jacob Robson. The rest of you will be the frontal attack force, which will consist of three squads. Each squad will provide two scouts every day. The scouts' job will be to range far and wide and find the Indian villages." He named the squad leaders and introduced Jenkins as his sergeant major. "You will all be getting further instruction as we go along."

"If I should become unable to continue as the leader of this campaign, your sergeant major will assume command. Your squad leaders will fill you in on your individual duties and you are required to follow their commands. From this point on, this is a military campaign. We will conduct ourselves in a military fashion. No military operation is successful without leaders and rules. Guards will be posted every night. The penalty for sleeping on guard duty will be severe. Now, does everybody understand our objectives and how we will achieve them?"

Many shouted, "Yes sir!" in a show of agreement.

"Squad leaders, you have five minutes to meet your troops, assign your scouts and hunters for today and be in position to move out."

Will carefully watched his company come together. When it appeared that they had answered his first command, he called, "scouts, front and center!" Six men left the ranks and rode to face Bowman.

"Today the main company will march northwest. We will travel at least twenty-five miles before we make camp. You and your partner are to stay together. Squad A, that's you two." He pointed to two men. "You range to the right. Squad B, you range straight ahead, and squad C, you'll do your scouting to the left of the company. You are to go out several miles from the company and scour the country carefully, but always stay in sight of your partner. Follow creeks and streams. They will camp near water. If you see any signs of tracks or where travois rails have gouged the dirt, follow them. Look to the sky from time to time. Investigate any buzzards you find. Buzzards will be around Indian camps. Do your best to conceal yourselves from any Indian sightings and get back to the company as fast as you can. Don't come back to camp in the evening till sundown. Any questions?" No one raised a question. "Men, be careful out there."

Will then turned to Jenkins, "Sergeant Major?"

"Yes sir?"

"Send out the scouts."

"Scouts away!" Jenkins called. The scouts spurred their horses into a gallop, each team to their assigned search area.

Will watched the scouts ride away, and then looked over the company of men. "Sergeant Major, give the order to march."

"All right men, column of twos, look sharp now. Forward, ho!"

CHAPTER 33

The first four days offered little for the troops but watching the countryside slowly pass by. Every evening before sundown Will retrieved his surveying instruments to take his readings to determine their new location and mark it on the map. Then after supper the squad leaders met with Bowman to mark their progress for the day on Will's map and go over the plan of march for the next day. The scouts also screened the map to look for water sources they would be investigating the next day. Will also drilled the leaders on the basic battle plan so that when they were ready, each could execute it exactly as defined.

On the afternoon of the fifth day on the trail, the scouts who had been sent west of the line of march came galloping back to the company. "We found some, Cap'n!" one of the breathless riders called from a distance before reaching the troops.

Bowman and Jenkins rode out to meet them. "How far away?" Bowman asked.

"Probably four or five miles or so. There's a bunch of teepees clustered along a creek next to some cottonwoods."

"How many teepees?"

One of the scouts looked at the other. "What you think, Sam, maybe around thirty?"

"Sounds about right," confirmed his partner.

"Bristow, you and Robson fall out over here," Will called.

Robson and I broke ranks to join him.

"Jenkins, have the company follow us at slow speed and look for a campsite with concealment," Will instructed. Then he looked back at the scouts. "Show us." He spurred his white gelding and fell in behind the scouts with me and Robson following him.

After following the scouts, we tied our horses inside a thicket of hackberry and bois d'arc trees a quarter-mile from a rise overlooking the village and walked the remaining distance. As we drew nearer, we dropped to the ground and crawled through the weeds to peer over the rise. The village was about four hundred yards to the west.

I counted the lodges. "Thirty-four lodges," I whispered to Will, who was looking through his spyglass.

The village was as the scouts had described. It was clustered along a bend of a stream running from the northwest to the southeast. The stream was edged with cottonwoods and willow trees. A half-dozen boys were tending a herd of about eighty horses just east of the village.

"That's not many horses for a village this size," I said.

"Not very many men outside the lodges," Will said, squinting through his glass.

"With the weather this nice, the men would be sitting outside their lodges, smoking and talking or working with their horses," I said

"There's just a few men scattered around and nobody but children around the horses. Look, there's plenty of women and girls in small groups working on hides or grinding something." Will said, still looking through his glass.

"I suspect that many of the men may be away on a hunting party," I said.

"We'll find out tomorrow morning," Will said, tucking his glass inside his coat and easing backwards on his belly with the rest of us until we were far enough behind the ridge to go for our horses.

That night the company dry camped three miles east of the village along the bottom of a small canyon. The canyon walls provided little relief from the cold north wind that had kicked up around dark. I spent a fitful night in Will's old tent with him and Tad, lying awake much of the night as soldiers had for centuries before a fight in anticipation of what the next day would bring.

We were all up well before daylight, saddling in the dark,

trying to work the stiffness from our joints. Each man took special care to pad anything that could make noise before we rode out of camp.

We left three men to look after the pack animals and gear we couldn't be bothered with during the fight.

We started taking our positions around the village when the pink first started showing itself in the eastern sky. Will positioned the bulk of the company on the south side of the village, beyond the ridge overlooking the lodges and out of sight of the village. His group waited about five hundred yards from the stream while the other units moved into position.

Robson's group, the right rescue unit that included Tad, moved northward quietly beyond the ridge along the east side of the village. A small group of five horsemen spun away from his group and silently worked their way toward the herd of horses that were grazing just southeast of the lodges. Tad and the rest of the unit continued to the north until they were well behind the lodges. They silently waited among groupings of mesquite brush.

I led my left rescue unit across the creek downstream of the lodges and rode well to the west of the sleeping village. We then turned north, ultimately swinging back toward the stream behind the village. While we rode, I tied my hat to my saddle horn to better prepare for whatever kind of riding the circumstances required. I also tested the strap I had woven into Prince's mane before we left camp. I positioned my men behind a growth of willows next to the stream and awaited Will's signal.

Each squad had planned and rehearsed our parts until each of us knew not only our particular responsibility, but we knew exactly what each other group would do during the raid. I knew that Will was waiting, nervously watching his men keep their horses still and quiet while Robson and I were getting our units in place. We all understood that every second he waited while we were positioning ourselves increased the chance of losing the element of surprise. When Will was certain that both the right and left rescue groups were in position, he was to execute the plan.

Gunfire broke the silence of the morning. Although I couldn't see him, I knew that Will fired the first shot as he spurred his horse into a full gallop. The rest of his troop was a half-beat behind him. All were yelling and a few were shooting as they raced over the top of the ridge, heading for the village.

I could visualize the men from Robson's group, waiting fifty yards from the Indian ponies, then spurring to a gallop when they heard Will's first shot. They raced between the village and the horse herd, driving the horses away from the village and into open country. The herd was beyond catching before the first warrior threw open his lodge flap.

People spilled from the lodges. As the warriors and young braves raced to respond to Will's frontal charge, women and old people gathered small children in their arms and pushed the older ones along toward the rear of the village, away from the attack. Many carried clothes and pulled blankets about them.

Will saw several puffs of smoke from rifles as twenty or so Indians reached the edge of the stream and realized their horses were out of reach. He didn't see any arrows fly as they were still out of range. He continued the charge until his soldiers were within a hundred and twenty yards of the Indians, then ordered a halt and dismount so the troops could fire. They dismounted and quickly formed two lines, one directly behind the other. Will watched the Indians race across the stream as his front line dropped to their knees and prepared to fire. "Fire high . . . fire!" he called. None of the Indians fell as bullets flew over their heads. The Indians slowed their advance as the first volley was fired. The first line of Texans traded positions with the second and reloaded. The warriors fired several arrows, which fell harmlessly short.

The Texans that ran off the ponies returned to the fight to make sure no Indians were able to retrieve their horses. Several young Comanches tried to go after the horses, but were turned back by the Texans' pistols.

I held my unit back behind the willows when I heard the shooting south of the village. I heard the women screaming and the panicked children crying before I saw them break into the open beyond the lodges, just east of my position. I looked carefully for any children or young women who didn't look Indian, but I couldn't tell their race because of the blankets and buffalo robes pulled about their faces and heads. A few young braves ran with the women and children carrying bows in one hand and arrows in the other. I patiently held my squad back as the panicked Indians ran to within fifty yards of our place of concealment. Then, when I was convinced that all of the women and children had cleared the lodges, I led the charge from the brush into the groups of rapidly scattering Indians. As my unit approached the fleeing Indians, I saw Robson's squad galloping toward them from the east. The Indians ran into the dried grass and sage to the north, the only direction free of white men. My group rode alongside the women and children as they ran, pulling blankets or buffalo hides from their heads and shoulders, trying to identify anyone with light hair and eyes or other features that didn't look Indian. We continuously looked behind and around us for youths with bows and arrows. Several times I had to fire at young braves who were stringing bows toward me or another horseman. I soon learned that charity toward those trying to kill me at close range wouldn't save my life. Several young warriors fell from a Colt's bullet before they could take down a white rider.

I raced toward a woman pulling a child by the hand to tear away their head covers. Suddenly a boy about eleven years old that was running between me and the woman stopped, turned to me and extended his hand upward to me.

Brown hair! I thought. *He has brown hair.* Then I realized the boy was begging to be pulled up behind my saddle. Once mounted behind me with one arm tightly clenched around my waist, he pointed with the other to the small figure being pulled along by the running woman. "Sister . . . sister," he cried in the

Comanche language. Then, pointing several more times, he struggled to say "sis–ter!" in English.

I spurred my horse toward the running woman and child. Approaching them from the rear, I reached over the side of my horse and yanked the blanket from the child's head, revealing a little blond girl about eight years old. The frightened child's cries became screams of terror when I, hanging almost upside down from my horse, pulled her away from the woman and brought her to my level, holding her tightly around her waist. Ignoring the woman's screams, I quickly transferred the girl to another rider and continued looking for other whites.

Our search was soon exhausted when we realized every other woman and child from the village were Comanche. My unit pulled back to the west and Robson did the same with his squad to the east. Both groups then circled back around to the south side of the village, well beyond the skirmish line. I sent a messenger to advise Bowman that we accomplished our mission and recovered captives.

Bowman and his troops fell back several hundred yards during the fight in order to keep the Comanches out of range while our two rescue units did our jobs. Upon receiving his message, he ordered a full retreat.

"So why do you think they won't come after us?" Will asked me as we rode back to the canyon where we camped the night before.

"Indians are savages, but they aren't stupid. They know they were outnumbered. They know we could have killed them any time we wanted to. With those odds and our superior firepower, we could have taken out the whole lot, but instead, they got just a few minor injuries. We didn't shoot to kill, even on the backside of the village when the young braves were after us with their arrows. When they learn that all they lost were two white children, they'll be happy enough. Tonight they'll be celebrating their great victory of running off a large raiding party of whites. By tonight, our numbers, from their exaggerated point of view, will be closer to two hundred than one hundred."

By the time we returned to camp, the boy had calmed his sister and I tried to talk with them. I asked in Comanche, "Do you want to talk in the People's language or do you want to talk in English?"

There was a hesitation while the boy tested his words. Then he slowly spoke in English. "Me and . . . Beth, we ain't . . . never talkin' Injun . . . no more."

I learned that his name was Henry Allen. He and his sister Elisabeth were taken when their farm on the Guadalupe River was raided two and a half years ago. They knew their father and mother were killed in the raid, but they thought they had an uncle somewhere north of San Antonio.

I asked whether they had seen a girl with curly red hair, but they just looked sadly at me and shook their heads. I'd learned to deal with disappointment about finding my sister, but it seemed the more that I tried to find her, every let-down became harder to swallow.

"Glad we brought that old tent," Will said after we had our supper and put the children to bed in the tent. "At least maybe they won't be quite so cold tonight."

"Just wish we had about twenty or thirty more of those tents," Tad said, warming his hands by the fire. "It's going to be a long, cold night."

CHAPTER 34

January on the Texas prairie is cold. Although the Bowman Company was well supplied and all the men had coats or blankets to wrap around themselves and some had small tents, the chill at night still went to the bone. It wasn't quite so bad in the daytime, and on some days the weather could almost be called pleasant, but when it turned cold again, the north wind was relentless.

The days blurred together as we maintained our northwesterly march. Every four to six days the scouts brought word of finding another Comanche village. We repeated the surprise attack process of running off the horses and having Will's group of riflemen hold off the Indian warriors while Robson's squad and mine searched through the running, panicked women and children looking for captives. Each time after a thorough search of the women and children trying to escape the frontal attack, I rode away without my sister.

Although I hadn't found Rosie, the operation, so far, was a success. Bundled in blankets and several confiscated buffalo robes and riding on pack animals were nine children under the age of twelve and two teen-aged girls.

On the evening of the twenty-eighth of January, I sat by the fire next to Will going over the map. Will pointed to a location north of the Canadian River.

"According to the readings I took this afternoon, we're right here," he said, tapping the map. That was the Canadian River we crossed yesterday and I suspect the flint outcropping we heard about in San Antonio is to the east of us." He moved his finger about an inch to the right. "Somewhere right around there.

"Andy, you know we're gonna have to turn around and head back soon. We promised the men we'd have them home in sixty days. It'll take us just as long to get home as it did to get here, maybe longer, depending on how many Indians we run up against going home."

"I know." I shook my head slowly. "Somehow I thought, maybe I was just hoping . . . ."

Will sighed. "Andy, there's gotta be hundreds of Indian villages out here, and not only Comanches. There's Kiowa, Cheyenne, Arapaho and Ute. Then there's the Sioux farther north, and it just keeps on going from there. The farther north we go, the farther we are from the settlements, and my guess is, the less likely we are to find many more captives. We'll keep looking north for three more days, till the end of the month, then we've *got* to head back."

"Thanks Will. I know you know how much this means to me. All I can say is thanks."

The next day started sunny, but by mid-afternoon, low, dark clouds covered the sky. The wind kicked up from the north and the temperature started dropping. I had my chin buried in my coat collar, but looked up to see two large tumbleweeds rolling toward the column. Looking beyond the tumbleweeds to the flat horizon, I saw two scouts galloping hard toward us.

Bowman rode ahead to meet them.

"Indian village up ahead," one of the men shouted.

"How far?" Will asked.

"No more than five miles."

"Robson and Bristow, let's go." He looked around, then pointed to his left. "Jenkins, take the company down in that draw over there. "Get out of the wind, and we'll be back directly. Make sure those kids are bundled up good."

Will, Robson and I followed the scouts north. After a half-hour lope into the blowing wind, the scouts drew up some distance away from a canyon rim. We dismounted and one of the scouts held the horses while the rest of us cautiously walked to the edge of the rim, dropped to the dirt and looked down. We saw that we were on the southeast side of a wide, horseshoe-shaped canyon. The village lay eighty feet below and six hundred yards away to the north and west of us on a flat valley with the canyon wall bordering the village on two sides. A stream with open prairie beyond it lay to the west of the village. About two hundred horses were located on the south side between the village and the canyon wall. After reviewing the layout, Will decided it would be better to drive the horses from the east along the southern wall and then out of the canyon to the west. He also decided it would be best to execute the frontal assault from the east side of the village as there was good access down the canyon wall and plenty of room for his unit to fall back during the rescue mission. Satisfied with our plan, we carefully withdrew from the canyon wall and rode back to the company.

Sometime during the night it started snowing. By the time the sentries started nudging us awake, there was three inches on the ground with more coming. The snowfall had been heavy, but the wind was calm. I saddled my horse and checked the strap still plaited in its mane and found it secure. I left my blankets with some of the children for the day as they would need them more than I would for the next several hours.

The company moved out well before daylight, as usual on the day of a raid, leaving the children asleep in tents and warm under piles of blankets and buffalo robes. Twelve men were left behind to ensure the children's safety.

A mile before we reached the canyon, we split into our groups and quietly continued through the snow to assume our positions. Will wasn't as nervous this time about being detected before we were ready. Although the snowfall was much lighter than it had been earlier, it would still muffle any accidental sounds of the separate units getting into our positions. We also had confidence that no one would be outside the lodges because of the weather to sound an alarm.

Daylight slowly pushed its way through the light snowfall as my men and I made our way around the southwest side of the village. We found the stream, layered with scattered thin ice and quietly crossed it. Several large ravines led to the water from the elevated level of the village. With hand signals, I directed my men to ride into them for cover until we were ready to advance. Once again I removed my felt hat and tied it to my saddle horn. I ran my fingers through my long, curly hair, fluffing it up in order to keep the snow away from my skin. I checked my pistols and my extra cylinders, then tugged on the strap on Prince's mane. I moved forward in the ravine so that I had a good view of the buffalo skin covered lodges. Smoke spiraled from smoke holes at the tops of the lodges, flirting with the few remaining snowflakes and then floating away. I was ready.

Soon, we heard the cracks of the first pistol shots and the faint yelling of the men on the other side of the village driving the Indian ponies away. In the next second the mixed sounds of rifles of different calibers and powder charges and the hollering of the main body of men sweeping down the hill to challenge the warriors echoed off the canyon walls.

Several seconds later, the first of the woman, children and old people started spilling onto the open ground between the village and the stream, running toward the water. I watched carefully from my cover, trying to see faces in the distance. I continued to hold back, waiting for more people to break away from the lodges. I looked for the young men who always ran with the women and children to usher them to safety. Several men ran with their bows, ready to string arrows. Finally, it appeared that most of the women and children had passed the lodges and were in the open.

I signaled my men to charge and rode out of the ravine in a gallop. I fired my pistol several times into the air to drive those who were scattering away from the main group back, so they could more easily be identified. I fired again until the pistol was empty, replaced it in the holster and reached for my second. With the reins in my mouth and the pistol in my right hand, I raced toward a group of women and children, jerking blankets from shoulders and heads, finding nothing but dark round faces, dark eyes and black hair. I spun and spurred Prince toward another group.

A burning pain shot through my left thigh. An arrow had entered my leg, glanced off the thigh bone and imbedded in my saddle. I spat out the reins, grabbed the arrow and freed it from the saddle. Ignoring the pain, I looked around. *Where is he? There he is!* I saw the warrior and was bringing my pistol around to fire when another arrow sliced into my horse's upper foreleg, causing it to fold under him while at full gallop. I flew over the horse's head onto the ground face first. Struggling to catch my breath, I looked up. The warrior was running toward me from my left. I raised my hand to fire. *Pistol's gone! In the snow! Where?* I looked. I felt for it. The warrior was almost on me. *Oh, God, I'm dead.* The war club arced toward my head.

There was a blur of movement from the right, a flash of red. Then, among blinding sparks of pain as everything went dark, I faintly heard,

"No! He's —"

CHAPTER 35

Something was snapping. Then it was a crackling noise. *Oh, my head. God, it hurts.* I brought my hand to my head. Something was wrapped around my head. I couldn't feel my skin. Warm. My face was warm. I lay on my back trying to understand the pain in my head and the sensation of heat. I turned toward the source of the heat and cracked one eye open. *Ow! That hurts too.* I realized that the snapping and crackling sounds and the source of heat was a fire. I watched the flames lick at the small sticks. They danced around the dry logs. Hands were feeding fuel to the fire. A woman's hands. Dark skin.

Libby? Is that Libby?

"Lib . . ." A raspy, whispered sound escaped my lips. *Was that my voice?*

I looked beyond the hands at the fire as the figure turned toward me. A leather skirt and top. Long black hair. A woman was kneeling at the fire, three feet from me. I started to move and she leaned to me and put a hand on my chest to still me. I looked into her dark eyes set in her round, expressionless face. She shook her head. It was just as well. I hurt too much to move. I felt toward my head again and probed the left side of my forehead. There was a large knot, the size of an egg.

The woman approached me again. This time she had a gourd of water in her hand. She put one hand under my neck and lifted me so I could sip a little. *Oh, it felt good in my mouth.*

My head was beginning to clear. It still hurt, but things were beginning to make sense. I felt the woman meant me no harm. She seemed to be taking care of me. I looked beyond the woman to view my surroundings. I was lying under a buffalo robe inside a circular hide lodge. *Why was I here?*

Then I started remembering. I should be dead. The last thing I saw was the large, stone-headed war club coming at me. Why didn't he finish me off? I felt my head again, beyond the wrap and ran my fingers through my hair. Why isn't my hair hanging off his belt or attached to his shield? I looked at the woman again. She could have already killed me if she wanted to. Maybe she has the answers.

I spoke in her language.

"Thank you for the water."

She looked at me. A slight smile slowly crossed her face.

"Why am I here?"

She looked at me for several seconds, then turned away.

"Who brought me here?"

She hesitated before answering.

"Evening Fire brought you here."

"Who is Evening Fire?"

"She is my daughter."

"Where is she now?"

"With her grandfather."

"Why am I here? What's going to happen to me?"

There was another long hesitation, "I don't know."

I saw movement in the shadows. I looked closer and saw that a man was sitting on a buffalo robe, leaning against some leather bags, watching me. It wasn't the young man that tried to kill me. This one didn't appear threatening. He was just watching.

One hundred and fifty feet away, in a different lodge, a discussion of another kind was underway. Outside that lodge, Evening Fire huddled inside a blanket wrapped around her. She leaned close to the slanted leather wall listening to the arguments inside. She had earlier spent hours pleading with her grandfather to argue with the other chiefs on behalf of her brother.

Never in her life did she think that she would ever be in this position.

Evening Fire's old life had been left behind. She loved her

brother and thought of him often during the first year with her new family, but with time her thoughts were occupied more with her new people and learning their ways. Also with the years flowing by, she forgot her old language and much of her past. She no longer looked for her brother when her people met those from other tribes.

After she learned the language, she told her mother how badly she and her brother were treated when they were first captured by the other tribe.

"Child," her mother said, "sometimes after a raid when children are taken, the warriors must quickly take control. The captives must immediately understand proper behavior. I'm sorry if it was a bad time for you, dear child," She stroked her daughter's head, "but that time was short and its over. Now you are surrounded by all these people who love you. You'll never be beaten again."

"What happened to my brother? Was he taken by a family like me?"

"Evening Fire," she hesitated a moment, looking for the right words, "older boys are not taken in to a family as you were. White boys your brother's age don't become Comanche. They are given work to do. Sometimes they die. It is best you not think of the old ways. It is against the People's way to talk of the dead. It shows disrespect. We will speak of your brother no more."

Evening Fire was accepted well by her tribe. She learned the language quickly and easily made friends with the other children. Now with the Comanche five years, she knew that she would soon be a woman. Two of her friends had already started their bleeding and she knew her time would come soon. She enjoyed letting the other girls take down her hair, comb it and re-braid it. It was hard for her to control her curls, but her friends laughed with her as they combed out the tangles in her long, red hair and worked it into braids.

She enjoyed going with her friends to collect cactus fruit and mesquite beans and wild berries for food because when they got out of sight from the village, they practiced dancing. She had been dancing with the tribe for years, but as she and her friends got older, they wanted to practice so they didn't look awkward to the boys and young men when they all danced around the fire at the feasts and celebrations. She'd noticed during the last several months that some of the boys were beginning to act differently toward her and her friends. Now the boys teased them when they rode their ponies past while the girls worked. They used to just ignore them.

She worked with her mother every day and could do everything a grown woman was expected to do. She had grown fast and was as tall as her mother even though she was only twelve-years-old. She made her own clothes and the beadwork on her dresses and moccasins were as intricate and colorful as any in the tribe. She lived a happy, carefree life — until that morning. Finding her brother alive and in the village had become a disaster.

She stood outside Standing Eagle's lodge, shivering in the cold, listening to the argument. She believed she had brought the trouble brewing inside. It had been a terrifying day.

She was awakened to the sounds of gunshots and yelling. Young men ran through the village shouting the alarm. "White men with guns are coming! Run, run to the west!" People fled their lodges in panic. Mothers, children and old people ran away from the shooting. Only a few teen-aged boys and young braves ran with them. Most of the men ran toward the sound of the guns. As Evening Fire followed her terrified mother out the opening of their lodge, she saw her father, Sharp Knife, run from his lodge toward the fighting, his bow and a quiver of arrows in one hand and his lance in the other. Following him was the old man, Laughing Crow, who pulled a blanket about himself as he ran from the lodge, but tripped on the lodge opening hole and fell into the snow. Evening Fire looked at her mother's back racing away, believing her daughter was behind her. The girl looked back at her grandfather who was trying to push himself from the ground and ran back to help him to his feet. When he got up, she grabbed his hand and led him toward the rest of the people running for their lives, scattering to the west, away from the village.

Suddenly riders appeared from the ravines, white men with guns, shooting into the air to divert their direction of escape.

Evening Fire looked for a route to run with her grandfather. The chaos was maddening as people ran in different directions, women screamed and children shrieked as the white riders shot their guns — but no one fell. Evening Fire watched as the riders raced their horses toward children only to pull blankets or robes away from their heads, take a look at their face, then race away to another group. One of the riders spurred his sorrel stallion across the snow, looking for another group of people with children. Evening Fire looked directly in the face of the young, blue eyed man with red curly hair as he rode past, no more than fifteen feet away.

From the corner of her eye, she saw Fast Thunder, a young brave, four years older than herself, draw his bow and let an arrow fly at the red-headed man. She watched as the arrow sliced into his leg and saw him gasp in pain. Fast Thunder rapidly strung another arrow, this time aimed at the sorrel horse.

Evening Fire let go of her grandfather's hand and watched, mouth agape as the young man tugged at the arrow in his leg to free it from the saddle, then flew over the horse's neck as the horse went down. She was overwhelmed with recognition and raw emotion as she saw her brother fly into the snow. Andy was on the ground between her and Fast Thunder. She saw him trying to push himself to his hands and knees. Her eyes moved beyond him to the young brave running toward him, pulling his heavy, rock-headed war club from his belt.

Evening Fire's blanket fell from her head and shoulders as she ran across the snow to her brother. Her loose, unbraided hair flew about her head as she and Fast Thunder both ran to the same figure. One wanted to kill and one wanted to save the man on the ground.

"No! He's my brother!" She screamed as she threw herself onto Fast Thunder's arm swinging the war club, crashing down on Andy's head. The three pound river rock attached to the heavy handle of the club was deflected from crushing Andy's skull and bounced off of the side of his head.

She fell on top of the prostrate figure, pulling her body over his bleeding head. "No, No!" she screamed again, looking up at the young brave hefting the club over his head for another blow. "He's my brother. You can't kill him!" The terror in her eyes met the blazing rage in his.

"Move away," he hissed, pulling the butcher knife from his waist band with his free hand.

"No! You're not touching him!" She cradled Andy's bleeding head in her arms.

Laughing Crow stood for a few seconds where Evening Fire left him. When the understanding of Evening Fire's screams penetrated his brain, he ran to her side. He grabbed Fast Thunder's wrist, above the knife.

"Go," he said firmly.

"That's my scalp, old man," the young man spat the words.

"Don't let him kill him," Evening Fire pleaded.

"There's no scalp today. Now go," Laughing Crow said firmly, looking into the young man's face, increasing the grip he held on the younger man's arm.

Fast Thunder looked into Laughing Crow's face and saw the force and determination the warrior Laughing Crow was as a younger man. Fast Thunder dropped the arm holding the club and turned to retrieve his bow and arrows. "This isn't over. I'll get my scalp," he called over his shoulder as he ran away to chase other white raiders.

The intensity of the argument she overheard inside the lodge jarred Evening Fire from her thoughts.

"It does not matter who he is. He was making war with us!" She recognized Standing Eagle, the war chief's voice. He was almost yelling.

"But, once again, I'm saying — no one was killed." Laughing Crow insisted.

"Laughing Crow," Standing Eagle said," we listen to you because you are the civic chief and elder of our tribe. We are brothers since childhood." He looked at the other elders sitting in a circle around the fire. Several of them nodded their agreement. "We respect you and we respect your granddaughter, but that man is our enemy. He came with soldiers to kill us. We should kill him."

"I saw him and the others with my own eyes." Laughing Crow answered, angrily flicking a finger against his eye. "They were to the west of the village," he pointed, "where the women and children and old people were running away. If they were here to kill us, why are we not dead? Look at me! I am not dead!" He pounded himself on the chest. "They could have killed many of us. But they killed no one. Instead of fighting, they were looking at children's faces and hair. That man did not want to kill us. He was looking for his sister, Evening Fire."

The lodge was quiet for several moments. Standing Eagle broke the silence. "Tonight we will have more council. The white man can speak. Then we decide."

Evening Fire realized the council was over and knew she must leave before she was discovered listening to the council from outside the lodge.

It was apparent that the woman was giving me no more information. She fell quiet when I asked more questions, so as long as I didn't feel threatened by her or the man lounging next to the lodge wall, I was satisfied to lie quietly, feeling my headache throb. I probed my leg, remembering the arrow. Someone had removed it and dressed the wound. I tensed the muscles in my leg. *Pain! That's gonna take a while to heal.*

I wondered if any more white children were taken today. I know I came up empty handed. I tried not to dwell on my fate, but I was bewildered by my treatment.

I heard a noise outside. Someone was running toward the lodge. I watched as the lodge flap opened and a figure wrapped in a blanket stepped through the opening and secured the flap. Once inside, the blanket was thrown aside and I looked into — Rosie's face.

I painfully bolted into a sitting position. "Rosie," I said in English, "is it really you?"

She slowly approached and kneeled beside me. She took my hand with both of hers and brought it to her cheek. She looked into my eyes as tears formed in hers. "I no longer speak the white man's words," she said in the Comanche language. "I am Comanche, but you will always be my brother. I am glad to see that you are awake. You were badly hurt."

"Oh, Rosie, Rosie," I cried, tears now streaming down my cheeks. "I didn't know if I would ever find you after all these years. I didn't know if you were alive or dead." I grabbed her and pulled her to me. I held her tightly as my tears fell on her shoulder.

"You must rest," she gently pushed me back onto the robe. Her hand lingered on my chest, then she brought her fingers to my hair, stroking and running them through my curls. "Like me." She said, smiling, exposing her even, white teeth and touching her own hair with her other hand.

"Just like you," I answered, returning her smile.

Wrinkles formed between her eyes, I could tell she was trying to remember something. She put her lips together, trying to form a word.

"B... Bub, Bubba," she said, her eyes widening.

"That's right. You called me Bubba because you couldn't say brother when you were little. But my real name is Andy."

"Andy?" She pronounced it slowly.

"That's right" I nodded.

"Evening Fire," she touched her chest. "My name is Evening Fire because of the sky."

"It's a beautiful name."

Our reunion was interrupted by another figure entering the lodge. It was an old, bent, gray haired man wrapped in a blanket and leaning on a staff. He walked to the center of the lodge and sat across the fire from me. The other man rose from his position and moved closer to the fire. I felt a flicker of recognition when I saw his face.

"Andy," Evening Fire said, carefully pronouncing my name, "This is my family." She nodded to the old man. "This is my grandfather, Laughing Crow." She gestured to the younger man, "This is my father, Sharp Knife." She turned and nodded to the woman. "This is my mother Running Stream. They are a good family. I love them very much. They are very kind to me."

I looked into their faces as she introduced me to her family. At first they were expressionless, but they each noticeably softened when she told of her affection for them.

She continued, addressing her family. "You know that he's my brother. His name is Andy."

The lodge fell silent as we all looked at each other. Each face reflected a warehouse of mixed emotions as we silently sorted out our cultural differences.

The old man broke the silence. "The women make food while we talk."

I waited for him to commence the conversation.

"Why did you come here with many white men with guns?"

"We came looking for white women and children that were taken from their families."

"What will you do when you find these women and children?"

"We will return them to their white families."

"So, you would steal them from us?"

"We would return them where they belong."

Sharp Knife leaned toward me. "My daughter belongs

here." He added emphasis by punching his finger toward me with every word. "You heard from her mouth what she said about her family."

"But I'm her family. She was taken from me. *You* took her from me. I remember you now. You were the one that bought her from Strings Bow Tight. You bought my sister for the price of a few trinkets. And I've spent the last five years of my life not knowing if she was dead or alive. You stole my sister and I came to take her back!" My chest was heaving with the release of the pent up anger.

Laughing Crow restrained Sharp Knife as he reached for his knife and started to get to his feet.

"There will be no killing in this lodge tonight!" Laughing Crow said firmly to diffuse the emotion. Sharp Knife glared at me for a moment, then returned to his sitting position but didn't take his eyes off of me.

Evening Fire stood beside her mother with her hand to her mouth watching the emotional exchange.

Laughing Crow leveled his gaze at me. "You must remember where you are and why you are here. You are our prisoner. Tonight our people will decide whether you will live or die. My granddaughter does not want you to die. I love my granddaughter and want her to be happy, so I have been asking that you be spared. You will talk for yourself later at the council."

CHAPTER 36

So that was it. I'd be defending my actions at council trial. Somehow I'd have to convince a tribe of Comanche Indians that even though I brought almost a hundred men to their homes to execute a surprise attack at daybreak by running off their horses and engaging their warriors in battle, (although a mock battle from our point of view), and terrorizing their women and children, my intentions were honorable and I should not be put to death— Whew!

I certainly did not get off on the right foot with Sharp Knife and realized I must try to do whatever I could to resolve our differences.

"Sharp Knife," I said with my eyes downcast in a subservient manner, "I need to ask your forgiveness for showing you a lack of respect. Instead of being angry for you taking my sister, I should be thanking you for giving her a good life with a good family that she loves. I was only a lowly slave and could have done nothing for her if she had stayed with me. It was all I could do to keep myself alive. Thank you for your generosity." Sharp Knife was silent, but he took on a look of satisfaction.

Laughing Crow spoke: "I see you are a wise young man to recognize Sharp Knife for what he is; a good man that loves his daughter. You and Evening Fire have much to talk about. You will be left alone with her. I do not fear your escape. You are unable to walk and I trust my granddaughter to sound an alarm if you should try anyway. Her mother, father and I will take our food in my lodge. We will all go to council meeting when we hear the drums." The three of them filled gourds with the stew that Running Stream had been simmering on the fire and left the lodge.

Evening Fire handed me a gourd of stew, took one for herself and sat next to me.

"I'm surprised they left us by ourselves," I said.

"My grandfather trusts me."

"I'm just so happy to find you. I really didn't know if you were alive. I didn't know if you were a slave like me. I just didn't know. Oh Ros— I mean Evening Fire, the only reason I managed to stay alive while I was with them was hoping some day I'd be able to find you."

"There are many here who want to see you dead."

"I suspect there are, and I can't really blame them, understanding what we put them through."

"The one who hurt you has vowed to kill you. He thinks he was robbed of your scalp. He even came back here to the lodge to kill you after we brought you here. That's why my father spent the day here. To protect you."

'While you were asleep, I cried and begged Sharp Knife and Laughing Crow to help me save you. I stood outside the war chief's lodge and listened to my grandfather ask the council to spare you. But tonight you must talk for yourself. I'm scared for you."

I saw the fear in her eyes. "All I can do is just try to explain myself the best I can." I said, enjoying the closeness of my sister but silently fearing for my life.

We spent the rest of the afternoon sharing some details of our lives. I told her a little of the difficulties of my life with the Comanches and of my escape. I shared with her how I became such good friends with the Jeffersons and Bowmans. I related the stories of the Council House fight, which she knew nothing about, and the Plum Creek fight.

I explained that my goal all along had always been to do whatever I could to find her. And I cried when I told her of the guilt I carried for all these years because I couldn't protect her like I had promised.

She cried with me when she relived being taken from me, but soon realized that she was being adopted by a loving family. She shared that she never experienced any of the abuse that I suffered, but was shown the way of the Comanche and made a part of the tribe. She cried when she told me that she thought I was dead, as she was told that older white boys don't adjust to the Comanche way of life.

We talked and laughed and cried the afternoon away and didn't notice the sky above the smoke hole at the top of the lodge had changed from daylight to dark. She was telling me about her and her friends riding their horses when we heard the drums across the village start their rhythmic beat summoning the tribe members to the council meeting. She and I looked at each other and a chill ran through me.

Her father, mother and grandfather returned to the lodge to escort us to the council meeting. Laughing Crow let me hang on his walking staff as they walked and I hobbled to the clearing. A fire had been fed with logs until it blazed six feet wide and seven feet high. Everyone fanned out on the south side of the fire. There was a line of older men standing with their backs to the fire. Most of them were in ceremonial dress. Some wore war bonnets. I was led to an area between the elders and the rest of the tribe and left by myself. Evening Fire, her mother and father joined the rest of the tribe and Laughing Crow joined the elders.

Standing Eagle stepped forward. He wore yellow elk skin leggings and a long shirt and had a wool blanket wrapped around him. The feathers from a war bonnet trailed down his back. The drums suddenly stopped their beat. The crowd grew silent waiting for him to speak.

The elderly chief looked around the villagers standing in the snow in front of him. All were wrapped in blankets or buffalo robes to ward off the chill in the air. He ignored me as he addressed the gathering.

"This morning, like every morning, before the Great Spirit lifted the ball of fire that gives us life into the sky, we slept. Our village was quiet. Our children were warm inside their robes. Our babies were at their mother's breasts. All things were as they should be.

"Then, many white men came. They drove away our horses. They attacked our warriors who were protecting their families. They ran down our women and children with their horses, terrorizing them. Then, as fast as they appeared, they rode away, all except one. This man here." He stretched his arm and pointed his finger at me. He stared at me before he continued.

"This man should be dead. Fast Thunder proved himself in battle today. The spirits were with him when his arrows flew straight. They guided his arm when he swung his war club. But his victory was taken from him. A girl and her grandfather stopped him. He respected a tribal elder more than he wanted the scalp. He let the man live. But these circumstances aren't normal. There were things about the raid that weren't normal. This man is Evening Fire's brother. He's lived with Comanches and knows our tongue. We have agreed to let him speak to explain his actions. Then we decide his fate." Standing Eagle returned to the line of elders, leaving me alone, looking into the faces of those I terrorized earlier in the day. I didn't really know what I would say until I started talking.

"I am a white man. But I lived with The People for four years. I learned much from you. We are different in many ways, but we are very much alike in some other ways. White people love their families and you love your families. Mothers and fathers love their children and we love our brothers and sisters. We fight for them. In some cases we die for them. When one in your family dies, you almost die yourself from grief. You slash yourself with knives. You cut off fingers. You bleed. You cry. You want to die. But you go on living.

"Evening Fire and I went on living when our mother and father were killed by the Mexican army. All we had was each other. We had no home. We had no weapons. We had no other family. We were both just children. I was all she had and I promised to take care of her.

"We were found and taken by The People but were soon separated. She came to your tribe and was adopted and loved by a good family. I was kept and made a slave.

"A day never passed that I didn't grieve the loss of my sister. I believed my sister must be a slave too, if she was alive. I knew that some slaves did not adapt well with the Comanche and died. I prayed to my God that if she was alive, that someday I would find her.

"I escaped from my captors about a year ago and have spent my time since then preparing myself to find my sister. During that year I met men who also had lost children or brothers and sisters to the Comanche. We agreed to come to Comanche country to find and be reunited with our loved ones.

"We also agreed before we left the settlements that we would avoid bloodshed wherever possible. There was already enough bloodshed when our people were taken. Did you notice this morning that no one was hurt when the horses were driven away? Did you notice that the line of white men firing their weapons always shot over your heads and then drew back as you advanced on them? Did you notice that those of us at the rear of the village fired our weapons only into the air as we approached you? Did you notice that all we did was try to identify any white women and children that may have been among you? We weren't trying to kill anyone. We were just trying to find our loved ones. We were doing exactly what you would do if we had your loved ones with us.

"So you see, we are very much the same as you. We just want to be with our families. And if we can't be with them, we just want to know if they are alive and happy. That's all. I mean you no harm. I just wanted to find my sister.

"I am truly sorry for any trouble I may have caused this morning, and I ask that you spare my life. I am guilty only of loving my sister." I looked into Evening Fire's face as I finished my plea for leniency. Tears streamed down her cheeks. She ran to me and embraced me tightly, her face buried in my chest.

She was soon followed by her family who escorted me back to her lodge to wait for my judgment. It was to be a long night.

CHAPTER 37

"I'm really having trouble with this, Will," Tad said. He put a dead mesquite log on the fire, adjusted his blanket around his shoulders and sat on a buffalo robe next to Will. His eyes were red from crying. "I don't know if I ever will get over it. I never had a brother and he had become as close as a brother to me."

"I'm having trouble with it too, Tad. We both got really close to him."

"He'd been through so much hell in his life. He didn't deserve this. Do you think there's any way . . . ?"

"No, you heard the reports from two of his men, both eye witnesses. They report the same story. He and his horse went down with arrows. They weren't sure how many arrows. Then a warrior went after him with a war club. They swore it looked like he got his brains bashed in. Then there were three on him. Our men said from where they were, it looked like they were scalping him. One of our boys tried to get off a shot, but his pistol was empty." Will paused. "Tad, they wouldn't have left him if they weren't sure he was dead."

Tad was silent for awhile, staring into the fire. "Will, did we do anything wrong that resulted in this?"

"No. This whole mission has been about doing something right, and Andy was the one behind the whole thing. Those kids over there," he nodded toward the children huddled around a fire under their blankets and robes, "they didn't ask to be stolen and brought out here. It's amazing they're still alive. Andy was just doing what he believed the right thing was for his sister and for those children. We all knew what the risk was before we left home. We also knew that the Comanches weren't playing by our rules."

No one slept much that night.

The wind was calm, the skies were clear and the early

morning sun glistened off the pristine snow. The children were eating their breakfast and looking forward to a warmer day, and the men were finishing their coffee before starting to pack up for another day on the trail when one of the sentries called out, "Riders approachin'! Looks like Injuns walkin' their ponies slow, carryin' a white banner."

Will and Tad dropped the bags they were packing and hurried to the north end of the camp, following the sound of the sentry's voice.

Will squinted as he looked across the blinding white snow. The Indians were still five hundred yards away, approaching slowly. As they continued their march toward Bowman's camp, Will counted at least ten riders, riding abreast in two rows. He looked beyond the riders approaching with the white flag.

An army of Indians were gathered a quarter mile behind those approaching. There were at least seventy to eighty mounted warriors holding their distance behind the advance party carrying the flag.

"Everybody hold your fire!" Will called, watching the Indians advance. When they were close enough to determine their features, it appeared that four older men were riding abreast, flanked by a young warrior on either side of the front row. They were riding so closely together, Will couldn't see the riders behind them.

Seventy yards away, they stopped. Will waited for them to make the first move. After several moments the four horsemen in the middle of the front row pulled their ponies aside to allow the riders in the second row advance to the front.

As the ranks opened in front of us, we rode between them to Bowman's camp.

My sorrel stallion slightly favored his left foreleg where a puncture wound had been treated. The bandages on my head and thigh reflected my injuries. Evening Fire sat next to me on a sorrel and white spotted pony. Her hair flowed over her shoulders onto a beautifully beaded elk-skin dress.

A cheer swelled from the throats of the men in camp as they realized a miracle had occurred. When Evening Fire and I rode forward, her father and grandfather, riding beside us trailed for a few feet, than reined in to watch as we approached the whites. Evening Fire briefly looked over her shoulder at the men behind her. Then she moved forward with me.

We rode to within ten feet of Will and Tad. When I attempted to slide from my horse, Tad rushed to me to help me to the ground. We silently embraced for a few moments. Then I turned to Will and hugged him.

I looked at Evening Fire and nodded with a smile. She slid from her pony and stood close to me, holding my hand.

"Friends," I said loudly for everyone to hear. "This is my sister." I gently took her hand and held it high in the air. "Her name is Evening Fire." I hesitated a moment, then lowered her hand. "My sister saved my life yesterday. Not just once, but several times. When you left the field, she took me to her lodge to nurse me. She and her family kept me from dying of my wounds. There were those from her tribe who wanted to kill me. She and her family protected me from them. When the council of elders debated my fate, her grandfather spoke on my behalf. Thanks to her and her family, I'm alive this morning.

"I asked all of you to come on this campaign with me so I could find my sister. All these years, I kept hoping to find her. But—" I hesitated as my voice broke and I struggled to contain my emotions. "But the little Rosie I knew is gone. I lost her a long time ago, and I'll never see her again. I've found someone I love just as much, I've found Evening Fire. She may have red hair, light skin and blue eyes, but her soul is Comanche. She doesn't understand what I'm saying now. It's just been too long. She will never leave the Comanches. They are her family now. They love her and she loves them. I have agreed to speak for her grandfather, who speaks for her tribe." I motioned for Laughing Crow and Sharp Knife to ride forward. They rode toward me and stopped twenty feet from Evening Fire and me. "The elder on the left is her grandfather, Laughing Crow. The other is Sharp Knife, her father."

The old man spoke and I listened carefully.

"He said that he understands why we came to his village and respects us for the reasons behind what we have done, but they do not like our methods."

Laughing Crow spoke again.

"He said that this is their land and we have no right here. He says that we must go and never return. There is nobody with them or any other tribe in this part of the country that doesn't belong with them. He wants you to look behind us and see that they have plenty of warriors to kill us all if we do not leave.

"Now that I have seen my sister and know that she is safe, happy and loved, I'm satisfied. I can give her no more than she has here. I don't belong here, but she does."

I turned to my sister and embraced her, whispering in her ear, "I love you. Don't ever forget me." I held her horse's bridle as she leapt on his back. I limped, holding her horse's mane as she slowly walked her horse back to her father and grandfather. I reached upward to the two men waiting for her and grasped their hands, thanking them for all they had done for my sister. I promised them that we would return to our homes without further harassment of the Comanches.

Evening Fire reached for my hand again and held it for the longest time, looking into my face. Then blinking away her tears, she pulled her hand away and looked beyond me to the company of Texas volunteers and former captive children. She lingered, staring at the blue eyes, fair skin and light hair of Will and the other Texans. After a long gaze at their faces, she smiled and waved at me and the rest of the Texans. I realized as she turned to ride away with her people that she had just said goodbye forever to her old life. She was returning to home and family.

The End

As a sixth generation Texan, Dan Vanderburg grew up listening to tales of his ancestors as they worked to build their farms, ranches and way of life on the Texas frontier. Those accounts lit a spark in Dan as a youngster to learn more about the people and events that built the American Southwest. He enjoys developing strong characters with their own stories to tell, then placing them in and around critical events in history. Dan Vanderburg lives and writes in Arlington, Texas.

If you enjoyed **Trail of Hope**, please consider leaving a review on Amazon. Thank you for your interest in the **Texas Legacy Family Saga**.

More books by Dan Vanderburg:
Legacy of Dreams (Texas Legacy Family Saga Book 1)
Freedom Road (Texas Legacy Family Saga Book 3)
The Littlest Hero

Coming soon: Little Old Ladies and Larceny and Other Humorous Short Stories and Captivating Poetry

You can find out more about Dan Vanderburg on Facebook, Instagram, Goodreads or Amazon

Read on for a peek at Freedom Road (Texas Legacy Family Saga Book 3) available now on Amazon.com

Freedom Road

New Orleans, March, 1860

CHAPTER 1

The sleek schooner glided slowly toward its berth at the New Orleans docks. Its huge sails were neatly secured and the deck made ready for landing by the anxious crew eager for a night of drinking and revelry. They wouldn't have trouble finding whatever suited their appetite at that port city. Whiskey, food and women were available at any of the many drinking dens along the docks. There were many places that provided cheap thrills at night and a guarantee of empty pockets and a headache the next day. The crew and passengers were more than ready to put their feet on firm ground. They'd been at sea twenty-nine days, sailing west on the trade winds, far south of their departure point at Plymouth, England.

A young man stood on the stern at the ship's rail, aside from the sailors and other passengers as the vessel slowly cut its way through the water. He looked out of place by himself on the deck. Standing several inches over six feet tall, he appeared to be well built. The man's handsome Negro features and clean shaven jaws were accented with clear, dark eyes. He was alone at the rail, taking in the sights, sounds, and smells of New Orleans as the ship slid through the waters. He looked no more than twenty-five years old and wore a fashionable, well tailored black suit of clothes. His white shirt had an upturned, starched collar and was set off with a carefully knotted dark cravat. A gold watch chain passed from a button hole on his vest to the pocket below his left breast. His wardrobe was topped off with a stylish gray, high-crowned felt hat.

A wide smile crossed his face as he acknowledged to himself the completion of this leg of his journey. He clutched the handle of his satchel a little tighter as he thought back on all the hard work of the last five years. The parchment document rolled up inside the canvas bag provided proof of his accomplishment and would pave the way to his future.

With only a little seasickness during the first few days, the voyage was what he needed. It allowed his body to rest. He'd worked hard, especially during the past year to finish his advanced studies in Scotland. During the voyage, he slept, rested and planned his future. Soon he'd be able to do what he'd been destined to do. He could finally teach.

The ship's bell interrupted his reverie, ringing four times, chiming the beginning of the early evening watch — six o'clock. He verified the time by slipping his watch from the vest pocket, popping the cover open and glancing at the watch. Time had become more important to him, now that he was getting closer to home. He'd been away from home and family such a long time.

He rubbed the filigree engraving on the surface of the watch cover as he thumbed it closed. He remembered the day Will Bowman presented it to him as a gift in this same town five years earlier after outfitting him with a new wardrobe at the beginning of his new adventure. Every time he looked at the watch, it reminded him of home, family and the Bowmans. He'd never owned a watch before and he'd never been without it since he received it as a special gift.

As darkness settled in, the sounds along the docks of the work gangs singing their chants as they loaded and unloaded heavy cargo died away. The bosses busied themselves re-attaching leg irons to the slaves for the evening march to their quarters.

The young man heard other voices from the street and buildings across from the docks. Laughter from the early drinkers in the pubs was carried by the evening breeze. The fish vendors made their final calls for the day as they shut down their carts. The lamp lighter moved from one lamp to the other as the sky darkened.

The familiar ship's stench of dirty bodies in close quarters gave way to a different scent. If the odor hadn't been so overwhelming, the young man may have thought it to be exotic. He recognized the smell as a combination of many factors that in sum was just the stink of a city by the water. He'd smelled cities like it in Scotland and England, but New Orleans had its own special aroma. It reflected the essence of the river; dead fish and rotting organic matter along with mud, wood smoke and horse droppings. A strong compliment of spices combined in food being cooked in that special way added a fragrance that only happens in New Orleans.

Three men watched and took inventory of the passengers and crew as the clipper glided into its berth, and the sailors held it fast to the moorings with thick ropes. The men hid themselves in the shadows against a brick wall of an alley that led away from the waterfront. Empty and broken bottles, garbage and bricks that had fallen away from the buildings littered the ground around them. They were looking for their next target.

New Orleans had more than its share of pickpockets and thieves. These were just three — too lazy to work as long as they found easy prey. There were always plenty of drunken sailors or transients passing through that were ripe for picking.

Although different in physical size, the three looked similar; dirty bodies and clothes that looked as if they had come from a rag bin, scruffy, unshaven faces, and not one bit of civility among the three.

"Whatcha think, boys?" Gaston, the tallest and leanest said. He spat a brown stream of tobacco juice on the ground, exposing several missing teeth in his gaping mouth as he moved his wad of chew to a new spot in his jaw. His long hair hung in oily strings under his dirty, slouch hat.

"I see a bunch of young sailors that we can take after they nurse their cups awhile," Charlie, the shorter, wiry one said.

"Yeah, but do ya'll see what I see?" Red said. Red was about the same height as Charlie but had a stocky build, appeared younger and wore a shock of bright orange hair and beard. "Look down by the stern, away from the others. There's a big nigger standin' over there all by hisself."

"Ooh, he *is* a big boy," Gaston said, grinning. "Why, lookie there. He's all gussied up like some high and mighty dandy. Where'd you think he got them clothes?"

"Stole 'em — where else?" Red said. "Wonder where his master is?"

"Don't see none," Charlie said. "You boys thinkin' what I'm thinkin?"

William Henry Jefferson, who'd been called Billy all his life by his family and friends, waited patiently as the other passengers disembarked from the ship down the gangplank. He followed the last passenger off the ship onto the wharf. His canvas satchel was in his right hand. In his left, he held a cotton bag with a change of clothes slung over his shoulder. He walked past the several carriages for hire that were boarding passengers. He had no need to leave the dock area as he would be seeking ship passage for the next leg of his journey in the morning. That night, he just needed food and a place to sleep.

While in Scotland, Billy experienced a limited opportunity to travel around the British Isles, and felt comfortable traveling. But in New Orleans, he considered himself in hostile territory — hostile for him, anyway. He was deep in slave country. An unaccompanied Negro man just didn't travel alone in the South.

He'd traveled through Texas, Louisiana and New England, and knew what to expect on the road, and how to get food and lodging. But then, he'd always been accompanied by a white man.

He believed, however, that his training, maturity, experience, appearance and demeanor as a gentleman would see him through. If not, the documents that he carried would provide safe passage.

He saw a sign for an inn about a block down the street. He knew that if the innkeeper used colored help, he may be able to negotiate a place to sleep in the servant's quarters and get a meal as well. He quickened his step to pass a couple of pubs and other businesses between him and the inn.

Someone suddenly crashed against him.

"What the . . . ?" The attack came from behind. Pain shot through his right arm as the thief wrenched his canvas bag away. He turned and swung the bag off his left shoulder, hitting the fleeing assailant and causing him to stumble, but he didn't go down. The wiry bandit ran back the way he came, clutching the satchel to his chest.

"Stop! Thief!" Billy called and ran after the man. Bystanders shrank away. The robber darted into an alley and disappeared into the dark. Billy followed and chased him about thirty feet into the alley. He stopped to listen. The running footsteps melted into silence. Darkness closed around him. He could see nothing. His own hard breathing echoed through the silence. His heart pounded against his chest. The dripping of leaking water into a puddle and the skittering of rats through the rotting garbage around his feet were the only other sounds he heard.

He sensed motion behind him. He started to turn but a crushing blow to his back caused his chest to fly forward. His head and arms were swept backward. He went to his knees. Before his body collapsed to the ground, he received another blow; this time to the back of his head. Billy's vision went black and he lost consciousness before his head hit the ground.

Gaston stood, breathing heavily as he leaned on the stout ax handle, minus the ax head, catching his breath and looking at the man at his feet.

"Woo-hoo! You took him down like a sack o' taters, Gaston." Red said, emerging from the darkness. Behind him came Charlie, carrying the satchel.

"You got 'em just in time, Gaston," Charlie said. "I couldn't hold my breath much longer back there. Grab that other bag and let's get outta here."

"You crazy?" Gaston looked up at the two men standing over him as he attempted to roll the large man over. "Whatever's in them bags is nothin'. The real prize is right here." Gaston nodded at the prostrate figure on the ground. "Look at this nigger. He'll be worth hundreds if he don't die on us. I whapped him purty good on the back of the head.

"You boys help me drag him further in the alley and get him turned over, then go get me a hand cart or somethin' to move him. He's too big to carry. I'll wait here an' keep an eye on him."

"We ain't got no cart." Red said as he helped tug the large body several more feet into the darkness. "Where we gonna get a cart?"

Gaston sighed and looked at his companions. "Red, what do

you do for a livin'?"

"Oh." Red said. "Come on, Charlie. Let's go get us a cart."

Gaston looked at Billy and the two bags. Going through the bags could wait. He couldn't examine them because of the darkness. He had, however, waited for his companions to leave to search the body on the ground.

"Nice," he said as he pulled the watch from Billy's breast pocket. He'd seen a glimmer off the gold chain from what little light made its way into the alley. He quickly unfastened the chain's fob from Billy's vest button hole and shoved the watch and chain into his own pocket. He felt around Billy's chest until he found a leather wallet. It was buttoned in the inside coat pocket. He removed it and took it to the corner by the boardwalk to find enough light to examine its contents. He opened it and found it loaded with cash. "Damn!" he whispered, grinning and thumbing through the bills. Counting it out, he found it to be a hundred and eighty dollars. He looked back and forth as he shoved a hundred and twenty into his pocket and tucked the remaining sixty back inside. The wallet also contained two folded pieces of paper that he left alone. Returning to the form on the ground, he replaced the wallet inside the coat, checked to see if the man was still breathing, grinned at his good fortune, spat a stream of tobacco juice into the dirt, and waited for the cart.

Fifteen minutes later he heard Charlie and Red rolling a hand cart through the alley. It stunk of old fish.

"We'd been back sooner but Charlie had trouble picking the lock on the chain," Red said, rolling his eyes.

"You ever tried to pick a lock that you ain't never seen before with a little ole piece of rusty wire?" Charlie said in his defense. "Well, I'll tell ya, it ain't easy, 'specially with someone whinin' in your ear that it stinks too much. The fishmonger's place is the closest I knowed where we could get a cart. Anyway, it's a damn cart and here it is. Now Red, quit your whinin'."

"Both of ya shut up and help me get him in there." Gaston

said. "Red, you get one arm, Charlie you get the other and I'll get his feet."

Within a few minutes they parked the cart outside the back door of an abandoned warehouse, three blocks off the water. The old building had once been a sugar warehouse. Deterioration had taken place over the many years it had been unused. The rotting roof had fallen away in several places in the front of the building, but those three slept in a corner room at the back of the building.

"Come on, bring him inside and get rid of the cart," Gaston said. "Red, take that cart back over to front street where the fish man will find it in the morning. Can't nobody say that I ain't got a warm heart — returnin' a man's cart."

"Why do I have to take it," Red whined. "You two gonna split up the kit while I'm gone, ain't ya?"

Gaston gritted what teeth he had left and balled his fist as he approached Red. "I'm tellin' ya to do it 'cause I'm damned tired of listening to your whining. Now get!" He spat a stream of tobacco at Red's back as he scooted out the door. "Damn idiot." Gaston lit the oil lamp, illuminating the room and turned to his new investment.

They placed Billy along a wall on the floor and started removing his clothes. "Charlie," Gaston said, "we're gonna need to secure him 'fore he wakes up. Go get them shackles we used last time while I start getting' these clothes off him."

Billy remained unresponsive as they wrestled him out of his clothes. Gaston checked him from time to time to verify that he was still breathing. Billy was rolled onto an old cotton picking sack and covered with a dirty blanket. Gaston inspected Billy's injuries as he got him undressed and found the blow to the back left a large bruise and swelling. He couldn't tell if there were any broken bones. He guessed maybe there could be some cracked ribs. He'd have some sore muscles though. The head injury concerned Gaston more than the back bruise. A large swollen area covered the entire back of his head.

Charlie soon returned with the shackles and restrained Billy's hands and locked a foot to a vertical support post.

Red returned from dumping the cart, anxious to see what bounty the young Negro brought them. "Now y'all ain't already looked in them bags did ya?"

"No, we saved all that till you got back." Gaston said. "First, I'll show you what I found in his pockets." He held his closed fist out, away from his body and let the pocket watch drop from his hand but held the end of the chain. Charlie reached for the dangling watch, popped the cover and examined the watch. "That's a nice one." he handed it off to Red.

Next, Gaston produced the long, thin wallet. "I think we ougthta look in here." He opened it with the enthusiasm of a child opening a Christmas present. First he pulled out the two pieces of neatly folded paper. Unfolding the first, he revealed the page filled with neat script.

"What does it say?" Charlie asked.

"How am I supposed to know?" Gaston said. "Just looks like scribbles to me." Then he unfolded the second paper. The writing contained flourishes and a much fancier style of script than the first paper. On the bottom margin of the page was a one-inch wide drop of red wax with a deep image pressed into it. The image looked like a lion's head with plumes and flags at the top and bottom.

"That looks mighty fancy," Charlie said, looking over Gaston's shoulder. "Wonder what it means?"

"Ah, it's just fancy paper. It don't mean nothin'," Gaston said and shoved the papers back inside the wallet. "Now this here does mean somethin'." His lips spread into a gapped-tooth grin. He reached inside, drew out the bills and counted the sixty dollars and waved them in the air. He divided it three ways and ʜ the others their share. Of course, he made no mention of ʜᴇᴅ and twenty dollars that he had already secreted

ʀ the satchel. Opening it he found a fourteen-inch-wide roll of thin, stiff, sheepskin parchment tied with a ribbon. Unrolling it, he found a rectangular shaped document with carefully scripted text, much more elegant looking than either of the paper letters. Some lines of words on the parchment were bigger than others. Along the bottom, underneath the words was another imprint sealed in wax. That wax seal was bigger than the one on the folded paper in the wallet, and it held a very elaborate imprint pressed into the wax. The three men examined it by the oil lamp. "That boy sure likes stuff with lots of writin' on it," Gaston said. "Now what'd you thank a nigger'd be doin' with that stuff?" Charlie and Red looked at each other, shrugged their shoulders and shook their heads.

Gaston reached in the satchel again and withdrew a soft cloth bag with a drawstring at the top. Loosening the string, he shook out the contents onto a table. They included a shaving brush, a straight razor folded in its cover, a mug with hard soap inside, a comb, a pair of scissors and a small rectangular mirror. Gaston grabbed for the razor, opened it, tested the fineness of its blade with his dirty thumbnail and pocketed it. "I'm keepin' this, 'case I ever have to slit a throat." He looked directly at Red as he spoke.

Next, he pulled out a fine, polished wooden box made of dark rosewood about ten inches wide, twelve inches long and four inches deep. When he opened the hinged lid, it revealed compartments for writing paper and accessories. Soft green velvet fabric lined the interior. Along with a supply of writing paper and envelopes, it contained a small ink bottle and wax to seal the glass stopper, a writing quill and a small pen knife. "I know what that is," Gaston said. "That's used for writin' letters to folks. I seen a man do it once. He dipped the feather in that black stuff and made his marks on the paper. It looked just like them other papers we seen."

"Now I'm *really* wonderin' 'bout that nigger," Charlie said. "He musta done killed some fancy man and took his clothes and all them papers and stuff. I think he done killed his master, an' that's why he's on the run."

"Betcha there's a bounty on his head," Red said, grinning and rubbing his hands together.

"We ain't messin' with no lawmen and bounties." Gaston said. "We'll get our money off this boy, but it won't be from no bounty."

He reached back in the satchel and found that the rest of the items inside were books — four of them. "Why lookie here," Gaston said holding one of the books up in the air. I seen one of them before. That's got holy words in it. That's what preachers carry around and preach about."

"I still don't get it," Red said. "What's this big nigger doin' with all this readin' an' writin' stuff? Everybody knows they can't read and write. Why, they ain't even real people like us. They's more like livestock. They ain't got no real brains like we do. They can't think for themselves. All they's fit for is hard work. Look at that boy there. That big ole buck there ain't made for readin' — he's made for workin'."

"Yeah, everybody knows that," Gaston said, "but whatever the case, he done brung us money. I know where I can sell all that stuff. What's in this other bag?"

Gaston fished around in the second bag and found it loaded with clothing. It contained a suit coat and pants, several shirts, some underwear, another pair of shoes and several pairs of socks. Holding up the suit coat to check for size and condition, he said, "Now look at this, he's not only wearing white man's clothes, he's carrying around a bunch more in this sack, just like what we took off him. That boy don't know it now, but he's gonna make us rich."

Freedom Road (Texas Legacy Family Saga Book 3) is ~~ble now on **Amazon.com**

~le Old Ladies and Larceny and Other
stories and Captivating Poetry